No Quest For The Wicked

SHANNA SWENDSON

ALSO BY SHANNA SWENDSON

Books in the Enchanted, Inc. Series:

Enchanted, Inc.
Once Upon Stilettos
Damsel Under Stress
Don't Hex with Texas
Much Ado About Magic
No Quest For The Wicked

CHAPTER ONE

I'd reached the part of my mission where stealth was most essential. One wrong footstep, one breath that was a little too loud, and the game would be up. The door ahead of me was ever so slightly ajar. It looked as though anyone could walk right through, but the door wasn't what kept out intruders. Anyone who tried to pass through that doorway would wake up in a body-shaped dent on the opposite wall.

Anyone, that is, who didn't have my particular qualities. For me, that slightly ajar door was the most challenging obstacle. I'd need to open it wider to get through, but there was the risk that would make enough noise to give me away. I slid my toe into the gap, shivering as I crossed the powerful wards. Moving my foot slowly forward, I eased the door open, bit by bit, then I paused and held my breath, listening carefully. The scratch of a pen confirmed my fear that the room was occupied.

At this time in the morning? How early did I have to get up?

At any rate, it was time to make my move. I slid my body into the gap in the doorway, edging sideways into the chamber. I'd made it all the way into the room when a crunching sound made me freeze. I glanced down and saw that I'd stepped on a wadded-up piece of paper. After holding my breath a few seconds without noticing any reaction from the room's occupant, I kept going, watching more carefully where I stepped.

I'd almost made it to the paper-and-book-strewn table in the middle of the room when the occupant said, without looking up from his work, "Katie, what are you doing here?"

I let out the breath I'd been holding in a disappointed sigh. "I was hoping to beat you here and surprise you with breakfast. But since you were already here, I thought I'd surprise you with breakfast. Now, I guess I've just brought you breakfast, hold the surprise."

"I'm surprised, really," Owen Palmer insisted, sitting up straight and stretching his back. "Mostly because I thought it was lunchtime."

I moved behind him to rub his shoulders. "It's seven in the morning. Have you been here all night?"

"Would you believe me if I said no?"

I came around the table to get a good look at him. "Well, you've changed clothes and shaved, so I might believe you this time. How early did you get here?"

He took off the cotton gloves he wore for handling rare books and rubbed his eyes. "Oh, I don't know. I did go home yesterday, and I got some sleep, but then I got up early and thought I might as well get to work."

"If you think it's lunchtime at seven, how early is 'early' to you?"

He blushed sheepishly, then changed the subject. "Did you bring coffee?"

"Coffee and cinnamon rolls."

"I think I can manage a break," he said with a grin. He shoved his chair back and stood, then hugged me and kissed me on the cheek. "Thank you."

We went from the sterile workroom that housed the fragile, old, and incredibly dangerous magical manuscript Owen was working on to the outer office that served as break room, where I'd set out the breakfast I'd brought. After serving him and myself coffee and rolls, I asked, "How's it going?"

"A lot faster now that I've got the idiosyncrasies of the language figured out. I got a couple of pages translated yesterday, some really interesting stuff about the Eye of the Moon—this incredibly powerful magical jewel that's been lost for ages. I think I found the directions for locating it."

"Really?" My spirits rose. "Does that mean a quest?"

"Not anytime soon. The directions are pretty cryptic, and I suspect they apply to situations and locations that nobody would recognize today. It goes back to Merlin's time."

Perhaps I should explain that Owen was a wizard. Or had been a wizard. I wasn't sure what his status was currently, since he'd lost his powers a few months earlier in a big magical battle. He still had all his training and knowledge as a wizard and probably knew more about magic than any wizard alive other than Merlin himself, but he was as lacking in magical power as I was, which meant he was so utterly lacking in magic that magic didn't affect him.

Although I was pretty sure he was still unhappy about that, he was taking advantage of the opportunity to study a rare manuscript that was so dangerous that no one with any magical power or susceptibility to magic was allowed to go near it.

"Too bad. A quest would have been kind of fun," I said. Certainly more fun than spending another day at my desk.

"The Eye is the sort of thing that should probably stay lost. I wouldn't want it falling into the wrong hands." He gave a little shudder as he took a sip of coffee.

"But you're finding good stuff—I mean, other than things that are too dangerous to share, right? This is worthwhile work?"

"I think so." He paused, then gave me a crooked grin. "And I'm about to get a lecture on obsession."

"A lecture? From me? Never. But tell me this: Do you know what day it is?"

He got a horrified deer-in-the-headlights look in his dark blue eyes. "Wait a second ... I know it's not your birthday because that was in May. It's September, so it's not a major gift-giving holiday I've missed. I haven't forgotten anything special, have I? That's not what this is about, is it?" He indicated the breakfast.

I took pity on him. "No, that's not what this is about. I was just seeing if you knew it was Thursday, though I'd also have accepted a calendar date. The breakfast was because I thought if I caught you before work, I'd stand a better chance of seeing you before you fell into that manuscript." I frowned at him in sudden concern. "You haven't been taken over by the manuscript, have you? Your powers aren't coming back without you realizing, so the evil thing can suck you in?"

With a laugh, he said, "No, nothing like that."

"So this is just normal obsession?"

"I'm not acting obsessed, am I?"

"Either that, or you've turned into a vampire, and you're just pretending to be obsessed so you'll have an excuse not to go out in daylight. And I'd prefer the obsession because I'm not into vampires."

"Okay, so I'm a little obsessed," he said with a shrug. "But this is an exciting opportunity, and I don't know how much time I've got. If my powers do come back, I won't be able to continue, and I'd hate to have to stop halfway through the project. I'm trying to get as much as possible done, just in case."

Owen was the only one who seemed to believe that his powers would come back, but I knew well enough to keep my mouth shut about that. If holding on to that hope helped keep him going, I didn't want to take it away from him. "That's why I'm not complaining," I said, reaching over to pat him on the knee. "I'm just checking on you."

"I do appreciate the company," he said with a smile that made me melt. "I sometimes feel like I'm in exile down here."

"Hey, I'm glad to do my part." I glanced at my watch. "I can even stick around awhile, if you like. I'm still way too early for work, and this isn't a busy day for me." The truth was, ever since we'd defeated the evil wizards behind our only competitor, there wasn't much for me to do as director of marketing for Magic, Spells, and Illusions, Inc. A trained monkey could market a near-monopoly. Heck, my ditzy assistant Perdita could probably do my job while filing her nails, chatting on the phone, and inventing new coffee concoctions.

He reached over to grab a container of wipes and cleaned his hands. "Sure, come on in and I'll show you what I've been up to." With another grin, he added, "I've got proof that I really haven't been using this as an excuse to avoid you."

I wiped my hands, too, knowing that bringing sugar or anything sticky into the manuscript room would be bad, then followed him back to his worktable. He pulled over a second chair so I could sit next to him, then sat down and put on the cotton gloves. He showed me a page covered in his textbook-perfect handwriting. "This is what I was working on yesterday."

I leaned over and read all about the Eye of the Moon and what it could do. "Yikes, I agree, that needs to stay hidden, and it's a good thing nobody with power can read this thing."

"Oh, they could read it, but they'd probably go insane."

"And is the whole thing written in verse like that?"

"Pretty much. It's all riddles and metaphors. Once I have it transcribed and translated, it'll probably take a committee of scholars years to figure it all out."

"That's if Merlin lets it go that far. What if it's not just the manuscript itself that's so dangerous? What if the magic *on* the manuscript is to protect the really dangerous information it contains?"

"That is a possibility. I suspect Merlin has a plan for what to do with my translation."

"I hope the plan isn't that anyone who knows what it contains has to be locked away for his own safety." I squinted as I read the page. "'Soaring while locked away in the clouds and under the narrow seat.' Maybe it's under a throne? One in a tower? No, that's not vague at all."

"It actually sounds better in the original language. I'm no poet, so I'm going for accuracy instead of beauty in my translation." He pulled the manuscript closer and pointed to the page. "See, here's that part."

The paper was yellowed with age, and the ink had faded to a dark reddish-brown color. The lettering was spiky, looking like something on a heavy-metal album cover, and I didn't recognize so much as a single letter. Even though the magic in the document couldn't affect me, I thought it *looked* evil. "I can't believe you spend all day with this thing. It wouldn't have to affect you magically to drive you nuts. What is it, written in blood on human skin?"

"It's not human skin," Owen said mildly, but I noticed he didn't say anything about the blood. Ew. If I were him, I'd be wearing rubber gloves under the cotton ones. Then he leaned closer to the evil document. "Wait a second, this can't be right."

"Maybe the inkwell bled to death," I said as a chill went down my spine.

"No, it's not an error in the manuscript. It's *changed*. This is the part I translated yesterday, the stuff about the clouds and the seat. It says something different now."

"It's rewriting itself?" I asked, leaning closer to look, even though I couldn't tell what might be different about the manuscript. "That's not entirely unheard of, though, is it?"

"No, and if any book could, it would be this one. But the events in this book happened so long ago that it shouldn't be changing."

"So if that part changed, that means this Eye of the Moon is in a different place now," I concluded. "That first description sounds like it could have been on an airplane when you translated it."

He looked up at me, and I could see from the pallor of his face how serious this was. "That would be bad," he understated.

"Well, where is it now?"

He turned back to the document, frowning as he studied it. "Let's see, there's something about glittering stars, cubical robins' eggs, a king's ransom in gold, silver, and jewels, guarded like a fortress, a place to break one's fast."

"Sounds like Tiffany's," I quipped.

"What?"

"The jewelry store. They have gold, silver, and jewels, and their boxes are kind of a robin's egg blue. I'm sure it's guarded pretty heavily. And then there's *Breakfast at Tiffany's*—you know, Audrey Hepburn staring longingly into the jewelry store windows as she eats her Danish on her way home from a night out?" His blank look told me he was sadly culturally deprived. "But of course, that's impossible, because how would some Dark Ages wizard know about Tiffany's?"

"What the Dark Ages wizard did was embed a spell that relays the current location of the Eye using certain possible descriptors. The Eye's been lost because the description of the original hiding place no longer matched what was there—the place had changed even though the Eye hadn't moved, and since it hadn't moved, the text remained the same. If it's been moved, then the text might use more updated references."

"So it really could have ended up at Tiffany's?" I put my hand on his shoulder as an idea struck me. "We should go! We could find out."

"I don't think so … I mean, it's been lost for centuries, and it shows up in Tiffany's? That's unlikely. It's probably just a bad translation on my part. I was doing that off the top of my head."

"Then translate!" I said, waving my hand at the table with a "get to work" gesture. "I can wait."

"This could take awhile. You should go to your office. I'll call you when I have something."

"You promise?"

"I promise."

"Okay, then." I leaned over to give him a kiss. "I'll leave the coffee and rolls outside in case you need another break." I then reluctantly headed up to my office, where I could do something exciting like alphabetize my pencil cup. Again.

On my way into the sales department, I smiled and spoke to everyone as I passed their offices. They were willing to chat, but they didn't need anything from me. In a way, that was good because it meant business was going well. Unfortunately, it also meant that I felt totally useless. I'm not sure that being busy would have helped much, though. While I'd hated my old marketing job before I learned about the magical world, I'd thought that was mostly because my boss was evil. It turned out that I just hated marketing.

I'd thought doing marketing was fun when I was working for my family's store back home. It was a nice break from keeping the books or working the cash register. As a day-to-day job, though, it wasn't my ideal. But what else could I do? I was twenty-seven years old, and I didn't know what I wanted to be when I grew up. My opportunities at a magical company were limited, since I didn't have magical powers or training. Most people like me worked in the verification department, seeing past any illusions meant to trick magical people, but that wasn't a very interesting job, either. I didn't want to leave MSI, but I didn't know where else I fit in there.

My assistant wasn't in yet, much to my relief. She was as bored as I was, and she dealt with it by talking to me. She'd taken to coming in later and later, and there wasn't any point in reprimanding her about it. I went to my desk and surfed Internet news sites. I didn't see anything that hinted at unauthorized magical activity going on anywhere in the world. Yay? It was bad that I actually hoped to find signs of trouble.

Then there was no point procrastinating further, so I did the one major task on my to-do list for the day, writing a new ad for the magical training program my friend Rod Gwaltney was putting together. I came up with three different concepts, annotated them, and e-mailed them to him. I checked my watch and found that I'd accomplished my entire to-do list before ten in the morning.

The ring of the telephone was the only thing that kept my forehead from hitting my desk. "I've translated that passage and then cross-referenced it in every related book I've got to make sure I was getting it right," Owen said.

"I'll be right down," I said, already rising from my chair.

"Don't bother. I was right the first time, more or less. The wording is slightly different, but the important parts are the same."

"So it really is at Tiffany's?"

"That's one possible interpretation of the translation of the text. There are a lot of other things it could mean."

"Like what?"

"It could be in a dragon's hoard."

"Would you want to have breakfast there?"

"The dragon would."

"We should go to Tiffany's, just in case."

"What would it be doing in a jewelry store?"

"It's a gem, isn't it? If it is there, we'd better get it quickly. Imagine what could happen if some unsuspecting customer bought it."

There was a long silence on the other end of the line, and even though I couldn't see his face, I knew what was going through his mind. He'd recently learned—along with the rest of the magical world—that his birth parents had been the previous generation's great threat to magical society. They'd been manipulated by the real villain, but the fact remained that his parents had tried to take over the world and they'd gone down in history as supervillains. Although Owen had never shown any signs of having inherited his parents' evil ways, he had been incredibly powerful before losing his powers, and there were people in the magical community who regarded him with suspicion. If he went after some dangerous gizmo known to make people superpowerful, there would be plenty of people who'd see it as proof that he was taking after Mom and Dad.

"If you don't want to go, I could go and check it out," I suggested when he didn't say anything.

"No," he said with a sigh. "It could be dangerous. This thing, it wants to be used, and it will draw people to it. Even nonmagical people will want to possess it. Only magical immunes will be safe around it. We'll both go."

"I'll be down in five minutes," I said. I had my purse in my hand before I hung up the phone and possibly broke some land speed records on my way to Owen's basement workroom. He was just locking the manuscript away in its safe when I burst through the doorway. "Ready to go?" I asked between gasps of breath.

He raised an eyebrow. "Are you sure this thing isn't beckoning you?"

"Come on, what woman wouldn't want the chance to go to Tiffany's and count it as work?"

"Does this count as work for you? It's not exactly a marketing activity."

"It's a very loose interpretation of my job description," I admitted. "But it would be a public relations nightmare if somebody tried to use this thing to take over the world." As we headed up to the building's exit, I asked, "Do you think we should tell someone about this?"

7

"I'd rather make sure before I report it. It would be embarrassing if I messed up the translation or the interpretation. We'll report it if we find it. Then Merlin will have to figure out what to do about it."

We took the subway uptown and then walked a couple of blocks to the jewelry store. As we entered, a polite salesman met us. He took in the two of us walking hand in hand and said, "Our engagement rings are on the second floor. The elevator is right this way." Owen turned bright red, and my face felt like it matched his, but to his credit, he didn't release my hand.

"Actually, today we're looking for something different," Owen said. "Something in rare gems."

The salesman nodded and told us we'd also find that on the second floor, while I tried not to get too excited about the fact that Owen had said that "today" he wasn't looking for an engagement ring. We hadn't been dating that long, and most of that time, we'd been busy fighting magical evil, but I already knew I couldn't imagine spending my life with anyone else, and I couldn't help but hope he was thinking along the same lines.

There was already someone at the counter when we got upstairs, and that alone told me that Owen's translation and my interpretation were correct because that someone was an elf. It was too much for coincidence that a member of a magical race was there. The elf was fair-haired—and highlighted, I guessed—with his hair blow-dried back from his face. Every item of clothing he wore bore a designer logo, and it was mostly in pastel shades. I'd thought preppies had died out with the eighties, but this one seemed to have survived.

We edged closer to overhear the conversation, but much to our surprise, the elf wasn't talking about a gem like the Eye of the Moon. He was talking about a Celtic-style golden brooch. "We did have something like that come in just yesterday," the salesman said. "Only, it has a gemstone set in it, a star sapphire."

"A sapphire? Are you sure? The piece I know had no stone," the elf said.

"Oh, it definitely has a stone in it, a rather beautiful one." The salesman's eyes glazed over. "So very, very beautiful."

"May I see it?" the elf asked, sounding a little too eager.

Owen stepped forward then and said, "It wouldn't have been a spherical dark sapphire, would it?"

"Why, yes!" the salesman said. "Do you know this piece?"

"I've heard of it," Owen said, warily eying the elf, who gave him a funny look in response. "But it's not set in a brooch."

"Let me go check. A piece that rare would be kept in a safe," the salesman said.

When he was gone, I asked Owen, "Is that it?"

"It sounds like it."

"But what about this brooch?"

"I don't know." He turned to the elf. "What brooch is this you're looking for? Is it of elven creation?"

"Ah, so you do see my true appearance," the elf said, giving a slight bow. "I am Lyle Redvers. I seek the Knot of Arnhold, which has been lost to my people for centuries. I had a vision of it here today."

"The Knot? Really?" Owen asked. To me he explained, "It's legendary. Supposedly, anyone who wears it is practically invulnerable."

The salesman returned, looking distressed. His eyes were red-rimmed, and he looked like he'd been crying. "Was this the piece you were looking for?" He showed us a printed digital photo of a golden brooch made of interlocked rings with a globe of sapphire set in the middle. The photo was crumpled, as though it had been clutched desperately in someone's grasp.

Owen and Lyle the elf both gasped so hard that it seemed to suck all the air out of the room. "Yes, that is it," the elf said to the salesman, his voice shaking. "I must have it."

"I'm afraid that won't be possible, sir," the salesman said with a mournful sniffle. "That piece was purchased this morning, almost as soon as we opened for business. It's gone." His voice broke in a sob. "We lost it." Then he pulled himself together with some effort and said stiffly, "Is there something else I can show you? We do have several other brooches of similar design. They aren't the same, but then, what is?" His voice trembled again, and there was a loud, wailing sob from the vault area. A bedraggled saleswoman with a blotchy, tear-stained face staggered out, grabbed the photo from the salesman, clutched it against her chest, then stumbled back to the vault, still wailing loudly.

"No, no thank you," the elf said, backing cautiously away from the counter, his hands clenching and unclenching. Then he turned and moved toward the elevator. Owen and I went after him. When we were out of earshot of the salesman, Owen reached to catch the elf's arm, but before he could do so, Lyle turned to Owen. "That stone was the Eye of the Moon, wasn't it?" he hissed.

"I believe so," Owen admitted.

"Combined with the Knot …"

Owen nodded grimly. "Somebody just bought ultimate power and invulnerability."

CHAPTER TWO

I grabbed Owen's sleeve. "Wait, so someone found this superpowerful, super-evil gem that's been lost for centuries, and then they combined it with a brooch that makes the wearer invulnerable? Who would be so crazy?"

"We can worry about that later. For now, we need to find it."

"Do you think whoever has it knows what they have?"

"Even if they don't, it'll affect them. Look at the way the sales staff is acting." The salesman had joined the wailing saleswoman, and their sobs carried throughout the store. "They couldn't have had it for long—definitely not long enough to use its power—and they're acting like they've lost the love of their lives. Anyone who gets this thing won't want to let it go, and that gives the stone the chance to work on them and take over. We've got to get it back."

"The Knot belongs to my people," the elf insisted.

"I'm not arguing with you there," Owen said. "The problem is that both the Knot and the Eye are currently in the possession of someone else."

"Who are you?" Lyle asked suspiciously.

"I'm with MSI," Owen said.

Lyle frowned at Owen. "You're Owen Palmer, aren't you? Is it true?"

Owen sighed wearily. "Is what true? There are so many rumors about me going around that I like to know exactly what I'm confirming or denying. I'm not evil, if that's what you're wondering, and I have no plans to take over the world."

"And yet you seek the Eye of the Moon."

"It wouldn't do me any good." Owen spread his hands helplessly. "No more magic. I found the location in the *Ephemera* I'm translating."

"You have no magic?" The elf quirked a slanted eyebrow.

"None whatsoever. I want to keep this thing out of the wrong hands. That's all. I need to report this to my boss. He should know what's

10

happening, and then we can decide how to handle it. This could be a touchy situation."

"You wizards won't take our Knot from us."

"That's what I mean by touchy. I'm not here officially, but my boss wouldn't want the Eye to fall into the wrong hands."

"I don't want the Eye in Merlin's hands, either."

"I don't think he'd want it. But he will know what to do with it."

The elf nodded again, as if in agreement, and then, moving almost too quickly for the human eye to see, he darted away and jumped into an elevator just as the doors opened. By the time we realized what he was doing and went after him, he was gone. Without magic, Owen couldn't do anything more to summon another elevator than push the button. Lyle must have done something to magically tamper with the elevators, because it took longer than I would have expected for another one to arrive.

I thought Owen would blow a gasket. "He played me!" he sputtered. "I should have known better."

To calm him down while we waited, I said, "He ran off without finding out who bought it. Something like that, you probably don't pay cash. There has to be a record of the sale."

"Yeah, but they don't pass out customer information like that to just anyone." He groaned. "I know how I could get it, but at the moment …" I patted him reassuringly on the arm, well aware of how much it bothered him to have lost his powers. Although he didn't use much magic in his daily life, there had been so many little magical things he'd taken for granted.

"Those two aren't exactly acting like your usual Tiffany employees," I said. I went back to the counter. "Excuse me," I called to the sobbing sales staff.

"I told you, it's useless. It's gone," the salesman sobbed.

"Curse you, Jonathan Martin," the saleswoman spat. "He'll never love it like I did."

"Or like I did," the salesman said, and then they collapsed on each other in tears.

I returned to Owen just as another elevator finally arrived. "Who needs magic?" I said with a grin. "Lyle may have a head start, but we know who bought it." When the elevator let us out on the ground floor, I grabbed Owen's hand and tugged. "Come on, the subway will be quickest for getting back to the office." While I guided him through the crowds on the sidewalk, he called the office to explain the situation.

When we got into the subway station, he kept staring up the tunnel, his fingers twitching like he was trying to magically summon a train. "Come on, come on, come on," he muttered under his breath.

"That spell doesn't work, trust me," I told him, taking his hand so he'd quit trying to use magic he no longer had. "I use it all the time, and for most of us, the more we want a train to come, the slower it will be. What did the boss say?"

"We're to see him as soon as we get back."

"You're not in trouble, are you?"

"I can't tell. I probably should have said something before we went, but I didn't know then, and it wouldn't have made any difference."

A train did finally arrive, and when we got back to MSI headquarters, we headed straight up to the executive suite, where Merlin was waiting for us in his office doorway. And, yes, this was *the* Merlin, the great wizard of legend. He'd been in a kind of magical coma for a long time, waiting to be revived for the magical world's time of great need. It turned out that he'd been revived for a bogus reason, but it looked like he was planning to stick around instead of going back into magical hibernation.

I'd seen Merlin go through a lot of stuff in my time with the company, some of it pretty hairy, but I'd never seen him quite so shaken. He appeared almost feeble. If I'd seen him around town looking like this, I'd have offered to help him cross the street. "Good, good, you're here," he said. "Come in, and we can make plans. I've already got Prophets and Lost tracking down the purchaser."

As soon as we were inside the office, Owen said, "I should have told you when I found the change in the *Ephemera*." He sounded like a schoolboy who'd been called to the principal's office.

"And I should have taken action when I sensed the Eye's arrival early this morning," Merlin said. "I thought I was mistaken. I'd hoped it was impossible."

"You sensed it?"

"You think I wouldn't have felt my own creation?"

Owen looked genuinely surprised. "You?"

"My greatest mistake," Merlin said with a sigh as he lowered himself onto a chair. "In the days when I was a young, inexperienced, and very foolish wizard, I planned to create a gem that would exude a subtle sense of power, so that when set in a crown, it would validate a king's authority. But the spell went horribly wrong. Instead, the gem created a thirst for power while giving its holder great power over others. I was initially able to resist its lure because my spell created it, but before long, it was even affecting me, so I knew I had to do something. I couldn't break the spell or destroy it magically. I tried every physical method I could find at the time to destroy it, from smashing it between rocks to throwing it in a blacksmith's forge, and it survived everything. By the time I created a container that dampened its effects and buried it where it could never be found—or so I thought— war had already broken out over it."

"And now it's back and loose in Manhattan, combined with a brooch that makes the wearer invulnerable," I said, wincing. "This should be fun."

"We must get it back before it does too much harm," Merlin said. "Technology has advanced significantly since my time, so perhaps it can now be destroyed once and for all. If not, it must be hidden again."

"What about the Knot?" Owen asked. "The elves do have a claim to it, and they won't want it destroyed."

"I'm sure they'll survive the disappointment," Merlin said dryly. "They're welcome to file a complaint against me if they have a problem with my decision, but holding on to the Eye long enough to find a way to break the enchantment that binds it to the Knot would be a bigger risk than I care to take."

"If the elves get it, they'll keep it, and I'm not sure I trust them to hand over the Eye—especially once they possess it," Owen said.

"That is why we must find it first. Even there, we will likely have to take it by trickery. The invulnerability of the Knot makes it unlikely that force would be effective in taking it from its new owner."

"Would a magical immune be affected by it?" I asked. "Would it turn an immune evil or power hungry?"

"It shouldn't," Merlin said.

"And what about the invulnerability from the Knot? Maybe an immune could get past whatever magical protection it gives."

"There is no record of anyone wearing the Knot encountering magical immunes," Merlin said. "They don't occur among the elven race, and the Knot was lost long before they began cooperating with mankind."

"So, it's theoretically possible that Owen or I could, say, punch someone wearing the Knot and take it away from them?"

Merlin stroked his beard thoughtfully, and he was quiet for so long that I started to worry about him. "Possibly, possibly, though it would require bare hands, as no weapons would work. Yes, that may be the only solution," he said at last. "Mr. Palmer, I know you regret the loss of your power, but it may be the saving grace in this. You're the only wizard who can be trusted with this mission. You must find and recover the Eye—before anyone else does. It cannot be allowed into the hands of anyone who can be affected by magic."

I tried to make myself invisible, hoping I could get away with tagging along, even though this mission had nothing to do with my actual job. Back when Owen was a powerful wizard, we'd often teamed up because his powers and my magical immunity allowed us to cover each other's weaknesses. Now that he was a trained wizard who was magically immune, I was redundant.

"You'll need help," Merlin said, "and I hesitate to assign anyone susceptible to magic." It took all my self-control not to jump up with my hand in the air and shout, "Ooh! Ooh! Pick me!" As if reading my mind, Merlin turned to me and said, "Miss Chandler is the obvious choice."

"I'd be glad to help, sir," I said, resisting the urge to salute. I knew this was likely to be a difficult and dangerous mission, but I couldn't stop myself from grinning like an idiot. It had been boring not being in danger all the time.

"I don't think we can do this with just immunes, though," Owen said. "The elves have magic. Katie and I can't compete against that. We'll need all the tricks, from the little things like getting through traffic and summoning trains to getting past building security or neutralizing bystanders. And then we may have to fight the competition to get to the brooch."

"This does present us with a dilemma, doesn't it?" Merlin said. "Magic will be essential for finding and reaching the brooch, but then it becomes potentially deadly once we obtain the object of our quest."

"What we need is a tranquilizer gun," I said. "We could have a magical person with us to help with the quest, but then knock him out as soon as we get near the Eye."

I'd meant it as a joke, but both Owen and Merlin turned to me with smiles. "Excellent idea, Miss Chandler," Merlin said, raising an eyebrow.

"I bet R-and-D can whip up something," Owen said, reaching for Merlin's desk phone. "The trick will be finding someone willing to work with us under these circumstances."

"Yeah, knowing you'll be knocked out just when things are getting interesting would be a real turn-off," I said.

"It would require a great deal of trust," Merlin agreed with a sidelong glance at Owen and a fleeting frown. I bit my lip, knowing what that probably meant. Although I had no doubt that Owen was a good guy, and Merlin trusted him completely, not everyone in the company was dealing well with the recent revelations about Owen's heritage. The loss of his powers was about the only thing that made his presence tolerable for a lot of people. There weren't many wizards who'd be eager to join Owen on a quest for one of the most dangerous magical objects ever created, and even fewer who'd be okay with Owen having the ability to knock them out. Even if they gave the tranquilizer job to me, I was so closely associated with Owen that it wouldn't make much difference.

Owen hung up the phone and said, "They've got something they think should work. And what about Rod for magical support? He'd trust me, and he's the best there is at illusion and charm." Rod Gwaltney was Owen's best friend from childhood. He ran the company's personnel department, and he was also an expert wizard.

"Good choice," Merlin said, nodding, as he gave a very subtle sigh of relief. "We can use the security gargoyles for aerial reconnaissance and support. They can track the elves while also clearing the way for your team. Gargoyles are less likely to be susceptible to the Eye. It takes a lot to affect a gargoyle magically."

Owen got on the phone to call Rod and Sam, the head of security. They arrived soon afterward and got a quick briefing. Sam the gargoyle was his usual unflappable self, but Rod was startled by the revelation about the Eye. He cast a worried glance at Owen as he said, "I can see sending the A team, but is this such a great idea? I don't doubt you at all, Owen, but you going after the Eye? It looks a lot like a bid for world power."

"I will deal with any fallout," Merlin said before Owen could answer. "There is no one better suited for this quest, as Mr. Palmer is the one wizard who isn't susceptible to the Eye."

Owen's former assistant, Jake, broke the tension by arriving just then with what looked like a pencil case. "Here you go, three tranquilizer darts." He opened the case to show three long, slender tubes. "You can either press them in directly, like a hypodermic needle, or you can throw them from up to ten feet away. They'll cause instant unconsciousness in anyone, and the effects should last about half an hour, depending on the person's size. Be careful with those. They're all we've got on hand, and it takes about twenty-four hours to brew the potion."

"We'll make them count," Owen said, taking the case from him and slipping it into the inside pocket of his suit coat. "But just in case, you should get started on another batch."

"Now all we need is a target," I said once Jake left.

Just then, Minerva Felps, the head of the Prophets and Lost division that managed the company's seers, swept into the office. If it had been anyone else, I'd have suspected her of lurking outside and waiting for the optimal time to make a dramatic entrance. Minerva had probably sensed five minutes ago when a good time would be. She carried a folder, from which she retrieved a stack of photos and documents that she spread out on the conference table. "Unfortunately, Jonathan Martin is a fairly common name," she said as we came over to the table. "This thing was probably pretty pricey, so I figured we could rule out busboys, bicycle messengers, and anyone else who doesn't earn at least seven figures. That still gave us a lot to sort through. The hackers and the seers ran credit card charges for this morning and looked for shifts in auras and came up with two very strong possibilities."

"Are either of them magical?" Owen asked.

"Would you believe, there isn't a single Jonathan Martin in the entire magical registry? We're in the clear on that count, at least."

"So odds are, whoever has it doesn't know what he's got and didn't buy it on purpose," Owen said. "We're not dealing with a power grab."

"Not a magical one, anyway," Minerva said.

"Can't we just check the manuscript again?" I asked. "If the text changed when it moved before, maybe it could give us an updated location."

"I'm not sure it would be much help, unless it stays in one place for awhile," Owen said. "Remember, someone had already bought it by the time we got to Tiffany's after I was sure of the translation. By the time I translate the new location and figure out what the cryptic, poetic language really means, it may have moved again. It'll probably be quicker to track down the owner, since we do have his name."

Minerva pointed to a photo of a steely-eyed man with close-cropped gray hair. "This one seems like our strongest candidate. His company took over another firm this morning, and there's been a major corporate bloodletting as he's consolidated power. The aura around him is really murky. It's not all-out evil, but it's not sunshine and puppies, either."

"Do you have an address?" Owen asked.

She handed him a printout. "Home, office, and his new acquisition are all on there. The strongest vibes are coming from the new office."

Owen scanned the sheet, then said, "It's just down the street. Let's go."

"I'll fly on ahead, see what might be in the way, and get my people to clear a path for you," Sam said. He waved a hand at a window to open it, then flew out. The rest of us went down the stairs.

We'd just left the building when Owen's cell phone rang. He listened for a moment, then said, "Got it. Thanks." After putting the phone back in his pocket, he said, "Sam says there's a commotion, but there aren't any elves in sight."

"Lyle left before we got the purchaser's name," I said. "Maybe they're still tracking it down the hard way."

I had to jog to keep up with the two guys as we headed downtown. I'd always thought that the way Owen carved his way through a crowd had something to do with magic, but he still managed it. He exuded "I'm on a mission" vibes that made people move out of his way.

When we reached the address, the commotion Sam had mentioned became obvious. A stream of people carrying cardboard boxes poured out of the building's front doors. Some of them were in tears, while others were livid with rage. "I don't think their human resources people are doing a very good job with this," Rod remarked. "It's going to leave a toxic atmosphere among the employees who are left."

"If this guy's on a power binge, he may not care. He'll want them living in fear," Owen said. "Think you can get us into the building and up to the executive floor?"

"If they're smart, they'll have beefed up security to keep disgruntled former employees from getting to the boss, but I can deal with that," Rod said. He whispered a spell and waved his hand, and we walked right past the lobby security guards to the bank of elevators. An elevator opened, and another group of box-carrying people got off. When the elevator was empty, we boarded, and then Rod did something to the control panel so that we went straight up to the executive floor, which should have required a special access key.

I had to yawn to pop my ears as the elevator shot upward. There was something wrong about this scenario, but I couldn't quite put my finger on it. As the elevator slowed, I said, "Would someone on a magical power binge fire everyone, or would he want more minions to do his bidding?"

The two guys looked at me for a moment, frowning. "He might want to choose his minions instead of taking what he got, or he could be testing their loyalty," Owen said. The elevator stopped and the doors opened before we could discuss it further. "You getting anything?" Owen asked Rod softly as we left the elevator.

"You mean like a sudden and inexplicable lust for power that's drawing me toward something? Nope." He raised an eyebrow and grinned. "However, I see something else that's drawing me."

I followed his line of sight and saw a buxom blond receptionist sitting at a desk that looked like it could control the space shuttle. I elbowed Rod in the ribs. "You're dating my roommate," I reminded him through clenched teeth.

"Sorry. I can't help it if my eyes still work." He adjusted his cuffs and straightened his tie. "Leave this to me." He put on his most charming smile and sauntered over to lean on the receptionist's desk.

As Owen and I stood back, watching him work, Owen said, "I was always impressed by how he does this sort of thing, but now I'm even more amazed." Part of Rod's success with women had to do with the fact that he used a handsome illusion to cover his rather plain real appearance. The rest of it was because when he turned on the charm, he did so magically. He'd supposedly stopped using an attraction spell on everyone when he started dating my roommate Marcia, but he hadn't let go of the illusion. I'd always seen his real face, and now that the illusion no longer worked on Owen, he had a best friend who looked totally different from what he'd known since college.

The receptionist tossed back her head and laughed at something Rod said, then he leaned closer and favored her with a huge smile before turning and coming back to us. "I don't think this is it," he said. "It feels wrong, and I don't think someone like her would be out here and happy about it if her boss had the Eye in his office."

Before he finished speaking, Owen was already on the phone to get the information on the other possibility. His magically enhanced phone worked even in the elevator rocketing downward, and when he ended the call, he turned to Rod. "Are you absolutely certain? Because Minerva said the energy around the other Jonathan Martin is happy."

"I'd be happy if I had ultimate power and invulnerability," I said.

"The boss did mention a container that dampens its effects," Rod suggested. "If they put it back in that box when they sold it, he might not be affected by it at all."

"That would make things a lot easier on us," Owen said. "It might also keep the elves from finding him if they're going by seers' signs instead of having a name."

In the building lobby, we got caught up in the mass of box-carrying former employees heading toward the exit. "It's too bad this one wasn't our guy," I said. "Then we might have been able to help these people by taking away his power."

"Then again, if this is what he does with power when it's not magically enhanced, what would he have been like with the Eye?" Owen said before jumping forward to help a woman get her cardboard box full of desk toys, photographs, and potted plants through the front door.

I shuddered. "Good point."

It was now lunchtime, and the downtown sidewalks were even more crowded. Sam led us to the next address by way of alleys and side streets. When he came to rest on the awning over the building entrance, he said, "I'm not seein' any elves around here. We may have beaten them."

"Or it may be the wrong place," Owen said wearily.

"Hey, chin up, kiddo!" the gargoyle said. "There's no point in givin' up this soon. You can't get a strikeout with one pitch."

This building's lobby was more posh than utilitarian. The building was relatively new, but the décor gave the illusion of stability and tradition, with lots of carved dark wood, oil paintings in gilded frames, and upholstered furniture. Rod's magic got us past the lobby security guards to the elevators and then to the restricted executive floor.

The executive lobby was even more posh than the main lobby had been. It looked like the sort of club where men meet to drink brandy, smoke cigars, and call each other "old chap." The receptionist's desk was so large that I had to wonder what the executive's desk was like. You could probably play table tennis on it.

This receptionist wasn't the office trophy wife type. She was the real wife type, which made me suspect that the trophy wife was at home. This was the kind of woman who served as an external brain for her boss, keeping track of all the little details of his life at the office and at home. She was middle-aged, conservatively dressed, and looked exhausted.

She greeted us with a wary smile. "May I help you?" she asked.

"We're looking for Jonathan Martin," Rod said, exuding his usual charm.

Either she was immune to magic or she just didn't waste time on smooth talkers, because she didn't melt the way women usually did when Rod hit them with the full whammy. Instead, she gave him a frosty smile and said, "Mr. Martin has gone to lunch. It's his fiancée's birthday, so I don't expect him back until late."

I thought I detected something familiar in her tone, so I signaled for the guys to let me handle this. "Sounds like his fiancée's a piece of work," I said sympathetically. "Let me guess, she acts like you work for her, too—and they're not even married yet."

She rolled her eyes. "I practically have to curtsy to Her Royal Highness while I'm picking up her dry cleaning and making appointments for her."

"Yeah, I've worked for one like that. And you know Her Highness has to go somewhere really special for her birthday."

"Naturally. I had to make the reservations for the Twenty-one Club weeks ago. He'll get all the credit, of course, though he did get the gift this time, which is an improvement."

Bingo! "Let me guess, something in a little blue box?"

"Nothing but the best for Her Highness."

A gift from Tiffany's looked like proof that this was our guy, and now I knew where he was. "Well, I guess we'll have to call on Mr. Martin later," I said. "Thank you for your help."

"Would you care to leave a message?"

"No, I suspect he'll know what we needed."

Once we were on the elevator, Rod gave me an appreciative nod. "Nice work there, and without even using magic."

I gave what I hoped looked like a modest shrug. "I recognized the look in that woman's eyes when she said the word 'fiancée.' It's the way our receptionist always looked when she talked about our boss." I gave an involuntary shiver. "Just looking at her gave me Mimi flashbacks."

"We still don't know if this is our man," Owen said.

"This one did buy a gift at Tiffany's," Rod pointed out.

"That would explain why the seers aren't getting the sense of power from him," I added. "If he bought it as a gift, he may be keeping it in the protective box. And that means we need to hurry uptown and snag it before he can give her the gift. I don't think we want a woman who can put that look in a receptionist's eyes to have this kind of power."

Sam was waiting for us outside. "We gotta get uptown, right away."

"We're way ahead of you, Sam," Rod said. "That's where we're heading."

"Yeah, but the elves are already on their way. My guys say they're movin' in on Fifty-first Street. Looks like they found it."

CHAPTER THREE

I'd thought we had a head start because we knew the purchaser's name, but apparently the elves could detect the Knot as soon as it came out of the protective box. "Uh oh," I said as I hurried to keep up with the guys, who were hurrying to keep up with a flying gargoyle. "If the elves' seers found the Knot, then that probably means Mr. Martin has already given it to his fiancée. And that means we'll get to deal with the scary dragon lady who now has extra evil power."

"We'll let Rod deal with her while we go after the Eye," Owen said.

"Wouldn't this be faster in a car?" I asked as we ducked down an alley to cut between two streets. "Or at least the subway?"

"We're doin' ya one better, doll," Sam said. "By the time we get back to the office, there'll be a carpet waitin' for you guys."

A flying carpet might have been fast, but it wasn't my favorite way to travel. When I flew, I preferred to have something solid like an airplane around me. Flying carpets were severely lacking in safety features like seatbelts. I was surprised, though, when Owen came to a complete halt and dug in his heels stubbornly. "No. Uh uh. No way on earth."

Rod stopped and turned around. "What?"

"I know how you drive, and I'm not getting on one of those things when you're in control."

"You're welcome to drive if you can find a way to do it without magic," Rod snarled defensively.

"It won't do us much good if we don't get there alive," Owen shot back.

Owen's anxiety was unsettling. I didn't want to do something that scared him this much. He didn't scare easily.

"I'll be careful," Rod said. "Yeah, I may have had a few mishaps, but I've grown up since then."

"Since last year?"

Sam flew back to us. "Boys!" he shouted. "We've got a quest to finish. And neither of you's drivin'. I got one of my people on the job."

That didn't make me feel much better. I'd seen the way gargoyles drove cars. I could imagine how they'd handle something that flew. Fortunately, the driver waiting for us wasn't a gargoyle. He was a small, pixie-like creature whose face was mostly obscured by a pair of plastic goggles. He'd tied two bits of the carpet's fringe around his body in a makeshift seatbelt, and I wasn't sure if that was a good or a bad sign. It might have meant he was safety-conscious, but it could also have meant that he was planning for a wild ride.

Owen helped me onto the hovering carpet, then sat beside me with one arm securely around my waist. I held on to the carpet pile with both hands as Rod climbed up behind the driver. Then the carpet took to the sky and I clamped my lips together so I wouldn't scream.

The driver proved to be very professional. He didn't show off or take unnecessary risks, unless you consider going ridiculously fast to be an unnecessary risk. Buildings sped by in a blur, making it difficult to tell where we were. It was probably the quickest trip uptown I'd ever taken, and we slowed to a stop within minutes. I slid gratefully off the carpet and was surprised to hear Owen's deep sigh of relief when his feet touched solid ground. That made me feel like less of a wimp for wanting to kneel and kiss the sidewalk.

Sam had flown ahead and was meeting with a cluster of gargoyles on a nearby railing. "Bad news, gang," he said as we approached. "The elves are already here."

"What about Martin and his fiancée—and the brooch?" Owen asked.

"It's kinda hard to tell," one of the other gargoyles said in a deep, gravelly voice. I couldn't determine if he was making a horrified face or if that was just the way he'd been carved, but his expression didn't inspire confidence.

"How is it hard to tell?" Rod asked. "It's either here or it isn't."

"It's hard to tell because we can't get inside," the gargoyle said, looking even more horrified. "Somethin's keepin' us out. Magically, I mean. We can't even get close enough to put a rock through a window. But it don't sound good in there."

"That probably means it's here," I said, then tried to swallow the nervous lump in my throat. If the gargoyles were being magically blocked, then that left Owen and me to go into the restaurant, with no magic to protect us.

"I'm not feeling drawn to power," Rod said. "Though it's possible that the wards are blocking its effects, or it could be back in the box."

"I can try to get in," Owen said. "I can get past the wards, and then I can find out what's happening."

"You mean 'we,'" I reminded him.

All of us headed for the restaurant entrance. The row of jockey figures overlooking us made me feel like I was being watched even though I knew they were a famous element of the place and had nothing to do with magic. The carpet driver took a tiny magazine out of his jacket pocket and settled down to read.

Owen and I made it past the iron gates and down the steps from the sidewalk to the entrance, while the others had to stop at the gates. From in front of the door, I could hear the noise the gargoyle referred to. It didn't sound like a typical lunch hour at a high-end restaurant. There was a high-pitched whine like a model airplane engine, along with repeated dull thuds and the occasional sound of shattering glass.

Owen winced at a particularly loud shattering sound, then put his hand on the door handle and glanced at me. "Are you sure you want to do this?" he asked.

"No," I admitted, "but who else can do it? Do you have a plan for once we get in there?"

"We find the Eye, then take it."

"Oh, *that* should be a piece of cake. I don't see *any* potential problems with this plan."

"Well, obviously it'll be more complicated than that, but that's what it boils down to. It will all depend on whether it's there, who has it, and if it's back in the box. And then we'll need to find whoever's warding the place and get them to drop the spell. It feels like elven magic, so my guess is the elves are trying to keep everyone else out until they find the Knot."

"You can tell the kind of magic being used?"

"You can feel magic, can't you?"

"Yeah, but just as a tingle. It doesn't have flavors."

"There are subtle differences in the tingle."

"And that's why it's cool to have a magical immune with wizarding experience. I'm guessing that the wards mean the elves don't yet have the Eye and the Knot."

"Probably not, or they'd be gone by now."

A cry of pain came from inside, and both of us winced. "Maybe we should be armed," I said.

"I've got a pocket knife."

"Oh, then we should be just fine."

"And remember, their magic can't hurt us."

"But flying objects can."

He grinned at that and said, "Ready?" In spite of my misgivings, I nodded, and he eased the front door open. We stepped into a reception area with a cocktail lounge off to the side. The maitre d' was slumped over the reception desk, and all the cocktail lounge patrons were snoring while sprawled on the sofas. It looked like Sleeping Beauty's castle under the sleeping spell. "They've been enchanted," Owen whispered.

"I hope I don't have to kiss anyone to wake them up. Bad things always seem to happen when I kiss someone to break a spell." I whispered my reply, even though I suspected I could have shouted without disturbing their sleep.

The noise was coming from the main room to the rear. We moved cautiously through the short hallway, then paused on the threshold, where I felt more wards. Directly inside the doorway was a pile of wrestling bodies that reminded me of a scramble for a loose ball inside the ten-yard line in a football game.

"It's definitely here," I remarked. "I don't think this sort of thing usually happens over lunch in a place like this."

Owen quirked an eyebrow, "Well, not until the third martini, at any rate."

Both of us instinctively ducked when a dinner plate flew at us, but it bounced off the wards, fell onto the pile of combatants, and then fell off them to shatter on the floor. "I'd bet it's either gone or back in the box," I said. "The activity seems too unfocused, more like people looking for something they lost than like people going after something they want."

"Let's hope it's here and in the box, and then we can get it and get out."

A small airplane that I suspected was normally one of the toys decorating the room's ceiling zoomed past and buzzed a group of elves working their way through the room. "There are the elves," I pointed out, "but I don't think they're the only magic users here."

"There were probably some wizards dining here. It's old-school and it takes a lot of money, which is a combination that draws wizards. Maybe they'll keep the elves occupied for us. We do have an advantage: We know who owns the brooch while they're going by feel. Do you see Martin?"

I didn't have a great view of the entire room from this spot, but I figured it was probably safest to check out the situation from this side of the wards. I'd had only the slightest glance at the photo of this Jonathan Martin when Minerva spread her dossiers on the conference table, and I recalled a fairly generic distinguished older businessman—the kind that would be a dime a dozen in a place like this.

It was also hard to spot any one particular person in all the chaos. In addition to the pileup on the floor and the battling wizards and elves, there was a man standing on his chair and demanding that "it" be given to him, and there were several people sobbing their eyes out. The only people behaving somewhat normally were a somberly dressed older couple sitting in a far corner and watching the proceedings with a distinct air of being Not Amused. They'd probably file a complaint with the management and write a strongly worded letter to the *Times* after this meal. They must have been magically immune, but I decided against trying to recruit them; they didn't look like they'd be much fun to work with.

Then I saw the man sitting alone at a table against the wall, weeping uncontrollably, his shoulders shaking. He looked a lot like what I remembered of the photo, though he seemed frailer than I would have expected. I tapped Owen on the shoulder. "I think that's our guy."

He turned to follow my gaze. "I believe you're right."

"It looks like his fiancée bailed on him."

"But he might know where she'd go, and he can tell us who she is. I don't want the elves getting to him, though—or the other wizards knowing what's going on. I'll create a diversion. You go talk to him."

"What kind of diversion?" I asked, getting an uneasy feeling. "You remember that you don't have powers anymore, right? You can't make it snow indoors, or anything crazy like that."

"I don't need magic. All I need to do is be here." He sighed. "These days, that's enough to get plenty of attention. I'll go in first. Wait until they notice me, then you go."

I was worried about how right he was. Although he'd done nothing to earn it, he was considered Public Enemy Number One by a lot of the magical world. I caught his arm before he crossed the threshold. "Be careful."

"I thought I was the one who was always saying that to you. And what is it you usually say to me? Oh yeah. 'Actually, I was planning to be reckless.'"

"But you usually *are* planning to be reckless."

Instead of responding, he straightened his tie, took a deep breath, and passed through the wards into the dining room. He neatly skirted the combatants still scrambling around on the floor and walked right up to the elves. When one of the wizards said, "Owen Palmer!" and all the elves and the wizards battling them momentarily stopped their fighting to turn to look, I figured that was my cue. I took a deep breath of my own and slipped through the doorway.

I was immediately met by a waiter who was making a visible effort to keep himself under control in the midst of the madness. "Good afternoon, miss," he said. "Do you have a reservation for lunch? I should warn you that things are a bit …unusual today. We might not be able to offer you our usual standard of service."

"That's okay," I told him. "I'm just here to meet someone."

"Very good, miss," he said with a polite nod. "But I do hope you return and enjoy a meal with us."

Since he was neither sobbing nor fighting, I suspected that there was another magical immune and I was tempted to give him my card and tell him to call me, but I'd never seen a waiter that dedicated, and I'd hate to interfere with a true calling like that. Besides, working at a place like this, he probably earned more than he'd make at MSI in the verification department.

I picked my way across the room, stepping around shards of glass and china. When I glanced over my shoulder to see how Owen was doing, I barely stopped myself from crying out a warning as the airplane dove at him. I remembered just in time that he was the diversion, and me shouting would defeat the purpose. He heard the sound and ducked, much to my relief. I forced myself to turn away and focus on my own mission.

When I got closer to Jonathan Martin, I saw that he had deep cuts down his face. He looked like a tigress had clawed him. No wonder the receptionist was afraid of the fiancée, I thought. "Mr. Martin?" I asked tentatively.

He turned to me with an expression that made me want to go read Russian literature to cheer myself up. "She took it. I bought it as a gift, but then it was too beautiful to give, and she took it away from me."

"Is she gone?" I asked. "Where did she go?"

"I don't know. She left. She said she didn't have to put up with this nonsense." He started sobbing then and barely choked out, "We hadn't even had dessert, and I'd arranged for something special."

I took a tissue out of my purse and handed it to him, then patted him on the shoulder. "It's okay," I told him. "Everything will be okay. Maybe it'll make you feel better to tell me about her."

He blew his nose into the tissue. "I don't know what I'll do without her."

"Surely she hasn't gone forever. You'll see her soon."

"She won't need me now. She has it. She can have anything she wants."

"I doubt that's true. Look at you, what woman wouldn't want someone like you?" Well, what gold digger wouldn't, but I was too nice to say that.

A tiny glimmer of hope shone in his eyes. "You think so?"

"Of course. I could even talk to her for you. Just tell me how I can find her." Really, all I needed was her name, but since I was acting like I knew her to get him to talk to me, I could hardly come right out and ask it.

"She has some thing tonight—one of her projects. That's why we had to celebrate her birthday at lunch."

Now we were getting somewhere. "What thing? She has so many projects, you know." I gave a little laugh, like I was well aware of the mystery woman's foibles.

"A gala. I'm not going. She said it was far too late for me to be out. Past my bedtime. My Sweetie-pie looks after my health, you know."

I tried not to wince. It sounded like the poor man needed an intervention. The woman must have been using his money to gain a social position for herself while cutting him out of society. "That's very considerate of her," I said halfheartedly. "You don't know where the gala

25

will be or what it's about?"

"Sweetie-pie said I shouldn't worry myself."

But what is Sweetie-pie's name? I wanted to shout, but I suspected that yelling at him would only make him cry. Surely it wouldn't be too hard to track down a billionaire's fiancée who was involved in a gala happening that night. I thought I'd try one last line of questioning where he might be more helpful. "When she took it away, was it in a box?"

"It was in a jewelry case lined with dark velvet." His eyes went unfocused as he added, "It was so beautiful nestled in that little box, the gold and the sapphire against the velvet. I never should have given it to her. It should have been mine." He broke down in sobs again.

There was a surge of magic from across the room, followed by a series of thuds, and I looked up to see the people I assumed were wizards slumping to the floor. The elves had just lost their distraction, which meant it was time to get away from Martin before the elves noticed me with him.

I gave Mr. Martin one more pat on the shoulder before standing up. He tried to hand me the tissue I'd given him, but I smiled and said, "You can keep it."

"Thank you so much," he sobbed.

"And you should probably see a doctor about those scratches on your face. You don't want those getting infected."

He clutched my hand. "You're so kind to care."

Feeling guilty about leaving him, I hurried back across the room to stand at Owen's side as Lyle Redvers, the elf from the jewelry store, said, "Palmer, I'm sure you didn't come here just to interrupt our search."

"Actually, I heard they serve a good lunch here."

"I know what you're after, Palmer."

"Yes, I realized that when you gave us the slip at Tiffany's, but we're both too late. It's not here."

"How do you know? I thought you lost the magic."

Owen gestured at the lingering madness. "Does this look like anyone's in possession of the Eye?"

I folded my arms defiantly across my chest and said, "Yeah, face it, Elvis has left the building."

"Did you let it go?" Owen asked.

"'Let' is not the word I would use," Lyle said with a haughty sniff. "I sensed its presence here, but I believe it had already gone before we arrived."

"Serves you right for tearing out of the jewelry store and trying to cut us out of things," I said.

"You would have done better?" Lyle asked, arching a slanted eyebrow.

"We don't have magic, and yet, we're here," Owen said. "This would probably work better if we cooperated. We have information on the owner, and we have people who are immune to the effects of the Eye. You can sense the Knot and use magic to help obtain it."

"What do you plan to do with the Eye?" another elf demanded.

"Destroy it."

"And the Knot?"

"Take that up with Merlin."

"How can we trust you?" Lyle asked.

"We could ask the same of you. The dangerous part of the brooch is ours, and we can't risk it falling into the wrong hands."

"You think ours are the wrong hands?"

"I think *any* hands are wrong."

"Other than yours, apparently."

"Like I said, no magic. I'm immune. It wouldn't affect me."

"How can we believe that?"

Owen shook his hands in frustration, looking like he was barely restraining himself from strangling the elf. "You saw all the power that the wizards threw at me and that you threw at me, and nothing happened. Not to mention the fact that I got past your wards. I can't use the Eye. I might even be able to separate it from the Knot, if it can be done physically."

"I will consider your offer and suggest it to the Elf Lord," Lyle said stiffly.

"Great. Now, drop the wards and let these people go."

"Do you think that is a wise idea?"

All of us looked around at the fighting or sobbing patrons. I imagined them being turned loose on the city to hunt down the gem. "Well, probably not," I said. "Maybe you could give them the Sleeping Beauty treatment, like you did to the people in front and to these wizards. You could throw in a little memory adjustment, while you're at it."

The elf gave me a surprised glance, then nodded. "Yes, we could do that." He waved his arms, and everyone in the room, aside from the elves, Owen, the waiter, and me, settled down into sleep. I was surprised that the stern-looking couple also fell asleep. I'd been so sure that they were immune. Maybe they just had a lot of self-control. "Now, we will return this place to its normal appearance. We know where to find you if we decide to accept your offer."

"Thank you," Owen said, then he took my arm and led me out of the club. I shivered as I looked at the people who'd fallen asleep in mid-squabble. If being in the same room with the thing made people that crazy, it wouldn't be easy to get it away from the future Mrs. Martin.

I noticed that Owen was bleeding from a cut on his forehead and asked, "Are you okay?"

He touched the cut, then frowned at the bloody fingertips he brought back. "I think so. I just had a bit of a Hitchcock moment back there with that airplane."

"You've seen *North by Northwest*, but not *Breakfast at Tiffany's*?"

"It had spies in it! That's different."

We joined the others outside, and I quickly explained what I'd learned from Martin, then Owen told them about the elves.

Sam snorted. "I don't trust elves."

"Really?" I asked. "We have lots of elves at MSI."

"Oh, I trust *them*. But these guys work for the Elf Lord, and he's a real piece of work. You can't believe a thing his people say. It may be the truth, but it's all spun up in riddle and different meanings for words, and stuff like that, so they can tell the absolute truth and still be dishonest."

While Sam ranted, Owen called the office to update Merlin. "They'll try to track down the fiancée," he said when he finished his call.

"What should we do?" I asked.

With a shrug, he said, "We may as well go back to the office and help. There's not much else we can do until we have a target."

"We'll keep an eye on the elves while you kids check in with the boss," Sam said. "I wanna make sure they don't get up to no funny business."

As we boarded the magic carpet, I glanced back at the club, thinking I'd seen something out of the corner of my eye. I hadn't counted the number of jockeys along the front of the building on my way inside, but it seemed like there were more of them now. And if I wasn't mistaken, one of them had a beard.

That was kind of weird, but the way this day was going, it only came in at about a four on a weirdness scale of one to ten. I was about to say something to Owen when I noticed something even more alarming, a man wearing a trenchcoat that was entirely too heavy for the weather, with a hat pulled low over his eyes. The carpet was already rising, so by the time I got Owen's attention to point the man out, we'd reached the end of the block.

"It's probably just one of my usual followers," Owen said with a shrug. "They want to make sure I'm not up to anything evil. I'm getting used to it."

"But if they find out about the Eye and learn it was there, they'll know you were after it."

"I don't intend to do anything with it that would give them a reason to worry. In fact, maybe it's better that I have official witnesses along the way. Then nobody can accuse me of anything." I would have expected him to say something like that with bitterness, but he was remarkably cool about it, if perhaps a bit weary.

Even though the restaurant was well out of sight by this time, I couldn't help glancing back over my shoulder to see if we were still being watched.

CHAPTER FOUR

Much to my horror, the flying carpet didn't let us off at ground level when we reached MSI headquarters. Instead, it stopped and hovered in front of the open window of Merlin's tower office. It was bad enough getting off one of those things when it was a few feet off the ground. Stepping from the carpet to a window ten stories up in the air was sure to give me nightmares for the rest of my life. Rod had the longest legs, so he made the jump into the building and then helped Owen and me across the terrifying gap. Once inside, I clung to Rod until I convinced myself that I really did have a solid floor under my feet. I'd never had a bad fear of heights, but if I had to travel by flying carpet too many more times, I thought I might develop one.

A tray of sandwiches on the conference table reminded me that it was lunchtime. I decided to wait until my stomach made it the rest of the way downtown before I tried to eat. Owen also looked a little green, but Rod leaned over and grabbed a sandwich and took a big bite before he picked up a plate.

Minerva Felps then burst into the office, making another dramatic entrance. "Unfortunately, engagements aren't a matter of public record, so we can't just get the documents from the courthouse, and not everyone gets a write-up in the *Times*," she said. "We're digging, though. I've got my people reading his cards, and then the hackers are looking for wedding registries and cross-referencing that with any galas happening tonight. Oh, and Katie? Your roommate's looking for you—the glamorous one."

No sooner had she left with Rod to do further research than Trix, Merlin's fairy receptionist, came in and said, "Katie, Perdita called and said Gemma was looking for you. She's at work."

While Merlin and Owen discussed possible ways to destroy the Eye, I used Merlin's desk phone to call Gemma. "Wow, you've been out of the office all morning," she said when she answered.

"I'm on a quest."

"In your line of work, I have a feeling I should take that literally."

"You should. What's up?"

"I checked the voice mail at home, and there was a call saying you need to pick up your grandmother at Penn Station."

"What?"

"You weren't expecting her?"

I shook my head, even though I knew she couldn't see me. "No. When did she call?"

"A few hours ago."

"My grandmother's been at Penn Station all morning? How did she get there?"

"I'm guessing on a train."

"Very funny. But my grandmother has barely left the county. There's no way she'd come all the way to New York without making a big production out of it. I'd have known about it weeks in advance."

"Hey, all I know was that there was a message from her saying she was at the station and she needed you to get her."

"Great. This is just what I needed," I said with a groan. I was about to hang up when I got an idea. Gemma worked in fashion at one of the designer houses, so she might know some of the local high-rollers. "Maybe you could help me with something. There's supposedly some big gala going on tonight, being put on by the fiancée of a financial big-wig billionaire named Jonathan Martin. She sounds like a real gold digging type—using a rich old man to buy her way into society, where she can soon enjoy a wealthy widowhood. I need to get her name."

"I know the type, but the name doesn't ring a bell. I could check around, though. Where should I call if I find something?"

"Owen's cell."

"Someday you'll have to join us in the twenty-first century and get your own cell phone."

"But then people could find me. Thanks a lot, Gem."

I got off the phone, still puzzling over what to do with Granny. She was a wizard, and if she'd chosen now to leave Texas for the first time in her life, I suspected it was because she felt there might be trouble. Had she sensed something about the Eye? Considering all the trouble I'd been through in the past year without her making the trip, that worried me. If I could get away to pick her up, I could probably leave her with Merlin while I was questing. She and Merlin got on pretty well and had a lot to talk about.

But before I could let Owen know about needing to get Granny, the office doors blew open and a slight fog billowed around the floor. The

Celtic version of elevator music tinkled in the background as three figures strode through the doorway and paused to pose against the backdrop of a golden light that couldn't possibly have been natural, given that there was no window behind them. A wind that couldn't have been natural, either, stirred the fog and made their cloaks billow dramatically.

Now back to his normal self, with no trace remaining of the feebleness he'd shown earlier, Merlin gave a casual wave, and then the music, light, fog, and wind disappeared, revealing three elves who would have looked pretty ordinary if it weren't for the pointed ears and slanted eyebrows. The billowing capes turned out to be trench coats that had been left unbuttoned and unbelted. One of the elves was Lyle, still looking like the height of eighties preppy fashion (he even had the collar of his coat turned up). The one in the middle appeared to be in charge. He had an eighties-vintage Michael Douglas look about him—slick, expensive suit, wavy hair blow-dried back from his forehead, and a firm chin. He gave the impression that he was ready to stage a corporate takeover at any minute.

The third elf seemed like part of a "which one doesn't belong?" exercise. He was younger than the other two—which meant he might have been only about a hundred years old while looking twenty-two—and instead of wearing expensive-looking clothes and a trench coat, he wore a faded *War Games* T-shirt and baggy jeans with an unzipped hooded sweatshirt. The points of his ears stuck up through messy hair. He looked more like a geeky college student dressed up as an elf for a science fiction convention than like an actual elf. I was tempted to see if the points of his ears came off.

If the elves were mad at Merlin for taking away their special effects, they didn't show it. They still posed as though the spotlight was on them. They seemed to be having a staring contest with Merlin to see who would blink first—or speak first. I wasn't sure if it was a defeat or a victory when Merlin finally said, "Sylvester, what brings you here?"

The head elf did blink at that. I got the impression that he and Merlin had never met and that Merlin wasn't supposed to know his name. "I heard Merlin had returned," he said. "You are he?"

"I am."

"Oh."

And then a wave of magic so strong it made the little hairs on my arms stand at attention swept the room, going back and forth between Merlin and Sylvester. It didn't feel angry or vicious, more like a testing. A nimbus formed around Merlin, making him glow and blur ever so slightly. As soon as it appeared, one like it developed around Sylvester. Suddenly, all the magic stopped. Merlin and Sylvester appeared entirely unruffled, but I felt like I had to catch my breath. Owen's gasp next to me reassured me that I wasn't the only one.

"You *are* Merlin," Sylvester said.

"Why, yes, I believe I said that earlier," Merlin replied with a thin smile. "Do come in and have a seat. Would you care for a sandwich?"

The three elves swept across the room. Sylvester and Lyle took seats at the conference table, leaving the third elf to stand behind them, shifting his weight uncomfortably from foot to foot. There were plenty of seats, so there was no reason for him to stand. "Go ahead and have a seat," I told him, giving him a welcoming smile.

"He doesn't need a seat," Sylvester said sharply, making the poor guy flinch. Then Sylvester narrowed his eyes at me. "I recognize Palmer, but who is she?"

"Miss Chandler works for me," was all Merlin said. "Now, was there something you wanted to discuss? I hear your people have been trying to find the Knot of Arnhold, which has been inconveniently bonded with the Eye of the Moon."

"Yes, that has been on the agenda today," Sylvester agreed, smiling thinly. "As you have been seeking the Eye of the Moon."

"That is rather a priority for us. You see, I remember the last time it was free in the world. Several wars began, killing thousands. I would prefer that not happen again. And why is it that you seek the Knot?"

"Because it belongs to me," the elf lord said through gritted teeth. "It was stolen from my people."

"There's no other reason, then?" Merlin asked mildly. "You wouldn't be planning to use it to gain invulnerability for yourself in, say, a power struggle?"

Sylvester gave another thin smile. "I have no immediate plans to use it. It is merely part of the traditional regalia of my office. Does the queen of England have a practical use for the crown jewels?"

"The crown jewels don't have magical powers," I muttered under my breath.

"Not anymore," Owen whispered in response.

I made a mental note to follow up on that later as the conversation between Sylvester and Merlin intensified. "I'm more concerned about your plans for the Eye," Sylvester said. "As you said, it is very dangerous."

"My plan is to destroy it or neutralize it so it can do no more harm," Merlin said.

Sylvester raised an eyebrow and smirked. "So you say now, but would you really be able to do that once you had it in your possession? I could imagine how tempting ultimate power would be for you. After all, you do need to consolidate your position in this century, when you're not so closely aligned with political power. It must be difficult for you not pulling a king's strings."

"I have no intention of going anywhere near the Eye," Merlin responded, sounding deceptively unruffled. I'd worked with Merlin long enough to recognize the signs of a calm that heralded a storm. "The people I've assigned to this project are immune to its power. To them, it's just another rock."

Sylvester glanced at Owen. "Yes, I'd heard that about Palmer. It's true?"

"I tested him," Lyle said. "If he were magical, he'd be dead."

The elf left standing opened his mouth as if to add something, but before he could speak, Lyle said, "We don't need to hear it, Earl."

"I suppose the girl is immune, too?" Sylvester asked Merlin.

"Yes. As I said, I can trust them to find the Eye without being tempted to use it."

"They may not be magically tempted, but it is still a valuable gem, even without power. Can they resist that temptation?"

"I'm actually not that big on jewelry," I said with a shrug. Turning to Owen, I added, "It does match your eyes, though."

"It's too gaudy for my taste," Owen said. "I prefer my evil accessories to be more subtle." Behind Sylvester, Earl smirked, then quickly straightened his expression.

"For now I'll take your word that your people won't use the Eye for themselves," Sylvester said. "But without magic, how will they destroy it?"

"We figured we'd climb Mount Doom and throw it in," I quipped, which earned a fleeting grin from Earl.

Ignoring my interruption, Merlin said, "It can't be destroyed magically. Believe me, I tried, and though magic has adapted over time, it hasn't fundamentally changed in such a way that we can do things now that were impossible then. Technology, however, has changed significantly."

Earl opened his mouth again, but Sylvester waved him to silence, saying, "We don't need your input, Earl." I wondered why they'd bothered to bring him. They must have needed something to step on to get into their car. I gave him a sympathetic smile, but he didn't respond. "And what of the Knot?" Sylvester asked Merlin. "What happens to it when you're destroying the Eye?"

"That would depend on which technology works to destroy the Eye," Merlin said. "If the two can be safely separated, we will return the Knot to you."

"Gold does have a lower melting point than sapphire," Owen said, earning another smile from Earl.

"We could give you what's left," I added.

Merlin gave us a stern glare before continuing. "But we don't even know how they were joined—are they merely joined physically, perhaps by a jeweler who was immune to magic and didn't realize what he was doing, or were they fused magically by someone who planned to combine their powers? Do you have any idea who stole the Knot?"

"It was long before my time," Sylvester said with a shrug, and I imagined that meant it was a very long time ago, indeed. "It is possible that the fusion was recent, and it is the combination with the Eye that made the Knot powerful enough for Lyle to sense." I couldn't read Earl's expression as Sylvester said this, but he definitely had an expression.

"I think the fact that this was done at all is of some concern to all magical races," Merlin said. "Who did it, and why? This is as important as retrieving the brooch."

"Your man—" Sylvester indicated Owen "—suggested we work together on this. Why should we assist you?"

"I rather thought of it as us assisting you," Merlin said mildly. "My priority is to find this thing and render it harmless as soon as possible. That's more likely to happen if we combine our resources. If you prefer not to cooperate with us, I would understand." His tone sharpened considerably as he added, "But rest assured, I will not allow you to keep the Eye if you do find it first. I will get it back, no matter what it takes."

Sylvester stared at him, unblinking, for a long time, but he was the first to break the gaze. He did so in the guise of shoving his chair back from the table. "It's good to know exactly where we stand. I'm sure we'll be speaking again within the next day or so." He stood, and Lyle popped up beside him. Earl barely got out of the way before they trampled him on their way out, then had to hurry to catch up with them. As they left the office, the golden light, Enya music, fog, and soft breeze returned, along with a faint peaty scent, but Merlin cut it off again with a gesture and waved the office doors shut.

He then turned to face Owen and me. "You will find it first." It was an order.

"Yeah, I have to agree with Sam," I said. "I don't trust this guy."

"He'd definitely keep the Eye and use it if he got it," Owen added. "I'm not even sure I want him in possession of the Knot."

"It belongs to him by right," Merlin said with a heavy sigh. "That's why it would be a real pity if it were destroyed along with the Eye."

Owen and I exchanged a glance. It sounded like we'd been given another order. "The elves won't like that," Owen said.

"If it can't be helped, it can't be helped, and they can take it up with me if they're unhappy. At any rate, we need to find it before we can destroy it."

My stomach growled, and I figured that meant it had finally rejoined me after the magic carpet ride, so I leaned forward and picked up a sandwich. "I wonder how Rod and Minerva are doing on tracking down the fiancée," I said.

Of course, that was the moment when Minerva opened the office doors and entered with Rod in her incense-scented wake. "This is not gonna be easy," she said. "Would you believe, several of the Jonathan Martins we've found are engaged, and we haven't yet figured out which one goes with which."

"Doesn't the fact that today is her birthday help narrow it down?" I asked.

"Not as much as you'd think. It takes a little more hacking to get that kind of info, and believe it or not, the Social Security Administration and the Department of Motor Vehicles have pretty good magical firewalls."

"Then you could look for the Jonathan Martin with the aura of having his life sapped out of him by an evil vampire woman."

She shook her head sadly. "Sorry, honey, but when you're dealing with wealthy old men, that doesn't narrow it down much. They're usually being drained by somebody. There are also a lot of charity galas going on tonight. Did you get from Martin whether his chippy is really running hers or maybe just on the board?"

"I got that he wasn't entirely sure what was going on, other than that he wasn't invited because it was past his bedtime and she was concerned for his health."

She tossed aside one of the sheets of paper she held. "That rules out that one. He's listed as a cochair. That would mean he's invited. One of the galas tonight is at Grand Central, but I guess that doesn't do you much good until then."

"Oh my gosh!" I gulped, clapping my hand to my mouth in horror as the mention of Grand Central triggered a recollection. "My grandmother's at Penn Station waiting for me to pick her up."

"Your grandmother came for a visit?" Merlin asked, looking far too pleased about that for my comfort.

"Not a planned one. I only just found out she was here. I don't know what's going on, but she's been there long enough to have caused all kinds of trouble."

"You had better go get her while we continue our research," Merlin said. "You could take the carpet."

I shook my head. "Oh, no, we don't want Granny on a magic carpet. She'd insist on driving. That is, if she didn't object to riding something so small and sporty. She'd insist on a room-sized rug."

Owen put a comforting hand on my arm—he'd met my grandmother and knew what I meant—and said, "We could take the carpet up there to get there faster, then send her back here in a cab. Odds are that any of these women will be uptown, anyway, so we'll be closer to our next stop when Minerva finds something we can use."

"We could always sic Granny on the elves," I suggested hopefully.

"I would prefer to be able to maintain somewhat cordial relations with them," Merlin said with a perfectly straight face. Only the twinkle in his eye gave him away.

"And I have no idea what to do with her while she's here. We don't have a guest room. Maybe Nita can get her a room in the hotel where she works."

"I've got a guest room," Owen said. "She can stay with me."

"Are you sure about that?"

"It won't be any trouble at all."

"I'll owe you, big time." I had no doubt that he loved me, but if he was willing to have my grandmother under his roof, then that was a true sign of devotion.

The flying carpet reappeared outside Merlin's window, and he said, "You should go to the station. We will notify you if we find anything. In the meantime, I will focus my efforts on learning who could have—and would have—stolen and fused the Knot and the Eye. Whoever that is would be very dangerous, and letting that brooch loose on the world may be part of a greater agenda."

As if I didn't have enough to worry about, I thought. It was almost enough to make the prospect of another magic carpet ride less frightening. It wasn't, however, enough to make stepping out of a tower window onto a hovering magic carpet less frightening. "You should install jetways for these things," I said as I screwed up the courage to make the jump after Rod got on and extended his hand to help me. The carpet wobbled alarmingly as I boarded, and then again when Owen got on.

"Penn Station, my good man," Rod told the tiny driver, and soon we were flying up Broadway. I suspected that in addition to the magical veil that kept people from seeing a flying carpet, there was a magical windshield that protected us from the full force of the air rushing past us at that speed—and from getting bugs in our teeth. My hair still blew around a little, but it was easier to conduct a conversation on a magic carpet than in a convertible with the top down on a highway.

"Why's your grandmother visiting?" Owen asked me.

"I have no idea. One of my family's weird magical powers is the ability to sense my stress levels so they can be sure to do something to escalate them. My mother was probably too busy to come bother me during this crisis, so she sent Granny."

"I don't know, I can't imagine your grandmother ever being sent anywhere by anyone. She either goes of her own accord or doesn't go at all."

"And you still want her in your house?"

"I'm used to Gloria, remember?" Gloria was his foster mother, an elderly wizard just as fierce as my grandmother, though in different ways. "Besides, when I was in Texas, she talked to me some about potions, and I'd like to pick her brains. There's plenty of potential research material there that doesn't require magic."

We passed over Union Square—or, rather, an open and partially greenish blur that I assumed was Union Square. I jumped and clutched Owen's arm when something suddenly appeared in the air beside us, matching our speed. It took me a second to recognize Sam.

"I think you've picked up a tail," he shouted.

I turned to look behind us. There were no other magic carpets in sight, and Sam was the only other flying thing I saw. "Where?" I asked.

"Look up."

All of us on the carpet—other than the driver, fortunately—tilted our heads back to see a hawk wheeling in the sky over us. "A bird?" I asked.

"The elves have got some tame ones workin' for 'em," Sam said. "Featherbrained turncoats," he added with a snarl.

"Do you know if this one is working for them?" Rod asked.

"Not sure yet, but better safe than sorry. Look out, and see if you can lose her."

The driver didn't say anything, but the carpet banked steeply to the left. I whimpered as I felt myself sliding, but the carpet soon leveled itself out as we headed straight up one of the avenues. "Why does it even matter if they follow us?" I asked when I caught my breath. "We're not on the mission right now. We're going to pick up my grandmother at the train station."

"They don't know that," Owen said.

"Yeah, but we'd be leading them straight to my grandmother."

"I have to admit, there's some appeal to that thought."

"We need to at least pretend to evade them," Rod said. "That's a big part of the game. They'll be suspicious if we make it too easy."

The carpet made another sharp turn and headed crosstown for a while before turning abruptly downtown. A few blocks later, we turned crosstown for a block and then back uptown. An overhead glance didn't reveal the bird, but I doubted we could hide from it for long. The carpet lowered, then stopped to let us off on a side street. There we blended as well as we could into the usual midtown crush of pedestrians and headed to the station.

"Do you know where you're supposed to meet your grandmother?" Owen asked as we approached the station.

"No idea. But if I know Granny, we won't have to look too hard. She'll be causing the kind of commotion that draws attention. I don't know how long ago she called, but she may even have been there long enough to take over. We might be just in time for her coronation."

Owen's cell phone rang, and after a brief conversation, he closed it and reported, "Minerva's people found a personal shopper reservation at Macy's for a woman with the same name as one who's engaged to a Jonathan Martin. They don't know if she's in any way connected, but since we're nearby, we may as well check it out after we find your grandmother." He checked his watch. "We've got about half an hour."

As we rode the escalator down into the station, I said, "Listen for someone loudly criticizing something. That'll be Granny."

"Do you know if she came in on Amtrak or on New Jersey Transit from the airport?" Rod asked. "That could help us figure out where she might be."

"I have no idea, as I said. For all I know, she flew in on her broom and thought this would be a convenient meeting place."

We'd reached the food court area of the station, and I started to fear that I'd been overly optimistic in assuming I could easily find my grandmother. Even as colorful a character as she was could be lost in these throngs and in this noise. She wouldn't even be the craziest person in this place.

But then I heard a piercing voice ringing above the din. "I think I've found her," I said, grabbing Owen's arm. The three of us followed the sound and found a group of young thugs cowering in a corner as a tiny old woman menaced them with her cane.

"Now, give the lady back her purse," she said, giving one of the guys a threatening poke with the cane. He nervously glanced at her before meekly stepping forward and handing a purse to the harried young mother standing next to Granny. "Everything's in there, right?" Granny asked him. He nodded mutely, and Granny turned to glance at the woman. "Check it out, honey," she said, more gently.

The woman opened the purse and checked through it. "It doesn't look like anything's missing," she reported.

"Okay, then, I won't shrink your manhood to the size of a boiled peanut," Granny told the guys, who all flinched. "Now, what do you say to the lady?"

"Uh, we're sorry?" one of the guys ventured.

"And?" The cane made a menacing move.

"And, um, we won't do it again?"

"That's right, you won't. And if you do, well, let's just say you'll have to buy smaller undershorts. I've already set the curse, so if you break your word, it'll happen, whether or not I'm around."

"Wow, her first day here, and she's already cleaning up crime," Rod muttered. "The mayor may want her to stay."

The thugs nodded wide-eyed at her, then slunk away. The purse's owner turned to Granny. "I don't know how to thank you," she said. "I don't know what I'd have done if you hadn't caught them. My whole life is in this bag." She opened her wallet, took out a bill, and tried to hand it to Granny, but Granny shook her head.

"No, I'm just looking out for my neighbor like the good Lord says to do. You go on and have a good day."

The woman shifted the baby on her hip, reshouldered her purse and said, "Well, thank you very much."

When she was gone, I stepped forward to approach Granny, but froze when a gruff voice behind me said, "So, now you're bringing in an outside wizard for the search. What do you have planned for when you get that brooch?"

CHAPTER FIVE

I slowly turned around to see a bearded gnome wearing a track suit with white pants, a yellow jacket, and a baseball hat. There was something awfully familiar about him. If those white pants were tucked into tall boots, if he posed properly, and if I saw him out of the corner of my eye, he'd look like … "You!" I blurted. "You're the extra jockey! I knew I saw something at the restaurant."

"Aw, you spotted me back there?" the gnome grumbled. "I thought that was a pretty good disguise, even if I hadn't also used some magic."

"Your magical veiling doesn't work on me," I said. "And I haven't seen too many jockeys with long, white beards."

"You saw him before?" Owen asked me.

"He was hiding among those jockey statuettes in front of Twenty-one. I guess I got distracted by that other guy I saw and forgot to say anything." To the gnome, I said, "But how did you find us here?"

"I've got my ways," he said, stroking his beard.

"The hawk works for you, not the elves," Owen concluded.

The gnome's bushy white eyebrows shot up. "You spotted the hawk?"

"I thought we evaded that hawk," Rod said with a scowl.

The gnome chortled. "Yeah, you thought you did."

"There you are, Katie," Granny said, spotting me. "Where have you been? I've been waiting all day."

I gave her a hug and a kiss on the cheek. "I'm sorry, Granny, but I only just got the message. I didn't know you were coming."

"It was an emergency. I didn't have time to call."

My heart leapt as I imagined all the horrible things that could have happened to my family. "Oh no! What is it?"

"I don't know yet. But something's about to happen to you, I can feel it in my bones, and you'll need me there when it does."

That was even more alarming. I reached for Owen's hand and clutched it as I said, "Something's going to happen to me? Something bad?"

"Good, bad, who can say? I just know that you'll need me here, and I want to be ready when the time comes." She turned to fix Owen with her beady eyes. "Good to see you again, boy." Then she frowned. "My, but you've changed. What happened to you?"

Owen winced. "It's a very long story."

"Granny, Owen has offered to let you stay in his guest room," I said, changing the subject before she could demand the whole story, right there in the station. "We don't have room for guests in our apartment, and Owen's place is nicer than a hotel."

"That's kind of you," she said, then she smiled at Rod. "And you're here, too. What a welcoming committee. I guess if you can't get here on time, you bring more people."

"And it's nice to see you again, Mrs. Callahan," Rod said smoothly.

She fluttered her eyelashes at him and extended her hand to let him kiss it gallantly. "It's good to see that someone in this city knows how to treat a lady."

"Hey, excuse me, but I wasn't finished!" the gnome said, elbowing his way into the middle of the group.

"Manners, little man," Granny scolded with a warning shake of her cane. "You don't talk to ladies like that—or gentlemen, either, for that matter. What do people teach their children around here?"

The gnome ignored her as he focused on Owen. "Now, as I was saying, I want to know what you people have planned for that brooch. It looks like you've got a whole operation going on here."

"We're trying to *find* that brooch," Owen said.

"I can see that, son. I've got two perfectly good eyes. I've also got a perfectly good battleaxe, and I'll start swinging it if I don't get a straight answer soon."

I bit down on my tongue to stop myself from telling him that we also had a perfectly good battleaxe, and that she was probably sharper and more dangerous than his. Granny might take offense at that.

"We want to make sure the brooch doesn't fall into the wrong hands, and when we do find it, we want to destroy the Eye to make sure it can never be used again," Owen explained patiently. "Now, what is your interest in the brooch?"

"It's an epic story of the sort that should be shared over food and ale."

"We don't have time for that right now. Short version?"

"Let's just say we have similar goals—and I'm here to make sure you people aren't the wrong hands. I'm also hoping that by following you, I might be able to find and catch some of those wrong hands."

"What's this brooch?" Granny asked.

"A very bad magic thing," I explained. "Makes everyone around it crave power while making the wearer extra powerful and invulnerable."

She snorted. "Any wizard worth his salt doesn't need that sort of trinket. If you can't do it on your own, then you don't deserve the power."

All of us turned to stare at her, and I gave an involuntary shudder. I'd only recently learned that my grandmother had magical powers, and now I had to wonder what, exactly, she could do.

"Why have you brought this powerful outside wizard?" the gnome asked. "Don't you realize that someone like her would be dangerous around the Eye?"

"She's not an outside wizard," I said. "Well, she is, but she's my grandmother, who picked a very interesting day for a visit."

The gnome turned to frown at her. "This is true, lady?"

She pulled herself to her full height, which wasn't much taller than the gnome. "Do I look like the sort of person who lies?" she said, her tone so icy it made me shiver. "I do my magic the old-fashioned way, without trinkets. If it doesn't come naturally, I've got no use for it."

He stared at her for a long time while she returned his stare, then at last he nodded. "You, I trust." He turned back to us. "This bunch, on the other hand …"

"Hey!" I protested.

Rod stepped forward with his hand outstretched and said in his most charming tone, "Rod Gwaltney, MSI. Glad to meet you."

The gnome frowned. "You're MSI?"

"All of us are," Rod said. "Allow me to introduce my colleagues. This is Katie Chandler, magical immune extraordinaire and granddaughter of Mrs. Callahan, our esteemed visiting wizard. The gentleman is Owen Palmer."

The gnome took a step backward, pulling a tiny double-headed axe from under the back of his track suit jacket. He hissed through his teeth as he glared at Owen. "Palmer? After the Eye? I don't like this."

Owen held his hands up in a halfhearted gesture of surrender. "I'm getting really tired of this," he said. "A: I'm not evil. Never have been, never will be. And B: No magic. None at all. I lost it completely. I'm even immune to magic. The Eye would be even less useful to me than a snowglobe."

"You know, we should probably get you a button saying that so you don't have to repeat it all the time," I muttered. "Or a T-shirt."

Granny nodded sagely. "Yep, I thought you looked different. What happened, boy?"

"I'll explain later," I whispered to Granny.

She addressed the gnome. "Do you think I'd let him near my granddaughter if I thought he was evil? Do you not trust my judgment?"

The gnome studied her for a moment, turned to look at Owen, then bowed to Granny and said, "I accept your wisdom." To Owen he added, "But I'm watching you, Palmer. Try any funny business and you won't be immune to my axe."

Owen gave him a thin smile. "Likewise. Now, if you'll excuse us, we have an evil piece of jewelry to track down before all of Manhattan is laid to waste, and we have about—" he checked his watch "—ten minutes to catch up with a possible lead."

The gnome re-holstered his axe, then said, "I'm coming with you. I figure you're more likely to find this thing first than those dopey elves are, so I'm throwing my lot in with you."

"I don't recall inviting you," Rod said, looming over the gnome, who only came up to his waist.

"I'm not giving you an option, kid." The gnome gave us a formal bow and said, "Thorson Gilthammer, at your service. But you can call me Thor."

I couldn't keep a straight face at the idea of someone who looked like a lawn ornament on a weekend trip to Atlantic City with his friends from the senior center being called "Thor." But he did carry an axe that would probably shatter my ankle, so I turned away and disguised my giggles in a coughing fit.

Granny didn't understand the concept of tact, so I worried that she'd start an interspecies incident, but all she said was, "Pleased to make your acquaintance, Thor. You can call me Granny. Glad to have you on the team."

"Um, Granny, you don't have to come with us," I said. In spite of what she'd said about not needing trinkets, I didn't like the idea of her anywhere near the Eye. "We were going to get you a cab. Merlin said he was looking forward to seeing you and offered to let you stay at his office while we're wrapping this up."

"You'll not get rid of me that easily, Katie Beth," she said, shaking her cane at me. "I'm not letting you out of my sight. That's the reason I came up here. That thing I felt could happen at any moment, and I *will* be there for it."

"Don't you have luggage?" I asked in a desperate attempt to find some reason she had to go to the office. "We'll need to do something with it before we can go wandering around town."

"Didn't bring any. It would just get in my way." She raised her enormous tote bag. "I've got a change of underwear and a toothbrush in here."

Thor gazed at her in admiration. "Now, there's a lady who knows how to go on a quest." He looked up at the rest of us and asked, "So, where are we going to track down this possible lead?"

"Macy's," Rod said.

"Good, I could use a new girdle," Granny said, heading out and plowing her way through the crowds. Although she'd never been to New York before, she somehow headed in the right direction. The rest of us had to hurry to keep up with her.

*

"Who are we looking for?" I asked Owen as our odd little party entered the department store.

"A Natalie Winters."

"We need a plan for approaching her," I said. "We won't be able to just walk up to her and ask if she got an interesting brooch for her birthday today. If she is our woman, we can't afford to make her suspicious."

"A personal shopper would help her choose clothes that flatter her and are suitable for her needs," Rod said. "If we can get to her before the real shopper does, it would be easy enough to ask if there's any accessory she wants to match."

"Looks like we've got a volunteer," I said.

"What? Me?" He shook his head. "No, no, no."

"You want *me* helping a woman choose clothes?" I asked, gesturing at my current outfit, which could probably best be described as "business bland."

He studied me, and I could tell he was wrestling with a diplomatic way to respond. "You don't look bad," he said at last.

"It took Gemma's help to get me this far."

"And I don't shop," Owen added.

A saleswoman approached us, gave Owen a dazzling smile, and asked, "Can I help you find something?"

Owen immediately turned bright red and started stammering. I'd almost forgotten about his shyness, it had been so long since I'd seen him outside the office basement. He could handle himself in an official capacity or with people he knew and trusted, but around strangers, he blushed and clammed up. It was really rather adorable.

Rod intervened, asking the saleswoman, "We were wondering about your personal shopper service."

"That would be on the third floor," she told him.

When she was gone, I said, "Owen also doesn't talk to strangers. Which leaves you. You're great with women." I didn't think that Granny or Thor would even be in the running for posing as a personal shopper.

"Okay, okay. If you think I can pull this off."

I patted him on the shoulder as we headed to the escalators. "Just pour on your usual charm, and you should do fine."

"I haven't used my 'usual charm' in ages. I've been trying to be good, but it's hard to reform when you people keep pulling me back in."

"It's all in the line of duty. You're playing Don Juan for a cause now, not for selfish reasons."

Up on the third floor, a frighteningly thin blond (probably fake, but with no roots showing) woman in a severe suit stood waiting, tapping the pointy toe of her high-heeled shoe impatiently, even though it was still several minutes before her appointment. "That's got to be her," Rod whispered.

"Do you feel anything that might be the Eye?" I asked him, also in a whisper.

He shook his head. "If she's got it, it's in the box. Do you think she'd be standing there, waiting, if the Eye were working?"

"Good point. Now, go get 'em, tiger. We're all counting on you. But no pressure!"

While the rest of us lurked behind mannequins, Rod dialed up the charm to maximum levels and approached the woman. "Ms. Winters?" he asked.

"Yes." She snapped out the word.

"I'm André, and I'll be helping you today."

"My appointment was with Cecile."

"I'm afraid Cecile had a family emergency, so she asked me to fill in until she could get here. She sent her most sincere apologies. Now, is there something in particular you're looking for today? Any big events you need to dress for or pieces you want to build an outfit around?"

She looked at him like he'd grown a second head. "Cecile usually pulls pieces and has them ready when I arrive. I told her what I wanted when I made the appointment."

"Oh, ah, um," Rod stammered. He sounded a lot like Owen. This was not a good time for him to lose his mojo and turn bashful. Then I felt an increase in magical use as he gave up trying to do this the hard way and hit her full-on with the whammy. "I wanted to add my personal touch," he said, his voice soft and seductive as he reached out to touch her hand.

All her frosty edginess melted away, and she looked more like what I was accustomed to seeing in women around Rod. In fact, it reminded me of when I first saw him, when I wondered if he was a rock star I didn't recognize because of the way all the women on the subway car looked at him. "Oh, personal is good," she sighed.

Still weaving his spell, Rod said, "I definitely think we should add more blue. I'd bet you look lovely in blue—like a sapphire blue. Please tell me you wear sapphires."

"I haven't before. But let's buy some!"

I put my hand over my mouth to suppress my giggles. I wished we were filming this because it was one of the funniest things I'd seen in ages. Then I noticed that Owen was staring at me, not Rod. "What's wrong?" he asked, frowning with concern.

"Wrong? What makes you think something's wrong? I mean, other than the killer brooch on the loose. This"—I gestured toward Rod— "is the best thing that's happened all day."

"Not now, at this moment, but in general. Something's up with you lately."

"What do you mean?"

"You're all lit up today, practically glowing, and you haven't looked like that in a long time. It's good to see, but it makes me wonder what's wrong the rest of the time. I know I've been kind of obsessed lately. Has that been bothering you?"

Owen acted like an absentminded professor, but he wasn't nearly as oblivious as he seemed to be. I wasn't sure what to say, though. Given everything he was dealing with, I felt like a whiner to complain about something so petty as being bored. "It's not your fault, really. Can we talk about it later, though, when we're not on a quest to retrieve the magical brooch that could plunge the world into war?"

"I'll hold you to that." His phone rang, and when he checked the caller ID, he handed it to me. "It's for you."

It was Gemma. "Sorry, I'm not having much luck," she said. "The profile you gave fits half our customers, and nobody remembers anyone's fiancé's name."

"Thanks for trying. We may have a good lead here." Since it had taken every ounce of Rod's magical charm to keep Natalie Winters from snarling at him, I thought she just might be our girl.

"Where did you find her?"

"Macy's. A woman engaged to a Jonathan Martin had a personal shopper appointment."

She laughed. "Oh, honey, that can't be the right one. The woman you're looking for wouldn't be shopping at Macy's."

"Really? It's my idea of a splurge. And she's got a personal shopper."

"*You* could get a personal shopper if you made an appointment. The woman you're looking for wouldn't shop off-the-rack. She might not even set foot in a department store. She's more likely to go straight to the designers for couture."

"Are you sure?"

"Yeah. We make our money dressing women like that."

"But she's super-thin and really blond. She looks like all the socialites in the newspaper."

"She probably aspires to be the kind of woman you're looking for, but she isn't there yet."

"Okay, thanks, Gemma." I handed the phone back to Owen. "We need to abort the operation. Gemma says there's no way this is our target."

I tried to get Rod's attention, but he was still working the whammy on

Natalie. A woman in a chic black suit came up behind him and said, "Natalie, I'm so sorry I'm late." She frowned at Rod. "And who's this?"

That got Rod's attention. It looked like Cecile, the real personal shopper, had shown up, and he was about to be revealed as a fraud. He started to edge away, but Natalie grabbed his arm while placing herself between him and Cecile. "I don't need you anymore. I've got André, and he will make me beautiful. I'm going to buy sapphires to match my eyes."

Cecile blinked at that, then glared at Rod. "You don't work here," she said. "What do you think you're doing, impersonating store staff? I'm calling security."

Rod was at an uncharacteristic loss for words. I couldn't blame him, as there wasn't a good explanation for what he'd done. It looked like someone needed to save the day. I left my hiding place and approached the group. "Excuse me, I'm looking for André, my personal shopper," I said.

"There's no personal shopper by that name working here," Cecile snapped.

"I meant my *personal* personal shopper," I said haughtily. "He's my new private wardrobe consultant, and I was supposed to meet him here."

Fortunately, Rod was quick enough to play along. "*You're* Natalie?" he asked.

"I'm Natalie!" the real Natalie protested.

"I'm afraid there's been a big mix-up," Rod said to Cecile. "I got the wrong Natalie. I'm so sorry." He took my arm and ushered me away, saying, "Now, darling, it looks like we have a lot of work to do with you. I don't even know where to begin."

"Gee, thanks," I muttered.

"Just playing my part. That was quick thinking." We rounded the corner, then joined Owen behind a concealing clothing rack. "She can't be our woman," Rod reported. "I don't think she's ever owned a sapphire in her life. Apparently, no one had ever told her she'd look good in blue. That must have been a new color of contact lens for her. If that was her real eye color, they'd have been putting her in blue from birth."

"And also, Gemma says that real billionaires' fiancées don't shop in department stores," I added.

He groaned and said, "I should have known that. I guess we forget how different they are from the rest of us."

"We'd better get out of here in case Cecile is still suspicious enough to call security," Owen said, tugging at both of us.

We'd barely stepped back into the aisle when a plaintive cry of "André? Where are you? I need you!" echoed across the floor. We leapt back into cover and headed for another aisle, crouching to keep our heads below the tops of the clothing racks.

"I guess I overestimated how much power to use on her," Rod said as

Natalie's calls continued. "I must be out of practice."

We crept out from behind a rack when the coast seemed clear, only to run into something thin and blond. "André, you shouldn't have listened to Cecile!" Natalie cried. "She's just jealous because she didn't think to tell me to wear blue. I need you."

He took her hand and stared directly into her eyes, and I started to scold him before he said softly, "Natalie, it's okay. You don't need me. Now, go let Cecile pick out some clothes for you."

"Yes, yes, I should do that," she said, nodding. Her eyes looked vague and unfocused. She swayed ever so slightly, and Rod steadied her, only releasing her when she seemed stable. She blinked out of it, stared quizzically at Rod, then nodded more decisively. "Yes, I have a personal shopper appointment."

"You do," Rod agreed, releasing her hand. "Have a nice day." As she walked away, he added under his breath, "And a nice life. Sorry." He turned to us and said, "Now, Owen is right. We ought to get out of here in case that real personal shopper didn't buy your story and has called security—or the police."

We'd nearly made it to the escalators when I realized that we were missing someone. "Hey, where are Granny and Thor?" I asked.

The guys glanced around. "I haven't seen them in a while," Owen said.

"Your grandmother mentioned needing a girdle," Rod said. "Do you think she was serious?"

"There's no telling. I think lingerie is on one of the higher floors. We could go check. At least it would get us off this floor."

We got on an up escalator. On the next level, as we stepped off and headed for the next escalator heading up, a woman dressed in black like the store employees gave us a startled look and then moved toward us. "Uh oh, looks like someone alerted security," I said. We'd be sitting ducks on an escalator, so we did an abrupt reversal and plunged into a jungle of clothing racks. The woman stayed on our tail, and when I looked back over my shoulder, I noticed that she wasn't wearing a store employee name tag. Either she was an undercover security officer or she was following us for some reason other than Rod's attempt to impersonate a personal shopper.

"The elevators," Owen suggested. None of us knew the store layout well enough to find them, so we wove our way around the floor, simultaneously looking out for our pursuer and for the elevators.

"There they are!" called Rod, just as a hand reached out from behind a rack and grabbed me.

CHAPTER SIX

I didn't get a chance to scream before a hand went over my mouth and I was pulled deeper into the clothing racks. I heard Owen and Rod calling for me nearby and struggled against my captor while screaming my lungs out from behind the muffling hand.

I then felt warm breath against my neck as someone whispered, "Hush, I'm not going to hurt you. I just want to talk to you." I didn't recognize the voice, even as I mentally ran through the voices of everyone I'd ever met. "I'll let you go if you won't scream. Will you scream?"

I figured I wouldn't go to hell for breaking my promise if he turned out to be dangerous, so I shook my head. He eased his grip on me, and I turned around. "Earl?" I blurted. "What are you doing here? Did the Elf Lord send you?"

The young elf glanced frantically around. "Shhhh! Don't talk about him! He doesn't know I'm here. I don't work for him. Well, okay, I do, but he's not the one I'm *really* working for."

"Then why are you here?"

"Because I want to help you find the Knot before the Elf Lord does."

"And grabbing me and scaring me half to death was the best way you could think of to announce that you want to be friends?" I asked, putting one hand on my hip and glaring up at him. "You're lucky Owen doesn't have any powers right now. He tends to go psycho when he thinks I'm in danger." I raised my voice and called out, "Owen! Rod! I'm okay. I'm over here."

Earl made a noise that sounded something like "Yrrggheeegg" while his eyes bugged out and his ears wiggled in panic. "Why'd you do that?" he moaned.

"If you've got something to say, you can say it to all of us at once." Then I remembered what we'd been running from and added, "And this might not be the best place to have this discussion. Someone's following us."

"I know. That was me."

"No, there was someone else, a woman."

Owen and Rod reached us, and Owen said, "Earl? Does this mean the Elf Lord wants to cooperate?"

"Actually, Earl's freelancing," I said. "But why don't we get away from here before we chat? My grandmother has been left unsupervised for far too long."

"We'll need a diversion because that woman in black is still out there," Rod said.

"I'm good at diversions," Earl said. He held out his hand, palm up, and a small orb of light formed on it. He blew on the orb, sending it flying, then said to us, "Go, and don't look at it." We ran for the elevators as the orb zoomed around just below the ceiling. The woman who'd been following us spotted us, but before she could make a move, there was a bright flash of light that would have been blinding if we'd been looking at it. We made it safely to the elevator, and Rod hit a couple of extra buttons so it wouldn't be obvious from outside where we were heading.

As I expected, we found Granny and Thor in the lingerie section. Thor was waiting uncomfortably while Granny harangued a saleswoman. "Did you find what you sought?" Thor asked us. Then he growled at the back of his throat when he saw Earl. "An elf? Are you double-crossing me?"

"You're working with *him*?" Earl asked.

"We don't yet know what's really going on with either of you," Owen said.

"I take it you didn't find what you wanted, then," Thor said.

"No, false alarm," Rod said.

Thor glared up at Earl. "So, elf, what's your game? Are you a lackey of the Elf Lord?"

"I am a spy in the court of the Elf Lord. My people want to make sure he doesn't obtain the Knot or the Eye. I believe the best way to ensure that is to help these wizards who plan to destroy the brooch."

"How do we know we can trust you?"

Earl shrugged. "How do we know we can trust anyone in this group?"

Granny came over to us, scowling. "I thought this was supposed to be a big store, but they don't have a proper girdle, just those Spandex panties," she said. "I don't hold with this Spandex stuff. Don't trust it at all." She noticed Earl and said, "My, I didn't realize they made your kind this big."

"Granny, Earl is an elf," I explained. "He's different from the wee folk back home."

"There are factions among the elves?" Rod asked Earl. "We hadn't heard anything about that."

"The Elf Lord would like a return to the old ways, when he held absolute power. Many of us would prefer that not happen. His office now is mostly ceremonial, and for some of us, even that is too much."

"You're trying to eliminate the position entirely," I translated.

"Not necessarily immediately, but over time. And that won't happen if Sylvester gets the brooch—and you can be assured that he won't hand the Eye over to the wizards."

"Maybe we'd better continue this discussion in another venue," I suggested. "Someone may be following us." Not to mention the fact that it was weird being with my boyfriend and my grandmother while surrounded by underwear. My grandmother was related to my mother, after all, which meant there was a strong possibility that at any moment she would suggest that I needed to pick up some nice things while I was there. Or worse, she'd ask me to explain a thong.

"In case we really are being followed, I suggest we take the escalator and spread out," Rod said. "Even if one of us gets caught, the others could still have a chance to get away."

Earl went down first to act as a scout. When he made it to the next floor below, Rod went. Thor and Granny followed after a group of shoppers went down. Although both Earl and Thor looked magically odd to me, I knew they were likely using magic to hide their nonhuman features from ordinary people. The other shoppers would only see a lanky kid and a little old man, even if I thought they looked incredibly odd riding an escalator.

As we waited for our turn to go down, Owen whispered to me, "We only have three tranquilizer darts."

I saw what he meant. "And we've got four magic users with us. Does it work on elves and gnomes?"

"Jake said it worked on everyone. And I would suggest not mentioning the darts to our new friends."

"And probably not Granny, either," I said. "I don't think she'd hurt me to make sure I couldn't knock her out, but then we don't know what she'd be like under the influence of the Eye."

"At least we can be sure of each other," he said with one of his shy smiles that made my heart go pitter-patter.

"Yeah, because I'd feel really bad if I had to dart you."

We stepped onto the escalator for the long ride down. No one seemed to be following us, and it didn't look like any of the other members of our party had been waylaid on their way down. As we got on the last escalator to head to the ground floor, I became more attentive. It occurred to me that maybe it would have been better to mix up the immunes and the magical people so there would have been someone to spot trouble and someone to deal with it, but I was so used to that being my partnership with Owen that I'd automatically teamed up with him.

When the ground floor came into view, I first saw Earl lurking near a display. Some dark suits milled around the floor at the foot of the escalator, but I couldn't tell from this distance if they were security, staff, or customers. Granny and Thor were hard to spot, since everyone else was so much taller than they were. It took me a while to find Rod, but when I did he was walking right past a throng of the black-suited men without drawing any attention. It looked like we were in the clear.

I glanced at the escalator steps to time my step off. Once I was on solid ground, I looked up and saw a wall of black suits closing in on us. "Uh oh," Owen muttered, and I knew he'd noticed them, too. "Act normal," he whispered, taking my hand. I clutched it desperately as he led me right to the black-suited people.

They didn't do anything as we approached and then walked past them. They didn't tell us to stop, didn't try to stop us, didn't grab us. All they did was fall into step behind us and follow us toward the exit. They didn't do it in an obvious, obtrusive way, though. If I hadn't been paranoid about store security and being followed, I wouldn't have noticed them at all. They seemed to just be going along with the flow of the crowd from the escalator toward the exit.

"I think they're watching us," I whispered to Owen.

"Let's find out." He tugged on my hand, pulling me toward a display. "Hey, look at this," he said more loudly.

Even while I pretended to look at whatever Owen was showing me, I saw out of the corner of my eye that the people in black had gone back to milling around. "What are they up to?" I asked.

"I don't know. Something seems off."

"Magic off or other off?"

"I'm not sensing magic."

"That's good, right? If wizards are watching us, it probably has something to do with the quest, and then we've got problems."

"Yeah, we're running out of room on the team. We've already got too many for the flying carpet or your average restaurant table."

"I was thinking more about those magical enforcers. They might not be happy about you being on this quest."

"I know most of them by now, and I don't recognize these people."

"Maybe they're wizards watching us so they can swoop in and grab the Eye as soon as we find it for them."

"It is reassuring that everyone seems to think we're the horse to bet on."

"Yeah, but I'd rather do this without an entourage," I said. "Teamwork is one thing, but it's hard to be stealthy with a crowd."

"I guess we'll have to lose them."

"How?"

"Like you said, teamwork. Come on." He took my hand again, and we went back to the main part of the sales floor, among all the fragrance counters. Rod and Earl were still lurking, and Owen caught Rod's eye as we went past. Rod's eyes then tracked the black-suited people following us, and he nodded, then wandered casually over to where Granny and Thor were arguing over a cologne that he liked but that she was loudly proclaiming that she thought smelled like a cheap whorehouse.

Owen then tugged my hand to lead me toward them. We walked past Granny. A moment later, I heard a startled cry followed by a thud. I couldn't resist looking back—since I figured that even an innocent person would have—and saw one of the black-suited men on the floor. Granny stood nearby, casually moving her cane to her other hand. A crowd formed around the fallen man, making it impossible for him to follow us. A nearby store staffer's reaction confirmed he wasn't an employee. This was a whole new party following us.

"One down," I remarked to Owen.

Now I spotted a couple of others coming after us, and they were being more obvious about it, elbowing people out of their way to get closer. "Head for the exit," Owen said through gritted teeth. "Let Rod and the others deal with them." He'd gone pale, and I could tell from the muscle jumping in his jaw that this was killing him. He was used to being the one to defend others magically.

One of the followers got so close that I could practically feel him breathing down my neck. We were next to the men's fragrance counter, so I whirled, grabbed a sampler bottle and said, "Have you tried our new scent?" as I gave him a thorough spraying, right in the eyes. I dropped the bottle back on the counter and ran after Owen, a smell like a spice factory explosion in a pine forest trailing me as relentlessly as the human pursuer, who stumbled blindly after me.

Rod rejoined us near the exit. "They're persistent. Who are they and what do they want?"

"They haven't tried to grab us, but they're following us," Owen said. "If we can't lose them in here, I'm not sure what we'll do outside."

"Head out," Rod said. "We'll cover you and waylay them."

We hurried toward the Broadway exit, but there was another man in black blocking the door. He could easily follow us when we left—or keep us from leaving. We turned to head for another exit, but yet another black-suited man appeared. As he approached Rod, a thin, blond figure flew at him, shouting, "Stay away from him!"

It was Natalie. She threw herself between them, then turned to Rod and said, "Go on, I'll hold him." With a smile, she added, "And I promise to wear blue."

"I thought you broke that spell," I said to Rod as we ran toward Thor and Granny, who'd been easily taking out their pursuers while maintaining the facade of being helpless elderly people.

"I did! I guess I'm just irresistible on my own."

I elbowed him in the ribs. "Remember, you're dating my roommate."

"Now what?" Owen asked. "They're covering the exits."

A pure, high, plaintive sound swelled through the air, and everyone in the store stopped to listen. It was as though the best Irish tenor ever had launched into a mournful folk melody in front of a bar full of Saint Patrick's Day drinkers, leaving them all crying into their green beer. Earl the elf was singing, that hauntingly beautiful voice disconcertingly at odds with his appearance.

"Ah, elfsong," Rod said with a nod, a tear trickling down his cheek.

"An interesting use for it," Owen said. "Let's go before it loses its effect."

Even the black suits stood entranced, their eyes welling with tears. Granny and Thor joined us, holding on to each other like a couple of drunks. Owen and I had to herd the group through the revolving door because the others didn't want to leave. Earl let the last note linger, then joined us. "I don't know how long the effects will last, so we'd better lose them before it wears off," he said.

Granny patted him on the arm. "That was lovely, son. Do you know 'Danny Boy'?"

"Granny, later," I said. "There's a subway across the street, or we could go back to Penn Station."

"Penn Station," Owen decided. "It's easier to lose someone there."

We ran the long block back toward the station. As we ran, Owen got out his phone and updated Sam on the situation. I didn't notice large groups of people wearing black following us, but I felt a lot more comfortable once we were in the station. "Now where do we go?" I asked.

"Away from here," Owen replied, putting his phone back in his pocket. We headed across the station to the Eighth Avenue subway, and a little of Rod's magic got us quickly through the turnstiles in time to jump on an uptown train just before the doors closed.

Our group stood in a cluster around one of the poles near the door. "I think we need to talk before this goes any further," Owen said.

"Yes, over food and ale," Thor agreed.

"I could do with a bite," Granny said.

"Come to think of it, I didn't get much lunch," Rod put in.

"You got more than I did," I said. "I didn't have much appetite then."

"Okay, we'll talk over food," Owen said with an exasperated sigh. We got off the train at Fiftieth Street and moved cautiously out of the station. Thor took the lead, moving one step at a time and glancing warily around before taking another step.

When he'd reached the sidewalk, a voice said, "It's okay, you're in the clear for now." Startled, Thor jumped backward, lost his footing, and would have fallen if Earl hadn't caught him. "Oh, sorry about that. Didn't mean to scare you," Sam said from his perch on a sign in front of the subway entrance.

Thor jerked himself out of Earl's grasp and straightened his jacket. "I was not scared. I was merely startled. I don't expect to see gargoyles at this level."

"Were they able to follow us?" Owen asked.

"Hard to say," Sam replied. "You know, in this city, wearing black doesn't make anyone stand out. For now, though, there's no one nearby that worries me. You've probably got a good half hour before anyone can track you down. What's your next move?"

"We will discuss our fellowship over food and ale," Thor said.

"Lunch," I translated.

"There's a diner just around the corner," Sam said. "It's probably safest if you split up and don't go as one big group. Just in case, you know."

The party left in twos. I was about to head out with Granny, but Sam caught my eye and shook his head, so I lingered with Owen. When the others were all gone, Sam said, "I figured that was the easiest way to get you two alone. I'd have kept Rod in, but someone we trust has gotta keep an eye on that bunch. And Katie, I thought your grandma was gonna go back to the office."

"That was the plan," I said with a sigh. "She refuses to go. She says she came here because something's going to happen to me, and she wants to be there when it does."

"She's powerful, so that might not be a bad thing." He escorted us to the diner, gliding as we walked. "So, you've picked up some new friends," he said.

Owen gave him a quick recap on the new party members and what we'd learned about the various factions. "At the rate we're going, I wouldn't be surprised if a manhole cover popped open and the Mole People came out to say they wanted to join our group," I added.

"It is reassuring that they have so much confidence in us," Owen said with a wry smile. "Do you have any idea who the people in black were? I couldn't tell what they wanted, and they weren't that aggressive. It was more like they were trying to hamper us or delay us than hurt us."

"We're lookin' into it. They aren't with the Council, I can tell you that much. The boss hasn't clued them in on all this yet."

"They're sure to find out sooner or later."

"And then they'll probably want to join our team," I said. "I don't suppose there are any other leads on the future Mrs. Martin?"

"None that I've heard."

"Who came up with the Macy's lead?" Owen asked, frowning. "Because we only got the tip a little while before we went there, and even though it was a false alarm, they were there in pretty significant numbers."

"A mole at MSI?" Sam asked.

"It wouldn't be the first time," I reminded him.

"I'll look into it. Now, you get something to eat and find out what the elves and the gnomes are up to. I'll stay in touch." He flew away, and we headed to join the others at the diner.

They'd pushed together two tables to seat our entire group in the nearly empty restaurant. Once we'd ordered, Owen asked, "Do any of you know who those people were in the store?"

"I thought you were running from security," Earl said with a shrug.

"Security would have done more than just lurk and follow," Rod said.

"No, they definitely weren't just store security," Owen said.

"Let's see, how many factions does that make so far?" I asked. I ticked them off on my fingers. "There's MSI. There are the Elf Lord's elves. There's whatever group Earl represents. There are the gnomes."

"We've got a couple of factions, too," Thor put in.

"And, of course, there's this mysterious fiancée," I continued. "Plus now maybe a group of wizards."

Our food arrived, and after devouring his hamburger, Thor said, "It's cards on the table time. If we're going to work together, we need to know where we're all coming from. I'll start." He cleared his throat and began, his voice taking on the singsong rhythm of someone reciting a story word-for-word from memory. "Great goldmasters the gnomes have been for many generations. Thus it was that the Elf Lord sought our aid for the greatest work of all: the wedding of the Eye of the World to the Knot of Arnhold."

"But the Knot has been lost for centuries!" Earl protested. "Sylvester didn't have it! Lyle only saw a vision of it this morning!"

Dropping out of bard mode, Thor shrugged. "Hey, all I know is that Sylvester came to our people with these two things and wanted them physically and magically joined. Someone must have found them for him." He cleared his throat, then continued his tale. "Though the gnomes had great skill, this task required great fortitude. The temptation would be great to seize power and invulnerability. Charms were cast and the goldsmiths worked two-by-two, no one ever alone with the gem when it was outside the box that shielded it. The most noble and upright guards kept constant watch."

Granny snorted. "Must not have done too good a job, since you're looking for it now."

"It was treachery!" Thor shouted, shaking his fist and then pounding it on the table. The fact that he was sitting in a child's booster seat made the gesture less intimidating than I was sure he intended. "The Elf Lord betrayed the gnomes, taking the great work without payment."

"That would be like him," Earl put in. "He's beyond cheap."

Ignoring him, Thor went on. "Our people could not stand for this. Gnomes tracked elven movements, watching for signs of the lost brooch. Seers searched the heavens." He launched into an in-depth description of the search. It was as though he'd memorized this story and couldn't deviate from it in any way, even if we didn't care about these details.

Out of boredom, I picked up the newspaper that had been left on an adjacent table and skimmed the headlines of the Life and Style section. There was a review of a new television series beginning that night that sounded interesting, although I doubted I'd be home in time to watch it. I turned the page and saw the society coverage. The photo accompanying the column about a fundraiser being held that night at the Metropolitan Museum of Art stopped me cold. Every single muscle in my body tensed.

"No, no, no, no, no, no, no," I muttered in sheer horror.

"Katie, what is it?" Owen asked.

"I think I've found our future Mrs. Martin. And we're doomed." They all turned to stare at me, and I had to gulp a few times before I could choke out the words, "It's Mimi."

CHAPTER SEVEN

The others stared at me, confused. Except for Thor, who scowled. "Now you've made me lose my place," he grumbled. "Let's see, where was I …" His voice returned to the formal, singsong rhythms of his storytelling. "The brooch landed on foreign shores, and new seekers joined the quest."

"What's a Mimi?" Earl interrupted.

"Hey, you can talk when it's your turn," Thor protested, then he groaned. "And now I've lost my place again."

I turned the newspaper so they could see the column. "Mimi Perkins is my ex-boss, before I joined MSI. And she's evil. I've met some truly bad people in my time, and none of them were scarier than Mimi."

Thor opened his mouth to continue his story, but before he could begin speaking again, Rod asked, "What does this have to do with the brooch?"

"According to the newspaper, Mimi is putting on a gala tonight, and the article mentions that she's engaged to billionaire Jonathan Martin. We've got our missing fiancée. Does nobody read the newspaper anymore? MSI research should have found this in five minutes." Of all mornings, this had to be the one when I'd gone to work before at least skimming the headlines. I'd have seen Mimi's photo and drawn devil horns on it, so I surely would have made this connection long before now.

"I thought she was engaged to someone named Werner," Owen said.

"Yeah, a year ago," I said. "She's obviously upgraded to someone older and richer."

"This looks promising," Rod agreed. "But what makes you so sure she's the one who has the brooch?"

"Because … because …" I trailed off. I knew what I feared, but was that the same thing as having good reason to suspect? "Because it's the best lead we've got," I finally said. "And, believe me, if it *is* Mimi, we're in huge trouble." They looked skeptical, so I added, "I know it sounds like I'm exaggerating, but the way you describe what the Eye does to people? That's her *normally*. She likes power and she's kind of passive-aggressive about it. She likes people being afraid of her while she pretends to be nice. She'll act like your best friend, but you never know when she'll snap and get ugly on you. Now, give her extra sway over people, more power lust, and invulnerability, and we've got problems."

Under the table, Owen gave my knee a gentle squeeze. I wasn't sure if he meant it to be reassuring or to tell me to chill. He said, "It is the best lead we've got, and from my one meeting with the woman, I have to say that we should at least rule her out." He turned to me and asked, "Where would we find her?"

"We know where she'll be tonight," Rod said, pointing at the newspaper.

I shook my head. "That'll be too late. She'll have started World War Three by then."

"She had the brooch in the box when she left the restaurant, so its effects are shielded," Owen reminded me. "Maybe she won't put it on until she gets dressed for the event—and if we're lucky, she doesn't know what she has."

"The sooner we get to it, the better," I said. I took a few deep breaths and forced myself to think clearly. Working for Mimi was the reason I'd been willing to respond to a very suspicious-sounding job offer in my e-mail, which led me to a magical company. I had to be desperate to even consider talking to someone about an unspecified job at an unnamed company, but they'd contacted me on a day when Mimi was at her worst, and I couldn't resist any opportunity to escape.

But she had no power over me anymore. She wasn't my boss, and her magic doodad wouldn't affect someone immune to magic. Not to mention, we were on a more equal footing now. My current job was on the same level as the job she'd held when I worked for her. She may have been engaged to a billionaire, but I was dating a millionaire who was much younger and way hotter.

And if I was right about her having the brooch, then it was my mission to defeat her. This had just become the best day ever.

Owen asked, "Where do you think we'd find her before the gala?"

"It doesn't sound like she has a day job anymore," I said. "I bet everyone back at my old company is thrilled about that." I frowned. "And I wonder why they didn't let me know. I'd have thought they'd invite me to the 'Ding, Dong the Witch is Dead' party."

"You were out of town for the first part of the year," Owen reminded me.

"Oh yeah. It's funny how long ago that seems. Well, if she's not at work, maybe she's at home. Do you think the office could get her home address?

I doubt any info I have would be current."

"I'll call," Rod said, getting up from the table as he reached for his phone.

Owen asked, "Any other ideas?"

"I think I was too successful at repressing that part of my life. I'm sure on the day she has a gala event she'd get her hair and nails done. I can't remember where she went, even though I used to make those appointments. Chances are, she's pissed those people off by now, anyway. She never could stick with one stylist for long. And I'm sure she's upgraded from wherever she went when she was paying for it herself."

Thor cleared his throat loudly. "As I was saying before I was interrupted, I joined the search when we learned the brooch was in our city."

Granny interrupted before he could get started again. "And you figured this bunch would be most likely to find it first, so you went in with them. It's a simple enough story. You don't have to make an epic out of it."

"But it loses all the poetry when you put it that way," Thor complained.

Rod returned to the table and said, "Apparently, she's moved in with her fiancé at his Park Avenue penthouse. I've always wanted to see inside one of those."

"We'll have to get past a doorman," I said.

"That's not a problem," Rod said with a shrug. "However, getting there could be a challenge. This group is too big for the carpet or for a cab."

"We could split up," I suggested.

"You're not going near the brooch without me," Thor growled.

"And I already told you I'm sticking with you," Granny added.

I tried not to sigh out loud before I said, "I meant we could take two cabs. Or two carpets. Could we get two carpets?" It was a sign of how urgent I felt this was that I actually hoped we could travel by flying carpet.

Owen was already on the phone. After he ended the call, he said, "They're on the way."

The waitress brought our check, and I was afraid it didn't bode well for the kind of teamwork we could expect to see on this mission that our group nearly came to blows over it. "We shouldn't split it evenly," Earl said. "I only had a salad and some water, while some people"—he glared at Thor—"had beers and a burger. I'm not paying for his meal."

"I provided the entertainment," Thor protested. "In decent company, I wouldn't have to pay for my meal at all after a story like that."

"Then your people need to get cable if that's your idea of entertainment," Earl shot back.

Thor snarled as he reached for his battleaxe, and then both he and Earl cried out in pain and jerked away from the table. Granny glared at them as she leaned back in her chair, holding her cane threateningly. "Now, boys, behave yourselves," she scolded. "This is no time for that nonsense."

Rod reached for the check and said, "I'll take care of it and expense it. We're on company business."

"If I'd known that, I would have ordered more," Earl complained.

"You elves don't know how to live," Thor said smugly as he drained the last of his second beer.

Earl started to rise to his bait, then glanced at Granny and instead got out of his chair and headed for the door. "I'll meet you there if you give me the address. I should limit my time with you, in case the Elf Lord's people catch up with you. My mission depends on maintaining my cover as his loyal employee."

He conferred with Rod, and as soon as he was out the door, Thor said, "Or maybe he is working for Sylvester, and he has to check in with his boss."

Owen and Rod exchanged glances, and then Owen hurried outside to have a quick conversation with Sam. The gargoyle flew after Earl as the rest of us came outside and found two magic carpets waiting for us. Both had little creatures piloting.

Granny took to carpet travel better than I'd expected she would. In fact, she seemed totally unfazed, while I clung to the carpet in a death grip. "Where do you put your groceries?" she asked after a particularly harrowing turn as our driver seemed to be trying to make sure no one followed us.

"We don't generally use these things for shopping," Owen explained. "They're more for rapid transit. They require too much magic for everyday use."

Granny leaned over the edge to look at the street below, and I fought off a wave of vicarious vertigo. "I can see how cars wouldn't be much use for getting around quickly here," she said.

We reached Park Avenue, and the carpets landed in front of an imposing apartment building. "Should we wait for Earl?" Rod asked after we'd disembarked.

"Here I am," Earl said, rounding the corner. "No other elves are present." Sam perched on the building's awning and gave Owen a nod that apparently indicated that the elf had come directly without stopping to report to Sylvester.

"Okay, now to get past the doorman," Rod said, rubbing his hands together. He gave the doorman a wave as he approached, and I sensed a surge of magic. Normally, people saw whatever Rod wanted them to see, but that didn't happen this time.

Instead, the doorman moved to confront us. "What is your business here?" he demanded.

Rod took a surprised step backward. Then he recovered and said smoothly, "We're here to see Mr. Martin."

"Is he expecting you?"

"We should be on the list."

The doorman stepped inside, then returned with a clipboard. Rod waved a hand at the clipboard as the doorman read it. "I don't see any guests listed here for Mr. Martin," the doorman said.

"There must be some mix-up," Rod said. He looked perfectly at ease, like this was no big deal, but I could hear the tension in his voice and I felt the magic as he gave it everything he had. Could the doorman be immune to magic?

The doorman then laughed out loud and said, "You think to fool me with your illusions? You MSI people don't know the first thing about magic."

Earl then opened his mouth, and the haunting sound of elfsong poured out. The doorman laughed at that, too. "You think that would work twice, elf?" he sneered. "We've forgotten more than you'll ever know about magic."

Thor unsheathed his battleaxe and stepped forward. "But how much have you forgotten about steel?" he asked, swinging the axe back and forth.

The doorman held out his hand, and Thor froze. Granny stepped up and swung her cane at him, but the cane bounced backward like it had hit something solid before it struck the doorman. Rod and Earl teamed up on a spell, but the doorman was apparently protected from it because he just laughed. Even Sam flying down from above wasn't able to get past the doorman.

"We do have tranquilizer darts," I said to Owen.

"I hate to use them when we aren't even dealing with the Eye. It's probably going to get much worse."

"Worse than getting our butts kicked by a doorman?"

He smiled ruefully. "Very likely. But a dragon guarding the gate is a good sign that the Eye is here, so we don't have much of a choice." He took the case from his breast pocket, removed one of the darts, then replaced the case. "I doubt throwing it would work. I'll have to get past his defenses, myself, then jab him directly. I'll need a diversion."

Thor was still frozen, but Rod, Earl, Sam, and Granny were giving it their all, each of them trying to get past the doorman to the side or above him or, in Granny's case, by crawling past him. He easily repelled all their attacks, shouting words I didn't recognize as he did so. "One diversion, coming up," I said. I then approached the doorman, smiling as he threw magic at me without having any effect. That disconcerted him enough that Owen was able to lunge at him and jab the dart in his neck. A second later, the doorman slumped into Rod's arms. Owen picked up his feet and the two of them carried him inside.

I glanced around, worried that even jaded New Yorkers would look askance at someone ambushing a Park Avenue doorman, but Sam said, "Don't worry, sweetheart, I had us veiled the whole time."

With some relief, I joined the others. Thor, who'd revived at the doorman's collapse, came staggering inside a moment later. Sam gestured the door closed behind him as he flew into the lobby.

"I'd say he wasn't the real doorman," Owen remarked, pointing out the bound man lying in his underwear behind the doorman's desk. Owen knelt beside him, checking for a pulse. "He's alive," he said. Rod magically untied the real doorman, then waved his hand and sent the ropes spiraling around the imposter's wrists.

"If somebody else got here first, we'd better get upstairs," I said. We squeezed the seven of us into the small elevator for the ride all the way to the top floor, where the doors opened into a private vestibule. It didn't look like there'd been a scuffle there. I glanced at Owen, and he shook his head.

"I'm not feeling any magic in use. Maybe the doorman was just keeping us away from the Eye."

"Does anyone feel a strange pull?" I asked.

"Nope," Rod said. "If it's here, it's in the box. So, how do we want to deal with this if she's home?"

"Let's pretend I'm paying her a personal visit," I said. "She thinks I'm useless and stupid—not remotely a threat. If she isn't wearing the brooch, I'll distract her, Owen can tranquilize her, and you guys go looking for it."

"And what if she has it on her?"

I flexed my fingers and formed a fist. "Then I'll punch her lights out and take it away from her."

Owen raised an eyebrow. "Make sure she has it before you hit her."

"Spoilsport. What happened to better safe than sorry?" I took a deep breath, and my hand only trembled a little as I reached out to ring the doorbell.

The chimes inside sounded like cathedral bells, echoing out into the vestibule, and I gestured for the others to move to the side, where they wouldn't be immediately visible from the doorway. There was no response for a long time, and I was almost ready to give up when the door opened a crack. A uniformed maid, complete with frilly cap, stuck her head out. She had the kind of fear in her eyes that I recognized from staff meetings with Mimi. She rattled off something in a language I couldn't identify. I glanced at Owen, our resident linguist, but he shrugged and shook his head. I figured it was just like Mimi to import a maid from some exotic locale— probably some place where they were used to living under the rule of tyrants and didn't know anything about human rights.

"Um, hi," I said. "Is Mimi home? I'm a friend of hers. We used to work together."

The maid said haltingly, "Sorry. No English."

"Okay," I said. In desperation, I tried charades, pulling my face into an exaggerated snarl and hissing as I raised my hands in claws.

The woman flinched but grinned in recognition as she nodded. She then shook her head. "Not home. Left this morning. Gone all day. Not back until late, late night," she said, pausing between words as though running them through a mental phrase book.

"I don't suppose you know where she'd be now," I said wistfully, but the maid just shook her head. "Well, thank you. You've been very helpful. And I am so, so sorry. We're doing everything we can to make sure it doesn't get worse."

After she'd closed the door, Thor asked, "Now where should we go?"

"If Mimi hasn't been home since lunch, she probably still has the brooch with her," I said. "And you can usually find Mimi by the trail of shattered people she leaves in her wake. I bet we could walk up and down Park Avenue and look for people who work in service industries who are either crying or setting things on fire. There could even be riots." Then I had an idea. "Or I could call Gemma and find out who the most exclusive hairstylist in the city is. Mimi would get her hair done before a gala like this, and we might find her there."

Owen handed me his phone, and I was already dialing before we reached the lobby. Gemma gave me the addresses of the top hair and nail salons, and I scribbled them on a notepad I had in my purse, then followed the others outside. As soon as I got through the door, I said, "I've got a few leads. It might be a good idea to split up to check them all out as quickly as possible, but surveillance only. We'll call each other before moving in if we find her."

They didn't respond, and it took me a moment to notice what they were looking at. The flying carpets were gone, and the two tiny drivers were lying on the sidewalk. "Wait, our carpets were stolen?" I asked. "They didn't even have radios in them. And I thought crime had taken a downswing."

"It's a safe bet they weren't joyriders," Rod said as he bent to check on the drivers.

"And they won't be stripping them for parts," Owen added.

"Someone is sabotaging us," Thor said, hefting his battleaxe in his hands. "I suspect the Elf Lord. He doesn't want his plot disrupted."

"This doesn't seem like Sylvester's style," Earl said. "He's more likely to let us find the brooch and then take it from us than to try to stop us from finding it."

"On the bright side, we're definitely on the right track," I said. "We've got to be if someone is bothering to get in our way."

"They tried to stop us at Macy's, and that wasn't even a real lead," Owen reminded me.

"The fake doorman knew Earl used elfsong earlier, so he must be connected to the black suits. Maybe that was about stalling us before we could figure things out and catch up with Mimi. Are the drivers okay?"

"They'll be fine," Rod said as he straightened.

Sam swooped in and landed on the awning. "Nothing in a three-block radius," he reported. "They're sending up some other carpets, but it'll take a few minutes. Maybe we should move on and have them meet us somewhere."

I checked my notepad. "One of the salons Gemma suggested is only about a block away. We could head there." I hesitated, then said, "But don't call the office to tell them where to meet us just yet."

"You're still thinkin' mole, doll?"

"Someone has been waiting for us twice so far today, and it seems to happen whenever we check in with the office."

As we walked down the street, I moved up alongside Earl and said, "You didn't get to tell your story."

He shrugged. "There's not much. From my time at court, I knew Sylvester was eager to solidify his power. When Lyle reported that he'd found the Knot, I decided to work with you to keep it out of Sylvester's hands. Knowing that Sylvester had the Knot all along and that he got the Eye and commissioned the brooch just verifies my suspicion that he's pulling an elaborate power grab. I have to make sure it doesn't work."

"No songs or poetry in the telling?" I asked with a smile.

He grinned in return. "There's a time and a place for that kind of thing. If I wanted to, I could tell it in a way that would make you weep—and not with boredom." I thought he looked more like a teenager than a bard who could keep his listeners entranced, but I'd heard him sing, so I didn't say anything.

"You don't think Sylvester stole it himself?" Owen asked.

"No, he's too frantic about it. He might play it cool in front of Merlin, but he went postal on Lyle when he brought him the news that it had been in a jewelry store. I believe the gnome speaks the truth."

"So, that means we have a power-hungry Elf Lord who had this thing made as part of a secret plot, and we have the domineering bitch who owns it now," I said. "I almost wish we could throw them into a secure room together and let them fight over it. It would be epic."

"You don't know Sylvester. It wouldn't be much of a fight," Earl said.

"You don't know Mimi," I replied, suppressing a shudder. "It would be the throwdown of the century."

When we'd visited the nearest hair and nail salons on our list without finding either Mimi or a record of an appointment for her, I said, "We're running out of time. Where are those carpets? If we don't find her soon, we'll have to catch her at the museum tonight."

Sam, who'd been flying surveillance loops, returned to us and hissed,

"Psst, don't look back. Keep walkin' casual-like."

"What is it, Sam?" Owen asked.

"I may be gettin' as paranoid as Katie-bug here, but I do believe you've picked up a tail. I mean, another one. This one's not a bird, and it's definitely magical."

Earl reacted first, leaping to flatten himself into a nearby doorway as he glanced anxiously from side to side. "Relax, kid," Sam told him. "I don't think it's an elf. And if it is, he's already seen you."

"But you're sure it's a wizard?" Owen asked.

"Keep walkin'. It's harder to shake a tail who knows you're onto him," Sam ordered. When we'd complied, aside from Earl, who refused to move from his doorway, Sam continued. "He's veiling himself, keeps changin' his appearance, but I noticed the steady wave of magic comin' after you. I don't know which person he is in all these crowds, but there's definitely someone there."

"Just one?" I asked. "And he's there now?"

"He's good. He's hanging back a bit—and don't look over your shoulder." He added this last part for Thor. Granny followed it up with a slap to the back of the gnome's head.

"How long has he been there?" Owen asked.

"I think he picked you up at the apartment building, but it's hard to say. He'd have to have been really good to follow you when you were flying."

"I wonder which faction he's with, or if we've got a new one," I said. "We practically need a chart to keep track of them all. This would be easier if everyone had uniforms or matching T-shirts."

"At least he hasn't offered to join us," Rod joked. "I guess we should go on with business as usual."

"I've got carpets waiting for us about a block away," Sam said.

"Should we try to lose this guy first?" I asked.

"Nah, it'll be easier to lose him in the air."

The back of my neck itched with the sensation that I was being watched, but I reminded myself that we weren't doing anything particularly important at the moment. Anyone who followed us would only get a tour of some of the top salons in the city. I glanced at Owen to see what he was thinking, and his eyes had taken on an unfocused look that was far too familiar. He was deep in thought, miles away. I hooked my arm through his because when he got like that, he sometimes needed someone to keep him from walking into lampposts.

He came to a sudden halt, nearly creating a minor pile-up on the sidewalk. I didn't stop in time and staggered backward, my arm still caught in his. "That's it!" he said.

"You've finally solved that global warming problem?" Rod joked.

Owen shook his head. "No, I know where I've seen those spells the doorman used. They're from the *Ephemera.*"

CHAPTER EIGHT

"You recognized those spells?" Rod asked.

"There was something familiar about them, but I wasn't sure why, and it's been bugging me ever since," Owen said.

"If they're from the *Ephemera*, does that mean they're evil spells?" I asked, shivering as my skin crawled.

"Not necessarily," Owen said. "The book itself is contaminated with evil enchantments, and a lot of the contents have spells embedded, but a good portion of the book merely records spells that were in use at that time. Those spells the doorman used were ancient, and he used the archaic forms."

"Does that mean someone else has access to the *Ephemera*, or is there another copy?" Rod asked.

"I don't know. Surely those spells were recorded somewhere else. We've moved so far beyond the magic from that time that even our historians don't generally go back that far in researching spells. But it would explain why we had so much trouble fighting him. It's like the way sometimes a really outdated computer can be more secure because the current viruses won't even run on that operating system."

"Keep walking," Sam interrupted. "You don't want our friend to overhear you or think you've made him."

We began moving again, Owen having to work to walk, talk, and think all at the same time. I held onto him to steer him around obstacles. Rod asked him, "Now that you know the source, do you know how to fight those spells?"

Owen shook his head with a groan of frustration. "No. Normally, I would have internalized the spells as I translated them, but since I can't work them right now, I only remember bits and pieces, and it's too risky not to go word-for-word. One variation and you might blow something up or fry yourself."

"And you can't carry the book around because it's too dangerous," Rod said with a nod.

"But the transcriptions of those parts could be safe. I should go back to the office and get them. You might have to go up against those people again."

"Do we have time for that?" I asked. "We need to find Mimi before she has a captive audience at this gala that she can recruit into her army of doom for taking over the city."

The two guys glanced at their watches. Rod said, "I don't want to face those spells again without some help. You go, and the rest of us will keep checking salons."

"I'll need Katie, though," Owen said. "She's the only other person who can get into the manuscript vault, and it'll go faster if we're both digging through the notes. That leaves you without an immune."

"We'll just do recon and surveillance. If we find Mimi, we'll track her from a safe distance."

As Sam had promised, there were two carpets waiting around the corner a block away. Earl was also waiting there, the hood of his sweatshirt pulled up over his head. "I didn't see anyone following you," he said, "and they didn't seem to be following me."

I tore the pages out of my notepad and handed them to Rod. "Here's the list of salons. You saw the newspaper picture, right? You're looking for a tall, curly-haired redhead with demonic eyes. The people around her will either be cowering, crying, or looking for weapons."

Sam perched where he could read over Rod's shoulder. "I'll check on a few of these for you. I may be able to do a fly-by."

Owen jumped onto one of the carpets, and when I followed him, Granny came with me. "I'm sticking with you," she said, her tone making it clear that there would be no point in arguing.

I gave Owen a helpless shrug, and he said, "It won't hurt for us to have a magic user with us." To Rod, he added, "Keep in touch and let us know where to meet." Once he'd helped Granny on board, he told the driver, "To the office, please, and we're in a hurry."

The carpet lifted, then soared skyward as it zoomed down Park Avenue. I'd thought we'd gone quickly before, but it seemed like we were close to breaking the sound barrier. I couldn't even recognize landmarks. I held on to Owen with one hand and the carpet with the other, and even Owen seemed tense. But Granny shouted with glee, "Woo hoo! Now, this is what I call traveling!"

We hadn't been in the air too long before I was pretty sure I saw the Empire State Building go by in a blur. We were heading straight down Fifth Avenue, about twenty stories up, and at a dizzying rate of speed. I felt like I should get double world-saving points for this adventure.

And yet, it was better than spending the day at my desk. That thought brought a smile to my face. I leaned back my head and joined Granny in a hearty "Woo hoo!"

A second later, something hit the carpet from below, knocking it sideways. If I hadn't still had a death grip on it, I'd have fallen right off. My clinging to Owen with my other hand was the only thing that kept him from falling, and his weight almost pulled me off. He grabbed the carpet just in time, giving me a chance to hold on with both hands. Granny had the head of her cane hooked over the side while the driver, tied securely onto the carpet with the fringe, fought desperately to turn it right-side up.

All the while, the carpet plunged downward. The wind, no longer deflected by whatever magical force field usually held it back, whistled fiercely around us. With the passengers hanging on to the edge of the carpet, it couldn't right itself. It was as though three people were trying to climb into a canoe at the same time.

Granny shouted something, but I couldn't make out the words over the roar of the wind. I didn't think she was talking to me, though. She seemed to be talking to the carpet, probably telling it to straighten up and fly right, if it knew what was good for it, because she had beaten plenty of rugs in her time.

Whatever she said, it worked. The carpet gradually rolled back to its proper position, with us lying across it. "Now, that's more like it," she said with a grunt of satisfaction. I pressed my cheek against the carpet pile and took several deep breaths before carefully sitting up. Owen and I took one look at each other and fell together in a one-armed hug—each of us keeping a hand firmly on the carpet.

"What happened?" I asked Owen as I clung to him. "I thought these things were supposed to be safe."

"This isn't the time for that sort of thing," Granny snapped before Owen could respond. "You two need to see this."

I reluctantly looked away from Owen to where Granny was pointing. A gargoyle flew toward us, but it wasn't any MSI gargoyle I'd ever met. This one looked ancient. It was nearly featureless from time and the elements wearing away the carving, and its stony skin was stained and mossy.

"That's not one of ours," Owen said, releasing me to reach for his phone. He flipped the phone open and said, "Sam, we're under attack. Fifth Avenue, probably around Madison Square by now. It's a gargoyle, and I don't think it's local." He closed the phone and returned it to his pocket as he said, "They're sending help."

I was afraid the help wouldn't arrive soon enough. The strange gargoyle wheeled around to fly straight at us, on a collision course. The carpet twisted out of the way just in time, like a matador's cape being whisked away from the bull's charge. For a moment, my fingertips were the only part of me still connected to the carpet. I could see the street directly below me. The ancient gargoyle's momentum sent it flying down a cross street while we barely jerked away before we slammed into the side of a building. When our driver had recovered from the near-miss and had the carpet back in the proper position, he poured on the speed.

To no avail. This gargoyle wasn't as agile as the ones I knew, so it couldn't turn on a dime, but it could build up some speed once it got started. This time, it came from above, dropping with its clawed feet extended. If it hit us, it would knock us out of the sky. To my dismay, our driver flew straight toward it on a collision course. At the last second, the carpet jerked to the side and practically came to a midair halt. The gargoyle shot past, unable to adjust its course in time. Our carpet sped up again, rising to fly over the roof of a nearby building, then dropping as we flew down Broadway. Our driver used the tall buildings as cover.

We reached Union Square without further incident. I let myself relax slightly, but then Owen called out a warning. The ancient gargoyle was back, approaching us quickly with its mouth pulled back in a rictus-like grimace. Our carpet sped up, and the gargoyle kept up, gaining on us. I couldn't bear to watch and turned to Owen. His jaw was clenched in frustration, and his cheeks flamed as his fingers twitched. I figured he couldn't possibly want to be able to do magic now more than I wanted him to.

"You get away! Shoo!" Granny shouted, waving at the gargoyle as it drew near. I wasn't sure what she did, but the gargoyle veered away, furiously flapping its wings. It looked like it had been blown off course.

"Hey, you're a wizard!" Owen said.

She shot him a withering glare. "Of course I am, even if I don't have all your fancy spells."

He shook his head. "Sorry. I'm just not used to not being able to do this for myself. Are you open to learning a fancy spell?"

"I'm always willing to learn," she said archly. "That's what keeps me young."

Owen addressed the driver, saying, "Take us out over the river. I don't want anyone below to get hurt." The carpet banked as it turned east down Fourteenth Street. I wasn't sure I wanted to be over the water, though I supposed it might be better than landing on the street if the carpet tipped again. To Granny, Owen said, "Repeat after me," and then he said a long string of something that sounded like mostly consonants.

She tried to emulate him, but got her tongue tangled. "Do you have to use such foreign talk?" she complained, absently waving a hand that deflected the pursuing gargoyle again. "What's wrong with good old English?"

"For this, yes, I'm afraid you need the foreign language. This is a pretty complicated process that's countering other magic. Now, try it again." He kept coaching her until he felt she wouldn't carry out an entirely different spell. All the while, our carpet rose, dipped, and zigzagged as it evaded the gargoyle attacker. I played lookout and shouted warnings to the driver while Granny practiced.

When she got it, Owen said, "Now here's the hand gesture." That one she picked up a little more quickly, though she didn't move her fingers as fluidly as he did. "The last part is all mental. You need to focus on the fact that the gargoyle is stone, that it shouldn't be flying. It shouldn't move at all. Can you do that?"

"That doesn't take much imagination," she said dryly. "It's the natural order of things."

"Okay, then, next time it comes at us, do it." We were over the river now, nothing below us but dirty water. The gargoyle plummeted toward us, its wings folded against its sides in a steep dive. If it hit us, it would drive the carpet—and its passengers—straight into the river. "Now!" Owen shouted to Granny. Then he instructed the driver, "Hold your course until I say otherwise."

Granny moved her hands the way he'd taught her while shouting that phrase that sounded like nonsense to me. I felt the tingle of magic, but the gargoyle kept dropping toward us. "Move!" Owen shouted to the driver. The carpet barely swerved out of the way as the gargoyle dropped like the proverbial stone. I couldn't resist a glance over the side to watch it fall into the river. I imagined I heard a splash, but that was unlikely from this height.

"What did I just do?" Granny asked Owen.

"You told it to turn back into stone. I got the feeling this one had only recently been animated, so it was easy enough to return it to its original state."

"Ha! Not so easy, since you needed me to do it," Granny said with a grin, poking him in the chest.

"But you needed my fancy spell to do it," he countered with a grin of his own.

"I'm sure I'd have figured something out eventually," she said.

"Don't try using that spell on our gargoyles," he warned. "I'm not sure it would even work, since most of them have been alive for centuries. It's more likely to just make them cranky."

"I bet I could figure something out," she said with a wicked gleam in her eye. "Then they'd better stay on my good side. Otherwise, I think they'd look real good in my garden. I could train ivy over them."

Owen's phone rang, and he winced guiltily at Granny's mischievous grin as he said, "Hi, Sam. No, we're okay, we got rid of it. We're on the East River. It looks like we're coming up on the Williamsburg Bridge." Then his eyes went wide. "Oh, no, Rod and the others could be in danger, too." He looked grim and nodded a few times as he listened.

"Are they okay?" I asked, clutching his arm as he ended the call.

"Yeah, Sam warned them in time."

"Someone really doesn't want us to succeed."

"And that someone seems to be a step ahead of us."

"On the bright side, our unknown follower couldn't possibly have kept up with us through all that, not on foot, and we'd have seen anything else in the air."

When we finally reached the MSI building without further incident, I asked the driver to take us to the front door. "I'm not getting off in midair this time," I said with a shudder.

Much to my relief, the carpet landed on the ground, and all of us let out a collective sigh. I sat there for a while, reveling in the knowledge that I couldn't fall from where I was. Owen stood first and extended a hand to help Granny up, then he pulled me to my feet and straight into his arms, where he held me in a fierce hug. I buried my face against his shoulder and hugged him back, enjoying the feel of solid earth beneath my feet and solid man in my arms. "I am never, ever getting on one of those things again," I said. "At least, not until they install seatbelts."

"Seatbelts sound like a very good idea," Owen agreed. Without loosening his hold on me, he spoke over my shoulder to Rocky and Rollo, the security gargoyles who had just landed beside us. "Someone's animating gargoyles. I don't know where they got that one, but it looked old and European. It even had moss growing on it."

I turned to see Rocky shuddering. "Moss? Talk about a personal hygiene problem! What kind of creep doesn't bother to scrape off the moss?"

"We'll look into it," Rollo said.

"Thanks," Owen said. "Now, could one of you escort Katie's grandmother up to Merlin's office?"

Granny gripped her cane with both hands and planted it firmly on the ground in front of her. I wouldn't have been surprised if it had grown roots. "I'm not letting Katie out of my sight. She's going to need me."

"I've already needed you," I said. "Maybe all that"—I gestured in the general direction where our aerial adventures had taken place—"was when I needed you, and you saved us."

She shook her head. "Nope. That's not it. I've still got the ache in my big toe, so it's still to come."

"But Mrs. Callahan," Owen began.

Granny cut him off. "You can call me Granny."

He blinked and blushed slightly. "But Granny, the thing is, we're going to be working in a restricted area that's very dangerous for anyone with magical powers. You can't go in there. And by that I mean you physically wouldn't be able to get in that area. It has nothing to do with wanting you there or giving you permission. We won't be there long, and I need Katie's help. Inside this building, nothing will happen to her."

"And you can hang out with Merlin," I added. "We need you to tell him what just happened to us. Maybe you could help figure out who in the company is working for the other side."

She glared back and forth between us for a long time, then nodded and said, "Well, alrighty then. I'll report to Merlin, and you two run along and do your thing." She waved a warning finger at us. "But don't take too long because I'll have to come looking for you." Then she turned and told the gargoyles, "Gentlemen, let's go."

With my grandmother temporarily out of our hair, Owen and I entered the building and ran down the stairs to the basement workroom. It seemed like days had passed since I'd brought Owen breakfast that morning. The coffee Thermos still sat there in the outer room, and I emptied the contents into a cup. The coffee was a drinkable temperature, though perhaps not as hot as I preferred. Under the circumstances, I wasn't going to complain about the temperature of my caffeine. I added a good dose of sugar and drank half the cup in one gulp before handing it to Owen. "Here, the sugar and caffeine will help after all that excitement," I said.

He obediently drained the cup, then abruptly hurled it across the room so that it bounced off the wall and then shattered on the floor. Bright spots blazed on his cheeks as he fought to get control of himself. "Did that help?" I asked him.

"Not so much." The red patches on his face faded, to be replaced by a pink flush that rose from his collar to his hairline. "I was so helpless out there. We would have died if it hadn't been for a little old lady with her folk magic. I had to teach someone else to do a spell because I couldn't work it myself."

I knew there was nothing I could say to make it better, so I didn't try. Instead, I said calmly, "It's about time."

"For what?"

"For you to admit that this sucks. You've been playing Pollyanna all along, acting like you'd practically planned to end up this way, and wasn't it great that losing your powers meant you got to do all this awesome research and kept the magical world from seeing you as a threat. I knew that couldn't be real. I mean, really, you were the most powerful wizard of your generation, and you lost all trace of magic. It's *awful*. It's like losing your eyesight, or an arm or a leg."

"Thank you for the pep talk," he said, raising an eyebrow.

"I'm not trying to cheer you up. That would be pointless. I'm just glad you're finally being honest with me—and with yourself." I hesitated, then asked, "Do you also really believe it will come back?"

He worried his lower lip in his teeth for a while, then whispered, "No." His shoulders sagged in defeat.

I stepped forward and pulled him against me in a big hug. "I'm so sorry, honey."

After holding me for a couple of minutes, he said, "So, now that we've dealt with my issues, are you ready to talk about what's going on with you?"

"Well, since I'm not throwing things, that's not an immediate crisis, and we have work to do."

He placed his hands on either side of my face, kissed me, and said, "Fine, but at some point, you're going to have to stop avoiding the discussion. I won't forget." Then the two of us headed into the manuscript room.

He pulled a stack of paper toward himself, lifted off the top half, and handed it to me. "I labeled it as I was transcribing. Look for the word 'spell' in the margins and pull those pages." I shuffled quickly through the pages, handing the "spell" pages to him as soon as I had a handful. From there, he turned the rest of his stack over to me while he read more carefully through the spells, sorting the pages into piles. After he'd gone through the whole stack, he picked up one of his piles. "These are the ones the doorman used and a few others that fall into the same era that seem like they might also be used for attack or defense."

"Is there anything in those spells that might give us a clue what this is about? Are they related to the Eye?"

"No, they're actually after Merlin's time, probably from one of his immediate successors. At the most, maybe two generations later. But they are all from the same era and I think they can be traced back to the same wizard. I'm not sure what that tells us, but there's probably some old grimoire out there from that time period, and the doorman could have read that. Now, let's go get your grandmother and get back to the others."

When we reached Merlin's office, he was standing at the conference table with someone I assumed, based on the beads, scarves, and scent of incense, was from Prophets and Lost. "Ah, there you are," he greeted us as we crossed the threshold. "I just heard from Mr. Gwaltney. They haven't found the brooch or Ms. Perkins yet. I trust your search was successful?"

Owen held up the stack of spells and opened his mouth to say something, but whatever he was about to say came out as "Ouch!" when Granny's cane jerked and rapped him across the shin so hard that the sound of it made me hop on one foot for a second.

She looked up at him with an expression of fake innocence. "Oh, dearie me. I'm so sorry. My muscles must still be twitching from all the excitement earlier. I can't seem to control myself."

The P & L person finished adding colored pushpins to a map of the city lying on the conference table. "There, those are our latest findings," she said. "Red is confirmed sightings. Blue is where we've picked up an aura that could mean something. Green is potential visions of the future." The pins spread over most of the Upper East Side, with a few blue and green pins trickling down to Midtown.

"Thank you," Merlin said. The woman nodded as she picked up her notebook and left, her scarves wafting behind her.

As soon as she was gone and the doors had closed, I whirled on Granny. "What was that for?" I demanded.

"Loose lips sink ships," she snapped.

I groaned inwardly and was about to tell her that just because someone dresses funny, it doesn't mean they're suspicious when Merlin said, "She is right about that, though I suspect she could have conveyed the same warning without resorting to physical violence."

I gestured to the doors where the P&L lady had exited. "You think she's the mole?"

"We've narrowed it down to that department."

"But why stop me from saying anything when you just said everything that was going on?" Owen asked as he straightened from rubbing his sore shin.

Granny grinned. "That's because we're setting a mole trap!"

CHAPTER NINE

"A mole trap?" I repeated dumbly, shocked to learn that my grandmother was involved in espionage. Not that I should have been at all surprised. She always did keep close tabs on everything my family and everyone else in my hometown did.

"Minerva is sending her staff members here on errands, one by one," Merlin explained. "While they are in the room, I take phone calls or have conversations about where our searchers will go next. Sam and his people are watching those locations, and if something happens in any of those places, that will reveal our mole's identity. But now that we're alone, what was it you wanted to tell me, Mr. Palmer?"

Owen sat at the conference table and handed the pages of spells to Merlin. "These are the spells that fake doorman used. I realized I'd seen them in the *Ephemera*. I'd guess they're from about a century before the Norman invasion, based on the language and syntax. We've been building on these spells for centuries, so there are now far more effective ways to accomplish the same things. No one uses these anymore, which actually made them difficult to counter."

There was a polite rap on the door, and Merlin waved a hand to open it. A young woman entered, and at first I didn't think she could be one of Minerva's mole candidates, since she was dressed professionally with her knee-length black skirt, medium-heel black pumps, crisp white blouse, and a chignon at the nape of her neck. "I've got some new readings for you, sir," she said, handing Merlin a folder.

"Thank you," he said, opening it. Then his desk phone rang, and he put down the folder to answer it, indicating with a gesture that he didn't want the woman to leave. "Oh, hello, Mr. Gwaltney," he said into the phone. "Ah, so no luck at the salons. Where are you now? Well, it's only a few blocks down Eighty-second from where you are on Lexington to get to the museum. Perhaps our best hope is to wait for her to arrive at the museum. Please keep me posted."

After he hung up, he smiled at the woman. "My apologies."

"I understand completely, sir," she replied.

He went back to the folder and flipped through the documents. "Is there anything you need to explain in here?"

"I'm sure it's all self-explanatory for you, sir."

"Very well, then. My thanks to your department for all your hard work today."

She nodded in acknowledgement and strode briskly out of the office. "Are you sure she works in P and L?" I asked when she was gone. Most of Minerva's department tended to dress like they were working at a carnival fortune-teller's booth, so she didn't look the part.

"Minerva says she's one of the best scryers she's seen," Merlin said. "And I believe she's the last one on the list. Now we wait to see where—if anywhere—our opponents go."

Owen's phone rang, and after answering it, he hit a button and set it on the table. "Okay, Rod, you're on speaker," he said.

"We've hit all the salons on the list and the good news is that we found Mimi's stylist," Rod reported. "The bad news is that the stylist is meeting her at the museum."

"I should have known," I muttered. "She'd want plenty of flunkies on-site."

"I'm afraid the first time we're sure of being able to get to her will be at the museum, possibly during the event setup. Do you think she'll show up to supervise, Katie?"

"Oh, yeah. She has to be there to micromanage and change her mind a dozen times."

"Then we'll go into the museum as patrons," Rod said. "We'll veil ourselves while they clear the regular visitors out of the exhibits and be in place to wait for her."

"How do we get in?" Owen asked. "You'll need us when it comes to getting the brooch."

"Sneak in with the catering staff. Surely she won't know everyone."

"The caterers will probably be scrambling to staff this event after everyone who's met her quits," I said. "It could work, but I'll have to avoid her while I'm undercover. Not that she'd pay enough attention to a catering waitress to recognize me."

"Did you find those spells?" Rod asked.

"Yes, and a few more they might use, just in case," Owen said. "I'll bring them with me. We'll be up there as soon as we can."

While Owen ended that call, Merlin's desk phone rang. "Yes, Sam?" he said, answering the phone. Then he frowned as he nodded somberly. "Are you certain? Have them followed. At the moment, I would prefer that they not know we're on to them." Merlin then dialed an internal extension. "Minerva?" he said. "Miss Spencer appears to be our person. Please bring her here immediately."

When Merlin hung up, Owen stood and said, "We'd better be going."

"I want to see this," Granny said, planting her feet solidly on the floor in front of her chair.

"I would prefer that you stay, for the moment," Merlin said. "It may help if you have firsthand knowledge of who is getting in your way."

When Minerva arrived, I was shocked to see the professionally dressed woman with her. She'd seemed too normal to be a magical spy. It didn't appear that she knew why she'd been brought to Merlin's office for a meeting. She carried a notepad and looked very much the way I must have once looked when I'd been Merlin's assistant and went with him to meetings.

"Please, have a seat," Merlin said to the newcomers with an expansive gesture. "Thank you for coming on such short notice on such a busy day."

Minerva sat across from Merlin and beckoned to her associate. "Come on, Grace, sit over here by me." She'd positioned the possible traitor so she'd have to get past all of us to get to the door.

"I thought it was a good time to update everyone on the status of our project," Merlin said. "We've run into a few obstacles, the first of which being that we appear to have someone within the company working at cross-purposes to our operation. Someone has provided misleading information to our team, has withheld useful information that should have been easily obtained, and is sending information about our team's activities to people who are interfering with and even attacking our people." If you didn't listen to his words, Merlin's tone sounded like he was starting any ordinary staff meeting. He even looked perfectly calm and neutral.

But as Grace heard his words, her face went as white as her blouse. She jerked back in her chair, like she was trying to shove away from the table so she could flee, but Minerva reached over and pushed her chair back up to the table. "Now, Grace, the meeting's just getting started," she said.

Merlin continued as though there had been no interruption. "Do you have any input on this matter, Miss Spencer?"

Grace stammered, then blurted, "I don't know anything about it."

"You brought me some reports not too long ago," Merlin said.

"Yes, sir, I did."

"While you were here, I took a phone call and discussed where our people would go next. Our enemies happened to converge on the spot I mentioned, very soon after you left my office. I find that interesting, don't you?"

Grace glanced from side to side, as though trying to decide whether she was more afraid of Merlin or Minerva, but she kept her mouth shut.

"And here's the interesting part," Merlin said. "They weren't really there. It wasn't a real phone call. What you overheard was bait."

"And you took it, honey," Minerva concluded, sounding more disappointed than angry. I recognized the tactic from the way my dad dealt with my brothers. The tone of disappointment was far more painful than anger. "Now, why would you go and do something so silly? I'm dying to hear who you're really working for. I've been under the mistaken impression that it was me."

A battle seemed to rage within Grace, as she wavered between continuing to play innocent and throwing herself on her boss's mercy. She went with an entirely different approach that I didn't think any of us saw coming. She straightened her spine and looked down her nose at Minerva as she said with a sneer, "Because I believe in true magic, not in power that is so bastardized by the modern age."

Owen reached for his pages of spell notes, a light dawning in his eyes. "You mean, the only good magic is the pure magic from the old grimoires," he said softly.

Her face lit up, losing the anger and wariness that had been there a moment before. "Yes! We are wizards. We have no need for technology. Long before anyone invented the engine or ways to generate and use electricity, we had power—true power. And we have weakened ourselves by not using it that way." Her eyes glittered with the depth of her passion, but then they turned hard and cold as she glared at Owen. "You're one of the worst—you, who took old spells and created new things out of them, taking away their purity."

"So, you're like magical Amish?" I asked. "Anything modern is wicked?" Now I saw her conservative business attire in a new light—and I came to the uncomfortable realization that I'd liked her outfit because it was almost identical to mine. Her hairstyle was more severe, and her blouse was buttoned up all the way, but everything she had on could have come from my closet. *I'm making Gemma take me shopping this weekend*, I thought as I surreptitiously unbuttoned another button on my blouse.

"I don't understand the reference, but we do believe that wizards have lost their way and should return to their roots."

Minerva raised an eyebrow. "And what the blazes does that have to do with your spying on this company and interfering with our efforts to retrieve the Eye of the Moon?"

Instead of answering her, Grace turned to Merlin and said, "You were one of the true wizards who created the magical foundations, and we knew that when you came back, you would restore things to the way they should be. But instead, you did this." She gestured disdainfully at the executive office, with its telephone, computer, and conference table.

She turned to Owen. "You're just as corrupt—even more so, because you were the one to corrupt Merlin, teaching him your wicked modern ways, infecting him with technology. And you were punished for it. That's why you lost your magical powers. Impurity must be punished!" Her voice grew shrill as her fervor overtook her reserve. "But we will purify the magical world!" As if realizing she'd said too much, she clamped her lips together and stared straight ahead.

Merlin leaned back in his chair and steepled his fingers. "Normally, I am very tolerant of other approaches to magic. There is certainly merit to the old ways, and it is good for us to remember how to work pure magic without the need for technology or other tools. But this isn't the time for a philosophical discussion. I want to know what the brooch has to do with this and why you're interfering with our efforts to contain it."

"I'm not seeing the link between the brooch and magical purity," I said, shaking my head. "Why would anyone want to stir up that kind of trouble?"

"Remember Bobby Burton, the volunteer fireman back home?" Granny asked me.

"The one they caught setting fires because he wanted to play hero and be seen putting them out?" I turned back to Grace. "That's it, isn't it? Your people stole the brooch from the gnomes, not Sylvester. Your plan was to create a threat to the magical world by setting that brooch loose, and then your people could swoop in when Merlin's team failed to save the day, proving that the old ways are the best and discrediting Merlin as a leader in the magical world—maybe then with your leader having the brooch so he can solidify his power."

"Only, everything would be ruined if we got there first and prevented the trouble, so you had to make sure that didn't happen," Owen said.

Grace tried to remain stoic, but she had a terrible poker face. She winced every time someone said something that must have hit close to the truth, which was as good as a confirmation.

Minerva turned to Merlin. "She came to work here very soon after the customer conference last summer when we officially announced your return. They must have planted her then to spy on you. I'm sorry, I should have seen this coming. After all, that's my job." She then asked Grace, "Did your people have the brooch then or were you merely being put in place to be useful someday?" Grace's lips twitched, and she bit her lower lip.

Owen faced Grace and said, "But do you really understand what you're dealing with in the Eye? How could you be so sure that you'd be able to save the day? What if you couldn't?"

"I created it, and I wasn't able to develop a way to resist or counter it," Merlin said. "I am concerned that this plan was poorly conceived, and that may put all of us at risk."

Grace went a little paler, and I noticed her throat move like she was swallowing a lump. Beads of sweat formed on her forehead and upper lip, but she didn't answer.

"There were people at the restaurant who didn't seem to be affected," I said. "I thought they were immunes, but they succumbed to the elves' spells. And they had a similar dress sense, as I recall. Is color wicked, too?"

Grace glanced down at her clothes, then cast a meaningful look at my outfit. One corner of her mouth turned up slightly, and I felt myself redden. On the upside, I figured I might be able to infiltrate their organization if it came to that.

"Don't get me wrong, I'm a big fan of the good old days," Granny said. "But there's something to be said for indoor plumbing and electricity, and magic's no substitute for either." She used her cane to leverage herself out of her chair. "And I've heard enough of this. We've got a plot to stop and a brooch to snag. Let's go, kids."

Owen and I glanced at Merlin, who nodded and said, "Now it is even more imperative that you obtain the brooch first and keep their plan from coming to fruition. I will brief Sam and Mr. Gwaltney about the opposition, and we will continue trying to get more information from Miss Spencer." Grace went a little paler at that.

We got up to follow Granny out of the office. "Wow, magical puritans. Who'd have guessed?" I said once we were in the reception area.

"I'd heard rumors of groups like that, but they're usually dismissed as crackpots," Owen said with a shrug.

"Crackpots can still be dangerous," I pointed out. "And it sounds like it could be really bad if their plan succeeds."

"Which is why we're going to stop them. How do we go about posing as catering employees?"

"Sadly, we're not too far off—for either caterers or magical puritans," I said with a grimace. He was wearing a black suit with a white shirt. "Lose the jacket and tie, and you're there. I'm already dressed for it." I frowned in thought as I studied Granny. "I'm not sure what to do about you, though, Granny. You don't really fit the catering waiter profile."

"But I could teach them a thing or two about cooking, I'd bet."

"Maybe a pastry chef, doing the finishing touches on-site?" Owen suggested as he folded his stack of spell pages lengthwise and handed them to me. "Can you put these in your purse?" Then he moved his phone from the breast pocket of his suit coat to the front pocket of his slacks.

"It's worth a shot," I said with a shrug.

"And if they don't believe me, I'll just hit 'em with a sleeping spell," Granny said as she took off for the stairs.

"Let's try to avoid the sleeping spell," Owen said to me. He handed me the case of tranquilizer darts. "You should probably keep this in your purse, too. Use them wisely."

I tucked the case away and gave him a mock salute. "Yes, sir." He rolled his eyes as he took off his tie. He left the jacket and tie lying across the chair next to Trix's desk. On our way out of the building, I said, "I know we're in a hurry, but I am not getting on another flying carpet. Probably never again, ever, but definitely not today."

"No, no carpets," Owen agreed with a shudder. "We can get an express train, though it'll be crowded at this time of day."

"Young people today have no sense of adventure," Granny said with a sniff as we headed for the subway station.

The train was crowded, with every seat filled and people crammed in like sardines. Even so, the train had barely started moving before Granny had a seat. Apparently, the young man who'd been sitting there discovered that there were more uncomfortable things than standing on the subway. I wasn't sure if magic was involved or if she'd just glared at him until his skin crawled.

I took the sheaf of transcribed spells out of my purse and handed them to Granny. "Here, you can make use of the time to read up on what you might face," I suggested. She put on her reading glasses and buried her face in the pages.

Meanwhile, I tried to remain aware of my surroundings. In that crowd, it was nearly impossible to tell if we were being followed. We'd caught our mole, but the bad guys were still out there. Most of the people in the car were wearing conservative black outfits, and the rest were wearing less-conservative black. For all I knew, everyone on the train was either a magical puritan or a magical enforcer from the Council. I leaned so that I could speak directly into Owen's ear. "Are you feeling any magic?"

"There's something nearby," he said vaguely. "More than on your usual subway trip, especially now that the magical Spellworks ads are gone."

"If it's someone following us, illusions and veiling won't work. We should notice."

"Do you recognize anyone?"

I glanced around again. "It's hard to say. There are some people who look kind of familiar, but is that because they've popped up everywhere we've gone today or because we work in the same part of town and see them frequently?"

"Our priority is getting to the brooch. We don't have time to take evasive measures like changing trains just to smoke out a tail."

"What if he's not just following, but trying to stop us from getting there?"

"We can sic Granny on him."

I couldn't help but grin at the mental image, even though I felt stressed and paranoid. Granny chortling to herself as she read the spells made it even funnier. "But that's just mean," I said, which made Owen smile, too.

By the time we got to the station nearest the museum, I was rethinking my position on magic carpets. We'd have been there a long time ago if we'd flown—that is, if we'd arrived alive and hadn't ended up as a damp spot on Fifth Avenue that disrupted rush-hour traffic after another gargoyle attack.

Sam met us on the sidewalk outside the station. "I got a full briefing from the boss, and he sent me to make sure you get there okay. I got nothin' against the Middle Ages, seein' as how that was when I was made, but lemme tell ya, it's nothin' to get nostalgic for, magic or not. Anyone who wants to bring back those times didn't actually live in 'em. And anyone who wants to turn the Eye loose on the world to make the boss look bad is clearly cuckoo."

"They'll want to keep us away from the museum, at any cost," Owen said.

"Don't worry, kiddo. I'll be with you."

That made me feel a little better, but fanatics willing to kill for their beliefs wouldn't be easy to stop. What *would* they do to keep us out of the museum?

Owen's phone rang, and after he answered it, he put it on speaker and held it out so we could all hear. "We're in the museum, and it's closed," Rod reported. "The event staff are coming in. They're setting up in the indoor courtyard of the American wing. So far, it's mostly the heavy lifting stuff—setting up tables and chairs and the like."

"Any sign of Mimi?" I asked. "She'd usually be micromanaging."

"She's here, but I haven't been able to get close enough to tell if she has the brooch. She's always surrounded by flunkies. She does seem to be on a power trip, though. She's made them move each of the tables about a dozen times, usually by no more than an inch each time, and it looks to me like they end up right where they were to begin with."

"That's not the Eye," I said. "That's normal Mimi. Has she yelled while doing it?"

"No. She's actually been pretty apologetic about it."

"Then that's *nicer* than normal Mimi." I looked up at Owen. "Is it possible that this thing has an opposite effect on someone who's already evil and power hungry and turns them nice and meek?"

"We can only hope," Owen said. Into the phone he added, "We're almost there. Be careful." As he put his phone back in his pocket, he glanced at Granny, and then stepped out to the curb to hail a cab. "We'll be running around enough tonight. We may as well stay fresh," he explained.

"And it'll be harder to tail you in a cab," Sam said approvingly.

Owen wasn't quite as efficient in getting a cab without magic as he'd been with it, but one stopped soon enough, and we piled into the backseat. A glance through the rear window showed Sam following us by air but no other followers. The ride was short, and Owen tipped the driver extra to make up for the low fare.

As we got out in front of the museum, I saw that a crew was setting up a red carpet and platforms for photographers on the main entrance stairs. Meanwhile, groups of people dressed in black skirts or pants and white shirts converged on the ground-floor entrance, where a man stood at the door, checking names and IDs against a list on a clipboard.

"Let's find another way in," I said.

"Give me a second, sweetheart," Sam said. "I'll see what I can find. There aren't too many buildings that a good gargoyle can't find a way into."

"Yeah, but remember that we can't fly."

"I'll find a door I can open for you."

We kept walking slowly, trying to give the impression of a couple taking an early-evening stroll by the park with an elderly grandmother. Owen's phone rang, and he had a brief conversation with Sam. I still wondered how the gargoyle used a phone. I'd never seen him with one and he didn't have pockets, yet we were always talking to him on the phone. Maybe he had a magical headset. The magical puritans probably wouldn't approve. Owen finished the call and said, "He thinks he can get us in through the parking garage."

We went around to the side of the building, following the driveway. Sam met us just outside the parking garage and flew alongside us as we went past the entry gates. "As far as I can tell, the coast is clear this way," he said. That didn't reassure me as much as I would have liked. There were too many places for danger to lurk, and as we made our way to the museum entrance, every little sound made me jump in anticipation of an attack.

It turned out that I was sorely lacking in imagination.

We reached the doors that led from the parking garage into the museum, but just as Sam went to magically unlock them, a tangle of vines burst out of the concrete floor, totally obscuring the doorway. "That wasn't one of the spells I found," Owen said with a frown, sounding insulted.

Granny stepped forward. "Don't worry, I know a thing or two about plants. Gardening is what I mostly use my magic for, anyway." She faced the vines, shaking her cane at them, and said firmly, "Now, you don't belong here. There's no sunlight, no good soil, no water. How do you expect to thrive? This isn't natural at all." The leaves on the vines started turning yellow and wilting and Granny nodded sadly. "Yes, that's what'll happen to you if you stay here. But isn't there somewhere better for you? I think you should go there now." Her voice turned to iron at the end, making that last statement into a command.

The vines receded, shrinking back into the ground as though they'd never been there. "No wonder your lawn always looks so nice," I said to Granny while Sam unlocked the door.

"Don't tell the garden club," Granny said with an impish grin. "I don't want to have to give back all my Yard of the Month plaques."

We'd just made it to the doorway when a group of men approached from the depths of the garage. "Looks like they weren't just counting on Mother Nature to keep us out," I warned, pushing Granny inside ahead of me. The men mouthed spells and sent them in our direction, but they had no effect on Owen or me, so we were still able to get through the door. Owen hit the elevator button while Sam sealed the door and put an extra spell on it. When the elevator arrived, Owen leaned in, hit a floor button, and let the doors close while he gestured us toward the stairs.

"Maybe they'll be waiting to ambush the elevator instead," he said as he led the way up. I'd worried about Granny's ability to climb the stairs, but she was practically running, confirming my mom's suspicion that she carried that cane as a weapon, not as a walking aid.

We reached the top of the stairs only to nearly run into a great wall of fire hanging in the air less than a foot away from the staircase, blocking us from entering the museum. I felt its warmth on my skin, so I knew it wasn't illusion. It was probably magical, since it was hanging in midair, didn't create any smoke, and hadn't set off the museum's fire alarm, but it would still probably hurt us. We had no choice but to remain in the relative safety of the stairwell. Then footsteps on the stairs behind us told me that the men in the garage had made it past Sam's spells. We were trapped.

CHAPTER TEN

"We've got puritans," I warned. "They're coming up the stairs!"

Granny whirled, pointed her cane at the stairs, and shouted, "Get on with you!" Vines sprouted from the floor and raced down the stairs and up the walls. Unlike the vines that had blocked the entrance, these had long, sharp thorns, and soon they formed a wall between us and our pursuers. "I know more about plants than you people will ever learn," Granny boasted. "And that's the oldest magic there is."

That still left the fire blocking the stairwell from above, as well as the puritans who must have cast the spell from within the museum. "Looks like we're trapped between a fire and a pointy place," I wisecracked, trying to keep my spirits up. It didn't work.

"The fire will burn out pretty soon," Owen said. "They're using elemental magic. It's very inefficient, so it's a huge power drain. They'll have to choose between maintaining the wall of flame and using other magic."

"Why don't we force them to use other magic?" I asked.

Instead of answering me directly, he called Rod on his cell phone. "We're in the stairwell coming up from the parking garage, and we're under attack," he said. "We could use some help. I'd like to hit them from both sides." Then he leaned his head against the wall and groaned. "And you don't have the spells that would help you fight these guys. Wait, I have an idea." He reached his hand out to Granny, and she handed him the pages. "Look out for a message. I'm sending the most likely ones to you now."

He lay the pages on the steps, then took pictures of them using his phone and sent them to Rod. "I should have thought of that earlier," he muttered as he worked.

"I think the fact that you didn't proves you aren't quite as modern and technologically corrupt as they think you are," I said.

"Yeah, but when you don't have magic, you'd better be technologically corrupt. I need to get used to it."

"I don't mean to alarm you kids," Granny said, "but we've got more problems." We turned to see water rising up the stairs. It had made it past Granny's wall of vines and was flooding the next step.

Sam was flying back and forth above us, talking into thin air. "Yeah, I mean now. What did ya' think I meant, whenever it's convenient for you to drop by and help in the attack that's happenin' *right now?* I wouldn't want to interrupt your dinner by being ambushed." I didn't see a phone, so I presumed I was getting a look at the way Sam communicated. "You'd better be here, 'cause if I die from this, I'll haunt you." He reached up a hand to tap his ear before saying, "Help should be on its way, assuming they don't get lost or sidetracked."

Owen's phone rang, and when he answered, Rod was shouting so loudly that I could hear his voice coming through the phone from where I stood. "You had to go after an army, didn't you?" he said. "There are hundreds of them. We can't deal with this."

Owen and I looked at each other, frowning. "How many do you see?" Owen asked me.

The wall of flame was fading, as Owen had predicted, and through it I could see the puritans. It was hard to count, since they were moving around, but there weren't hundreds. "Five, maybe six," I said.

"Yeah, that's what I've got." Into the phone, he said, "There are only five or six. The rest are illusion. Just hit them with something."

"And he'd better hurry," Granny said. I glanced down to see that the water was two steps below where we stood. It wouldn't drown us unless the wall of fire held it in, but it could make it very difficult for us to stay out of the flames.

"I am definitely coming in late tomorrow," I said. "I so deserve comp time for all this. That is, if we survive."

A moment later, there were shouts of horror from the gallery at the top of the stairs, and the wall of magical flame vanished entirely. We ran up the rest of the stairs, the rising water at our heels, and into the museum. "What did you do?" Owen asked into the phone.

I overheard the response as Rod said, "I gave them a little Hitchcock treatment."

"Very nice bird illusions," Granny said with a satisfied nod. The puritans ducked and flailed their arms as they fended off attacks from imaginary birds. That gave us an opportunity to make a run for the adjoining gallery, aiming for the Great Hall.

We'd almost made it when the bad guys realized that we were getting away, and apparently their mission was more important to them than their fear of a swarm of vicious birds because they came after us. We reached the entrance to the next gallery and found more puritans blocking the way. We were surrounded—again.

Then there was a guttural roar as Thor rushed out of the adjacent gallery, swinging his battleaxe and hitting one of the puritans on the kneecap. Another puritan rushed at Owen and me, and Owen swung a fist, hitting him squarely in the jaw and knocking him down. Owen shook his hand and grimaced in pain as he resumed running.

We made it into the next gallery, where Rod and Earl were waiting among a forest of Greek and Roman statuary, and I turned to see that Thor was escorting Granny through the remaining magical puritans toward us. I shouted a warning when I saw one of them closing in, but Sam swooped down on him, hitting him in the head with his stone talons.

The two remaining puritans came after us. Rod fought back with everything he had. "Hypocrites!" he gasped in between shouting spells. "I recognize that spell. It's a recent MSI offering. They're using the modern magic they supposedly want everyone else to give up." He raised his voice and shouted, "And I bet you've got a computer and a cell phone, too!"

A rushing noise above made me look up, and then I cried out in joy when I saw that it was gargoyles. Our reinforcements had arrived! They flew the length of the gallery, but instead of attacking our opponents, they came straight at us, and not in a friendly greeting way. They were nearly upon us before we realized they were the enemy—more stained, mossy, old gargoyles like the one that had attacked us earlier. Now we were the ones ducking and taking cover from an aerial attack, only the attack on us was real, not an illusion of birds.

I swatted away a gargoyle that pulled at my hair, grazing my knuckles on the rough stone. A second later, someone knocked me to the ground and rolled me out of the way. I heard a thud as something hard and heavy hit the floor where I'd just been, then I looked up to see Owen leaning over me. "Oh, hi," I said to him, a little dazed. I blinked to see that he'd moved me behind a headless Greek statue, and nearby a mossy old gargoyle with a chipped face was staggering on the floor, struggling to fly again. "Wow, thanks," I added.

"Are you okay?" he asked. I was just sitting up when I heard another rushing sound above. I ducked, crouching against the wall and protecting my head.

I heard Granny shouting the words of the spell Owen had taught her earlier for turning the antique gargoyles back to stone. But before she finished the spell, Owen shouted "Wait! Don't! Our gargoyles are here now." I opened my eyes and looked up to see that Sam's reinforcements had arrived and were engaging the enemy in aerial combat just below the gallery's soaring ceiling. They moved around so fast and were so entangled with the other gargoyles in fierce dogfights that it would have been impossible to target the spell.

A mossy gargoyle mistimed a dive and hit the floor. "Granny, you know what to do!" Owen said. She shouted the spell while waving her hands at the gargoyle, and it turned back to lifeless stone.

"That's one down," she said, brushing her hands as she smiled in satisfaction. Then she raised her head and called out, "Sam, send them my way!"

The MSI security gargoyles double-teamed the mossy attackers. One headed toward the puritans, as though going on an attack run, and got the enemy gargoyle to give chase, with another MSI gargoyle flying behind to herd the enemy past Granny so she could cast the spell. Soon, there were lifeless stone carvings interspersed among the ancient Greek statuary. I was impressed with her precision as she avoided hitting any of the artwork—or any of us—with the falling gargoyles.

"It's too bad we aren't in the medieval art department," Rod said as he surveyed the gallery. "These don't look right here."

"I wonder if that's where they came from," I said. "The curators are going to wonder how they escaped." That made me think of something. "Hey, where are the security guards? You'd think that with the museum having an event and all the event people traipsing in and out, they'd have guards. And you'd think they'd have noticed all this."

"We'll probably find them tied up, unconscious, in their underwear, if these guys are true to form," Owen said.

The MSI gargoyles now had enough of an upper hand for us to flee. "Finish 'em off, boys," Sam instructed before we ran out of the gallery, Sam flying above us.

We followed Rod through the Great Hall and into the medieval art exhibit—which was distinctly lacking in gargoyles or even empty spots where gargoyles should have been—and then turned into the Arms and Armor galleries. We entered a larger space, and at first I thought a medieval army was coming at us. A group of knights on horseback filled the middle of the room. When we got closer, I saw that they were just empty suits of armor made for horses and men. But then they went into motion, the armor clanking as the empty metal shells drifted across the floor, moving as though they were filled with horses and riders.

I cried out in shock, but Rod said, "Don't worry, they're on our side. I set this up earlier." The knights rode to the gallery entrance and lowered their lances, blocking the way. "How's that for medieval magic?" Rod crowed.

We ducked into a side gallery and circled up for a conference. "I doubt those are the only people they have here," Owen said. "Not only do they want to keep us from interfering with their scheme, but they'll have people here to make a big show of defending the world against the owner of the brooch. That's what this whole plot is about, after all."

"They're setting up the gala just through there," Rod said, pointing toward a nearby doorway. "I'll give you a disguise illusion so you can blend in as staff. That should get you closer to Mimi and the brooch. The rest of us will split up and watch the entrances to keep out as many of the puritans as possible." He waved his hands at Owen and me, and I tingled from the magic, but since the illusion affected the viewer and the magic didn't work on me, I couldn't see any difference in Owen. However I looked, I was glad that Mimi wouldn't recognize me. Facing her while dressed as a catering waitress would be humiliating. You never want your ex-boss to think you've failed in your career.

We jumped at the sound of clanging metal behind us and moved to peer back into the larger hall. The magically animated knights were engaged in a fierce battle against puritan attackers. "They'll figure out how to break my spell sooner or later, so you two had better go," Rod said.

"Okay, then, let's get this over with," Owen said. It wasn't the most rousing pep talk I'd ever heard, but it was what we were all feeling. He glanced at Granny and added, "I don't suppose I can persuade you to stay with Rod and the others."

She shook her head firmly. "Not on your life, son. I'm sticking with Katie."

"It could get ugly in there, and if you show any sign of having been compromised by proximity to the Eye, we'll have to deal with you," he warned. Since I had the darts, I knew I'd be the one to deal with her. I wondered if I could bring myself to tranquilize my own grandmother. It was too bad my mother wasn't here. She'd jump at the chance.

"You do what you need to do," Granny told Owen. "I trust you to do the right thing."

"Then I'd better disguise you, too, in case they've had a good look at you," Rod told her.

"I can fix my own face," Granny said. "I've been doing this sort of thing since before you were born." I raised an eyebrow at that. Of course, I'd never have noticed, but I couldn't help but wonder why my grandmother would ever need a disguise.

I couldn't tell what she'd done, but Rod grinned. "Yeah, that should hide you," he said. "Now, go get that brooch."

The event space, an indoor courtyard, was connected to the small arms and armor gallery. Round tables were scattered about the space, with chairs arranged around them. Although the room was being set up, the staff were busy taking tablecloths off the tables and pulling cloth covers off the chairs. They didn't look too happy about it.

Someone passed us, talking on a cell phone. "Yes, I know that's what she ordered," he said. "But this is what she says she wants. I don't suppose you have that order in her handwriting or have her on video making that order? Yeah, she's claiming this is what she ordered and we're the ones who messed up. See what you can do on short notice, and we may need extra hands once we get the right colors here. Thanks."

"Mimi strikes again," I whispered to Owen as we moved away from the guy on the phone. "Now you see why it was so easy to recruit me away from her."

"Do you see her?" he asked.

I scanned the room, then shook my head. "Not at the moment. Maybe she's getting her hair done. Or she's out back, biting the head off a puppy. Do they have medieval torture implements on display here? We might find her in there, shopping."

Everywhere we turned in the room, there was more evidence of Mimi's influence. A gorgeous ice sculpture of a graceful woman in a flowing gown stood on one of the tables, and a man nearby muttered to himself, "Not thin enough, huh? Give me a blowtorch, and I'll give you thin."

A woman wearing an apron with a florist's logo on it cleaned up a scattered arrangement that looked like it had been angrily knocked off a table as she muttered, "Not fresh! The roses were cut this morning! They still had dew on them! And if you order flowers that have to be flown in, they can't be same-day fresh. I could scatter dirt and seeds. *That* would be fresh."

Nearby, other people in the same aprons glanced at her worriedly while they rearranged the floral displays, pulling out individual stems. Another woman ran in with a bucket full of flowers. "You wouldn't believe the mess back there," she said. "They do know there's an event tonight, right? Because it looked like they were doing maintenance on the entrance from the parking garage." She set down her bucket. "Okay, let's see if these suit Her Majesty." Then she bit her lip and glanced around guiltily. The florists went to work sticking those flowers into the arrangements.

"I don't think she's been wearing the brooch," I said to Owen. "Wouldn't that make people *have* to follow her? Instead, we're getting rebellion. At this rate, she'll need the Knot to get out of here alive. They're a hairbreadth away from pitchforks and torches."

"Is there a chance that she really doesn't have the brooch?" he asked, his forehead creasing. "The puritans could have set us up to believe this is it and get us off-track so they can create their big show with the real owner."

I shook my head. "No, remember, the elves were at the restaurant where Mimi got the brooch, and they're magically tracking the Knot, not following sketchy research. They also weren't at Macy's when we were following the false lead."

Rod, Thor, and Earl were in place now, with Rod guarding the main doorway and the other two lined up at the sides, where they could keep an eye on the room. I caught Rod's eye and shook my head. He nodded acknowledgment.

We looked conspicuous by not doing anything when everyone else was rushing around busily, so Owen and I joined in pulling tablecloths off tables. One of the women working with us kept up a nonstop stream of grumbles. "Seriously, can anyone tell the difference between ivory and cream linens? I bet we'll get the new ones on, and she'll scream that we didn't change them. Maybe we should leave one table the same and see if she notices the difference." The others laughed at that, and I joined in. We'd once done a similar thing when I worked for Mimi, and she hadn't noticed. She just liked making people jump through hoops. We'd learned that all we had to do was pretend to make the changes she ordered and let her think she'd forced us to obey an order.

A sharp voice cut through the general hubbub, saying, "You would not believe the difficulties I'm having here. Absolutely *everyone* showed up with the wrong things. It's a disaster—the wrong color linens, wilted old flowers, an *obese* ice sculpture. How hard is it to get an order right?"

Speak of the devil, I thought. Mimi was entering the courtyard, talking on a cell phone. I caught Rod's eye and gestured toward her with my head. He nodded and signaled the others.

As soon as she got fully into the event space, Mimi took one look at the preparations and snapped, "Why aren't the tables set up? You can't have a black-tie, celebrity-filled gala with bare tables! There should be tablecloths and chair covers! Those have to be on before we can do the centerpieces and name cards! What is wrong with you people?"

I expected the man in charge of the table linens to remind her that the tables were bare because she wanted different tablecloths, but he didn't stand up to her at all. Instead, he fell on his knees. "I have failed you," he said, bowing his head in shame, his hands clasped in front of him in supplication.

Surprised, Mimi took a step away from him, her face screwing up in distaste. As much as she'd always wanted that kind of response, she must not have expected it. "Well, yes," she said. "But when will you get the right tablecloths and get them on the tables?"

"Soon! Now!" He gestured to the staff, indicating for them to hurry up stripping the tables, and then he got on the phone and yelled at whomever was bringing the new linens.

Mimi moved on to her next victim, the florist, who jumped to attention. "We're almost done, we got new flowers, see, the centerpieces are done, and we'll get them on the tables as soon as the tablecloths are on," she babbled. "I hope the arrangements are to your satisfaction." She bobbed an awkward little curtsy. Mimi was so stunned that she didn't even complain about the new arrangements and make the florists put them back the way they'd been.

"She must have the brooch on her, but I don't see it," I whispered to Owen as we kept pulling cloths off tables. "But why aren't they scrambling to get at it? Shouldn't there be a big fight like there was at the restaurant?"

"She seems to be using it," he replied. "Unfocused, it creates the chaos we saw at the restaurant, but when someone is actually wielding it and using its power, then the user can control people and keep them in line. People with a thirst for power will still be drawn to it, but most will just be put under its thrall."

"This is disturbing on so many different levels," I muttered, then I glanced over at Granny and saw a frightening gleam in her eye. "Uh oh," I said, elbowing Owen.

He turned to look, then winced at what he saw. He bent and took Granny by the shoulders. "I need you to focus, Granny," he said.

"That doodad y'all are looking for must be nearby," she said, her speech a little slurred. "My, but that's powerful."

"Can you resist it?" he asked. "If you can't, I need you to get away from us."

She pulled herself together and gave a disdainful snort. "I've never had a weakness for jewelry. But I do want to take it away from that biddy. I don't like her."

I looked around the room to see how everyone else was reacting. Most of the event staff were treating Mimi like she was the empress of the universe. They practically bowed as she passed, trailed by a pair of clipboard-bearing assistants. Rod had flattened his back against the wall, and even from across the room I could see that he was breathing heavily.

I pointed that out to Owen. "We'll have to keep an eye on him," I said.

Earl seemed less affected. He looked bored. I didn't see the gnome. His head didn't come far above the tables, so he'd be easy to lose. "Do you see Thor?" I asked Owen and Granny.

Owen shook his head. Instead of a response from Granny, there was a "thwap" sound and then a thud. A glance at the floor showed Thor lying on his back, his axe in his hands. Granny stood over him, holding her cane out like a weapon. "He was trying to sneak up on her," she said.

Owen leaned over him. "Are you carrying out the mission to retrieve the brooch, or are you under its influence?" he asked.

"I think a little of both," Thor admitted groggily, rubbing his head. "It is our property. But, boy, is it ever enticing. I could really use a piece of that."

"The ownership is currently disputed," Owen said. "Sylvester owes you for the work, but the brooch doesn't actually belong to your people."

"Still, I'm on assignment. Can't blame me for trying."

"As long as you don't blame me for making sure you don't try again." Owen used one of the discarded napkins to tie Thor's hands behind his back and then rolled him under the nearest table. "He'll probably be able to work his way out eventually, but that should keep him out of our hair for a little while." Then he frowned and said, "Hey, what's this?"

He bent to pick up a brooch of ornate Celtic knotwork in gold, with a spherical sapphire set in the middle of it.

"The Eye! It must have fallen out of his pocket," I guessed excitedly. "But how'd he get it? He must have been on his way back from grabbing it, and we didn't notice."

Owen shook his head. "I don't think so." He raised it to the light and turned it from side to side, then wrapped his hand around it. "I don't think it's real," he said. "They must have made a duplicate and he was going to try to pull off a swap. I wouldn't be surprised if they'd planned all along to give Sylvester the fake." He held it in front of Granny. "Does this do anything to you?" he asked.

"Not a bit," she said with a shake of her head. "I don't have the slightest desire for it."

"It's definitely a fake," Owen concluded.

"You're good at sleight of hand," I said as an idea took shape in my head. "How are you at pickpocketing?"

"I've never tried."

"Well, maybe we can use this—see if we can get a chance to swap this out. It might buy us time if Mimi doesn't realize the real one is gone."

"But we'd have to find the real one first," he said.

We both turned to watch Mimi as she continued yelling at everyone who displeased her. Although she'd seemed surprised by the subservient responses at first, she now looked like she was enjoying the power and had gone into full-on czarina mode. Then I noticed that she kept putting her right hand in the pocket of her suit jacket. Every time she did so, a look came over her face, as though touching whatever was in there gave her strength. I pointed it out to Owen. "Does it look to you like she's got a 'my precioussss' thing going on with something in that pocket?" I asked him.

He watched her for a while longer, then said, "Yeah, I think that's where it is. Let's see if we can move in on her. You and Granny create a diversion, and I'll make the switch."

I looked up to signal our colleagues, but I couldn't find Earl. He was too tall to disappear easily. Then I saw him crouching and darting from sculpture to sculpture, on his way to the exit that led into the Arms and Armor section. A glance at the other entrance explained why: Sylvester, Lyle, and a few other elf flunkies had entered.

"Oh, fun, the gang's all here," I said.

"We need to get it before they do," Owen said.

Rod gave Owen a "What should I do?" signal, and Owen waved for him to stay back. Owen and I headed closer to Mimi. As we moved, I thought of ways to distract her. I wondered if I could signal Rod to drop my illusion disguise. Seeing me pop up here would certainly distract Mimi, but I preferred not to resort to that.

I picked up one of the flower arrangements that looked like it was meant to be a centerpiece and carried it toward Mimi. My plan was to "accidentally" drop it right in front of her so she could be distracted by the need to berate me. I figured I might even be able to shock her by not falling on my knees or begging her for mercy. If she was enjoying her newfound power over people, she might find open defiance disconcerting.

Oh, yeah, this was the best mission ever.

I was already anticipating sweet revenge when something stopped me in my tracks.

I smelled something familiar—a scent like a spice factory explosion in a pine forest. That was the cologne I'd used as a weapon in Macy's. It came from the assistant to Mimi's right—the same side as the pocket she kept touching. The smell was so strong that either the guy had marinated in it or he'd recently been hit in the face with a heavy blast of it. I suspected it was the latter.

The puritans had infiltrated Mimi's inner circle. We didn't stand a chance of getting close enough to her to make the swap.

CHAPTER ELEVEN

I tried to warn Owen to abort the mission, but he was so focused on finding an opportunity to pickpocket Mimi that I couldn't get his attention without also drawing the attention of both Mimi and her puritan protector. All I could do was not create the diversion Owen was waiting for. I returned the centerpiece to the table and hoped Owen figured out that there had been a change of plans.

I watched helplessly as he edged closer and closer to Mimi. Once he was in position, he glanced around, looking for the expected diversion. When he finally saw me and gave me a "Well?" look, I shook my head. He frowned, shrugged, and then wandered casually back to me.

"What happened?" he asked when he was close enough that we could speak without being overheard.

"The assistant standing by Mimi's critical pocket is a puritan."

"How can you tell? Do you recognize him?"

"I smelled him."

"Smelled him?"

"This guy reeks of that cologne I sprayed all over the guy chasing us in Macy's. I mean, way more than 'I don't have time for a shower, so I'll just put on some extra cologne' levels. You know they'd have someone close to the brooch to be ready for making their grand saving-the-world show, so it all adds up. I doubt you'd have stood a chance."

He glanced at Mimi and her minions, his brow knitted as he chewed his lower lip. Then he turned back to me and sighed softly. "You're probably right. Good catch. But now what do we do?"

"I'm not sure we should do anything at the moment," I said, nodding toward Sylvester and the elves, who were heading for Mimi.

He turned to follow my gaze, then he winced. "We should probably do something," he said. "We can't let them get to it first."

97

I caught him by the elbow as he started to move. "No, wait. Those puritan guys aren't going to let the elves take it, either. Maybe we could let them fight it out."

He gave a grin that was so close to evil that if the people who were convinced he would follow in his birth parents' footsteps had seen it, they'd probably have insisted on having him arrested immediately. "Nice thinking. Be ready to act once they're distracted."

But the elves walked right past Mimi. They acted like they were sniffing the air but hadn't yet homed in on the scent—and I didn't think they were tracking the minion's cologne. "They don't know who has it!" I whispered to Owen, clutching his sleeve where I still held his elbow. "They didn't see her at the restaurant, and she's not wearing the brooch. They must have sensed the brooch was here, but how accurate are they at close range?"

"I guess we'll find out." We went back to work messing with tablecloths but paying far more attention to what was going on with Mimi.

It turned out to be Mimi who approached the elves. "The band seems to be here," she told one of her minions. "Check that off." Then to Sylvester, she said, "Good, you're here. They've got the stage set up over there." She quirked an eyebrow as she took in an eyeful of Sylvester and Lyle's vintage eighties attire and added, "I believe I mentioned on the phone that black tie would be required, so I hope you're planning to change into your tuxes after you've carried in your gear." When the elves didn't move, she glared at them and said in a dismissive tone, "You can go set up now." Without waiting for a response, she and her minions headed off to deal with the next item on her list.

Lyle turned and started to move away, obeying the order, but Sylvester caught the back of his shirt collar and kept him from going anywhere. Meanwhile, the Elf Lord's eyes narrowed as he watched Mimi's rapidly retreating back. One of his slanted eyebrows slowly rose, and he smiled slightly to himself.

"He's figured it out," Owen whispered to me as he pulled a cover off a chair and added it to a growing pile of rejected linens.

We both turned when someone new ran into the room. It was Earl. He skidded to a stop when he reached his supposed boss. "My lord!" he panted. "I got your message."

Sylvester didn't bother telling him to shut up. He merely raised his hand without turning to look at Earl. Earl made a face at the back of Sylvester's head, then turned to us and gave a helpless shrug. "He is really on our side, right?" I whispered to Owen.

"He's probably trying to keep his cover. At least, I hope so."

A funny gleam in his eyes, Sylvester slowly followed Mimi, moving like a sleepwalker. He hadn't released Lyle's collar, so his sidekick was forced to go with him. The other elves glanced at each other, then followed their boss. Earl trailed behind all of them. Sylvester raised his hands in front of him to shoulder height—at least, he raised his left hand. His right was still holding on to Lyle. He realized this when his right hand didn't fall into position, and he quickly released Lyle and resumed whatever he was about to do. Earl called out, "Uh, your lordship?"

"Not now, Earl," Sylvester hissed through clenched teeth without taking his eyes off Mimi. Behind him, Earl gave a "Well, I tried" shrug.

Sylvester's lips moved, but I couldn't hear what he said. I felt a slight tingle as the sense of magic in the room built, but nothing happened. Sylvester frowned and brought his hands up in front of his face. "What?" he growled.

"I tried to warn you, my lord," Earl said. It was a sign of how stunned Sylvester was that he allowed Earl to speak more than two words. "It's the Knot. It—"

"Shut up, Earl," Sylvester said, returning to his senses.

"A magical attack wouldn't work any better than a physical one on someone in possession of the Knot," Owen said softly to me.

"So we've got the advantage here, since we can physically attack her," I said.

"If we can get past her minions." He grabbed another tablecloth and added it to the pile on the floor.

Mimi hadn't noticed the magical attack, but she did notice that the "band" hadn't gone anywhere. She whirled on Sylvester, her eyes taking on the mad wildness that I used to think of as "Evil Mimi" and that had made working for someone who literally turned into an ogre every so often seem not all that scary in comparison. "I thought I told you to set up," she snapped. "We don't have much time, and I don't want you doing sound checks after the guests start arriving. You will begin playing five minutes before the doors open. Is that understood?"

The elves took a step backward, and then they all turned as if to go. A second later, Sylvester shook his head and snapped out of it, turning back to face Mimi while catching Lyle by his collar again. The Elf Lord pulled himself to his full height—which seemed to grow a little—and loomed over Mimi. "Do you know who I am?" he thundered. "Who are you to give me orders, little woman?"

Mimi put one hand on her hip and gave him the full Evil Mimi glare. "I know exactly who you are," she said in a voice that could have preserved the ice sculpture in a kiln. "You're a soon-to-be-unemployed musician. Do you know how many talented musicians there are out of work at any given time in this city? With one phone call I could have dozens here competing to take your job." She turned to her undercover puritan minion and said, "Start making calls."

"You are no one to dismiss me," Sylvester said.

She put her hand in her pocket, drawing power from the Eye. I could hear that power in the tone of her voice. "Let's see, I'm the fiancée of a museum trustee, I'm on the board of the foundation benefiting from this event, and I'm the chairwoman of this gala. I am *definitely* someone to dismiss you."

Sylvester's fingers twitched, and then he seemed to remember that wouldn't work, and his hands formed into fists at his side. "You are in possession of my property," he said.

She raised an eyebrow. "You didn't even bring in your gear, so don't expect to get paid."

With an animal-like snarl, he leapt forward, aiming for the pocket where the brooch apparently was. The puritan minion moved to intercept him, but Sylvester's magic worked on him, knocking him aside. Unfortunately, Sylvester was foiled by his own brooch because he was unable to even touch Mimi's clothes.

"That's good to know," Owen commented to me from behind the chair cover he'd just removed. "We really may be the only ones who can get it off her. It should be safe from the elves."

"I don't think he's going to stop trying, and we can use that to our advantage," I said. "Let's get into position for the next time he knocks aside Minion Number One."

The courtyard was now so full of staff setting up the event that it was easy to blend in with all the people moving back and forth. We simply found something that needed to be carried from point A to point B, with point B being near where Mimi and Sylvester stood arguing.

Sylvester made another go at the brooch, this time neutralizing the puritan minion before starting. Owen reached for Mimi's pocket under the cover of Sylvester's attack, but someone else got there first.

With a bloodthirsty battle cry, Thor, who must have freed himself from his napkin bonds, rushed at Mimi from behind, swinging his axe at her knees. Instead of touching her, the axe hit the air about half an inch away from her, but he responded as though he'd swung his axe with all his strength at a steel beam. His whole body vibrated along with the axe, his vibrations moving him away from Mimi.

Owen reached down, grabbed his jacket, and slung him under the nearest table. Meanwhile, Mimi shrieked at Sylvester, "This is the second time you've attacked me. What is your problem?" She raised her voice and shouted, "Security! Is security here? Get over here, this instant!"

Several men in uniform rushed forward. Sylvester raised a hand, stopping them in their tracks. The guards wavered, caught between the compulsion to obey the owner of the Eye and Sylvester's spell holding them motionless. It didn't help when Mimi shouted again, "Well? I *said* get over here. Deal with these men. They're trespassing." I worried that the guards would spontaneously combust from trying to simultaneously obey two mutually exclusive compulsions.

Owen used this latest outburst as an opportunity to make another attempt. He had the fake brooch in his hand, ready to slip it into Mimi's pocket, but the puritan minion came to his senses at the worst possible moment and turned just in time to notice Owen. He caught Owen by the arm, grabbing him hard enough to make him wince.

I looked around for help. Thor was still vibrating under a table, Earl was pretending to be Sylvester's loyal servant, Rod was on the other side of the huge room and visibly fighting off the desire to go after the Eye, and I couldn't see Granny anywhere. That had me almost as worried as the fact that Owen had been caught. Owen was pretty good at taking care of himself, with or without magic, but I wasn't sure what Granny might be up to or how the Eye was affecting her. I didn't want to find myself in a situation where I'd have to take down my own grandmother to save the world from her tyranny.

Sylvester inadvertently came to Owen's rescue. He'd apparently decided that going with the fiction of being the band for the event was his best chance of staying near the brooch, as he got up in Mimi's face and said, "You wouldn't dare fire us. You wouldn't be able to replace us. How many of the unemployed musicians you have on call can do this?" Then he opened his mouth and sang.

I'd thought Earl's singing was sublime, but this was beyond that. Earl's voice still existed in the mortal realm. It was beautiful, but there were human singers who could do almost as well. Sylvester sounded like I'd always imagined angels must sound. The security guards quit struggling, Owen's captor released him, and everyone in the room stopped what they were doing so they wouldn't risk missing a note.

Once he realized he had the room in the palm of his hand, Sylvester signaled to his flunkies, and they joined in, creating an otherworldly harmony that soon had everyone in the room in tears. The magic of it didn't affect me, but I still found it breathtaking. My brain didn't seem to want to work anymore. It just wanted to listen to this lovely sound.

"That was close," Owen said, rejoining me after escaping the minion's grip and propelling me behind a sculpture.

"Hush," I told him. "This is gorgeous."

He frowned in concern. "The elfsong shouldn't affect you."

"Elfsong or not, it's good music. Oh, wow, but Sylvester can sing."

"Huh. Tenors get all the girls."

"Baritones are nice, too, and you've got a good voice. But you're not an elf."

The question was, how did this affect Mimi? The music was getting to me in spite of my magical immunity, so even if the brooch shielded her from the magical effects, it shouldn't have kept her from being stirred. Then again, I wasn't sure Mimi had a soul or that whatever shriveled, dark thing she had in place of a soul was capable of being affected by such pure beauty.

She listened for a moment, then said, "That's not at all what was on the demo you sent. You were supposed to be a jazz combo, not an *a cappella* vocal ensemble."

My jaw dropped. Seriously, that was all she could say about this? I'd actually been joking about her having no soul, but maybe I was right. I turned to see that Owen looked equally astonished. "I thought you were exaggerating about her," he murmured. "I owe you an apology."

Then Mimi sighed heavily. "But I suppose you'll do. It'll certainly be different. Everyone does jazz combos and string quartets, and if I have to hear another harpist I'll take a knife to the strings. People will definitely be talking."

When they aren't crying, I thought. I wasn't so sure that elfsong made the best dinner music, but I doubted Sylvester and the elves—which would make a great band name if they ever decided to perform—would stick around that long.

Which reminded me, we were there to get the brooch. I shook my head to clear the last strands of elfsong-induced cobwebs. "What are we up to, Plan C?" I asked Owen.

"Just Plan B, I think. We made two attempts with plan A, unless you count the one Thor interrupted. I won't be able to make another go, though, since they already know I'm after it."

"I don't know if I've got the skills," I said. "Maybe we could get Rod to change your illusion."

"Oh, come on, don't tell me you didn't learn to slip stuff into or out of your brothers' pockets," he teased.

"No, not really. I just got to be pretty good at knowing when they were trying to slip something into mine. It helped that most of the things they tried to slip into my pockets tended to slither."

"All you have to do is wait for her to take her hand out of her pocket, then when she's distracted, bump or brush up against her. Grab the real brooch, drop in the fake one, then get away quickly. There will still be something in her pocket, so she won't immediately assume she's been robbed."

"That is, until she doesn't get whatever power surge that thing's giving her."

"She doesn't know where the power's coming from. She'll feel a loss, certainly, but she wouldn't know it's the brooch, since she doesn't know about magic—that is, unless she's learned something since you quit working for her."

"You'll take care of the diversion?"

"Trust me. Now go look busy. Do something that takes you back and forth by Mimi a few times before you move in, so they'll be used to you being in that area." He handed me the duplicate brooch, then pulled me close for a quick kiss on my temple before sending me off with a playful swat on my behind that I was glad my grandmother wasn't there to see. Where was she, anyway?

I kept an eye out for her while I looked for a job to do that would help me blend in. The new linens had arrived, so I joined the group picking up stacks of tablecloths and napkins to distribute to the tables. I had to agree with the people who'd been talking earlier—there was no discernable difference between these and the ones we'd removed. It was typical Mimi, only magically amplified.

Taking the linens to the tables gave me the opportunity to walk past Mimi several times. She didn't seem to notice my existence, which was also typical Mimi. I was more concerned about her minions. They'd recovered from the elfsong, and the one reeking of expensive cologne had gone on full alert. Even if whatever illusion the elves used to mask their true natures worked on the puritan, he still had to know that something magical was afoot. I couldn't tell if the other minion was part of the scheme. He mostly focused on his clipboard, jotting down every request Mimi made. If he was smart, he'd be recording everything she said because when she changed her mind, she thought the new thing was what she'd always wanted, and written evidence wasn't good enough proof for her.

I definitely didn't miss that job, even if my current job was boring most of the time and dangerous the rest of the time.

I'd made several trips past Mimi and her minions—which would also make a great band name—and I figured it was almost game time. I'd noticed both Rod and Owen on their phones, so I supposed they were concocting something. I just wished I knew where Granny was. I didn't like wild cards—like, say, Thor and his battleaxe. Granny was an even bigger wild card than Thor, both literally and figuratively.

I spotted her on the far side of the room, where pastry chefs were putting the finishing touches on a giant cake shaped like a wheelchair. I wasn't sure that was in good taste for a charity focusing on helping people with spinal cord injuries, but it was certainly visual and memorable. Granny was supervising the placement of flowers around the cake wheelchair's spokes. That meant we might be safe from interference for a while. Granny didn't need a gem to make her bossy, and this opportunity to be bossy held even more allure for her than any magical brooch.

I gave Owen a nod to signal that I was ready to move in for my mission, then headed to get one last armload of linens to carry to the table nearest where Mimi currently stood. Then, as though she was picking up on my brainwaves and doing exactly what I least wanted her to do, Mimi headed over to inspect the cake, bringing her within range of Granny.

My initial plan thwarted, I changed course to go to the table nearest the cake. I thought it would be best if I were in position to intervene in case Granny did something strange. Well, stranger than normal. Even before she'd been open with me about her magic, I'd thought she was extremely eccentric.

"What is this supposed to be?" Mimi demanded when she reached the cake.

The cake decorators cringed and cowered, looking like dogs being scolded for making a mess on the carpet. That left Granny to face Mimi. She looked up at Mimi and snapped, "It's a wheelchair made out of cake. Any fool can see that. What did you think it was?"

Mimi was struck speechless. I wished I had a video camera because that wasn't something that happened often. Her mouth opened and closed a few times, but nothing came out. She coughed, then sputtered, "I meant, why isn't it the way I ordered it?"

"And how did you order it?" Granny asked, her hands tightening on the top of her cane and her voice taking on an edge I recognized all too well. When her voice got that tone to it, even my mother quit arguing with her— and my mother's main hobby, aside from trying to make me wear more makeup, was arguing with her mother.

Mimi was distracted enough for me to slip in close to her, but her brooch pocket was too close to the cake table, and then she put her hand in her pocket, presumably to draw strength from the Eye so she could deal with Granny. "It—it was supposed to have a more metallic look in the icing," Mimi eventually managed to say.

Granny nodded. "Yes, I can see where that would be important. Metallic icing is just what's keeping a cake shaped like a wheelchair from being tasteful." The cake decorators grinned and clustered around Granny.

Even from where I stood, I could see the lump in Mimi's pocket where she formed a fist around the brooch. When she spoke, her words were tinged with power. "Do it as I ordered it."

Granny stared her down in silence. The cake crew started to cower again, but then drew strength from Granny and straightened defiantly. When Mimi began twitching anxiously, Granny said, "Well, alrighty, then. Girls, throw on some silver glitter. Don't worry about how it'll make the cake taste. Taste is obviously not a concern here. Want us to add some streamers to the handles? That'll really jazz it up." Behind her, the crew took some little vials of silver cake décor and began sprinkling it on the metal parts of the wheelchair cake. They hadn't even waited for Mimi's reply.

I couldn't believe what I was seeing. Either the Eye had met its match and found the one force in the universe that was more powerful than it was, or Granny was drawing power from the stone without actually being in possession of it. She was in total control of the situation, even while Mimi desperately clutched the brooch. I supposed it helped that Granny knew exactly what she was dealing with and maybe even knew how to channel its power, while Mimi had no idea what was going on other than that touching the brooch made her feel stronger.

I moved so that I could catch Granny's eye over Mimi's shoulder. If Granny was channeling the Eye, then maybe she could get Mimi to obey her. When I was sure Granny was looking at me, I mimed taking something out of my pocket and handing it over. Granny didn't acknowledge me, but she stared Mimi down again and said, "Why don't you show me that pretty thing you've got? Maybe we could work the design into the cake. That would be nice, wouldn't it?" Her voice had softened, taking on the tone of someone trying to get a toddler to hand over her candy, but it still had an edge of command to it, very much like the tone Mimi got when she touched the brooch.

Mimi's hand slowly moved out of her pocket. I couldn't see from my angle, but it looked like she was taking the brooch out. She held her palm out to Granny, and Granny leaned over to look at it. "Ah, very nice, isn't it?" she said sweetly. Then her voice hardened and she added, "Give it to me!"

The puritan minion jumped forward to intercept, but he wasn't fast enough. Mimi's arm moved as though she was really going to do it, but then she jerked back, clutching the brooch against her chest and crying, "No! It's mine!" Her minion breathed an obvious sigh of relief. Mimi shoved the brooch back into her pocket and kept her hand in there. It had come so close to working, but now I didn't stand a chance of getting it away from her anytime soon. She'd be extra-clingy.

I headed over to where Owen had watched the whole incident while spreading cloths over tables. "That was …interesting," he said.

"I think Granny was using the Eye," I said, running my hand across the tablecloth to smooth out a wrinkle. "Is that possible?"

"Maybe. There had to be a way of overpowering the owner and taking it over, or it wouldn't have stirred up so much strife. The owner could have just commanded everyone to back off. A powerful person who knows what she's doing might be able to use it from nearby without actually touching it or possessing it."

"Then maybe we could just keep Granny close to Mimi, and she can counteract or minimize the damage until we can find a way to make the switch. She already stopped Mimi from abusing the cake decorators."

"That may work for a while, but it won't be enough later in the evening."

"Why not?"

"When this event starts, this room will be filled with billionaire and millionaire philanthropists, celebrities, and politicians. Now, think about those kind of people surrounding the Eye."

"That's when the real trouble will start," I said, nodding as I imagined the likely scenario. "That's probably what these magical puritans have planned—a big scuffle breaking out that they can resolve."

"Or worse, one of those people with real power getting the brooch away from Mimi. Imagine what might happen if a senator got that thing and took it to Washington. That's when the real trouble would start that they could step in and save us all from by plunging us back into the Dark Ages."

"Yikes," I said, shuddering. "Okay, then, we've got to get the brooch and get it out of the museum before the event starts." I turned to watch Mimi fleeing from Granny to go micromanage something else, trailed by her minions. "Maybe we should use one of our darts on the puritan minion, get him out of the way, and then we can go for the brooch."

"Okay, let's do it that way. Give me a dart and I'll deal with the minion."

I took the case out of my purse, handed him a dart, and said, "I'll distract him."

I picked up a flower arrangement and headed past Mimi and her minions. When I thought I was in the perfect position to distract all of them, I pretended to trip, dropping the arrangement so the vase shattered on the floor, the water splashed everyone nearby, and flowers flew in all directions.

That triggered a patented Evil Mimi hissy fit outburst. "I do not believe the incompetence I've seen here today!" she shouted. "This is a world-class institution. I am trying to put on a world-class event. And yet you people can't do anything right. You can't get the linens right, you can't get the flowers right, you can't get the cake right, you can't even walk across the room without dropping something. I'm *terrified* of what the food is going to be like. You, stop that!" she shouted at me as I bent to pick up the fallen flowers. "Don't do another thing. Don't touch anything else. I want you out of here, right away. This instant! Do you hear me?"

She seemed to expect me to fall down and grovel or else scurry away in fear, but instead, I stood up and faced her, stepping toward her in a way that showed I wasn't the least bit intimidated by her. I might not have been able to channel the power of the Eye the way Granny did, but I wasn't influenced by it, either, and I had taken my last verbal abuse from Mimi almost a year ago. She had no power over me anymore, and it felt really good to know that.

She stared at me. I figured she was baffled by the idea of a catering staff member not being cowed by her. But I didn't expect what she said next.

She frowned as if in disbelief, then said, "Katie Chandler? What are you doing here?"

CHAPTER TWELVE

It was my turn to be stunned speechless. Mimi wasn't supposed to be able to recognize me. I was magically disguised! I glanced over at Rod and saw that he was on the phone. Behind Mimi, Owen was also on the phone, so I assumed they were conferring about this very situation. Either Rod's illusion on me had slipped, or the brooch made Mimi immune to magic and not just magical attack.

"Well? Explain yourself!" Mimi snapped.

I turned back to her as if just then remembering she was there—which was halfway true—gave my best mysterious Mona Lisa smile, and said, "That would be my business."

"You're working for me, so that makes it my business."

"Actually, I'm not." I had to bite the inside of my lip to keep from smiling. This was way too much fun.

She waved her hand dismissively. "You may work for the catering or event company, but I'm the one hiring those companies, so ultimately, you work for me."

"Isn't your foundation the one paying the bills?" I asked in mock innocence.

"I'm the one signing the check," she shot back. There was a slightly frantic edge to her voice, like she wasn't quite sure how to deal with this situation. I'd never dared to openly defy her when I worked for her. She'd probably thought I was a meek little mouse then. I was a meek little mouse then, but saving the world from bad magic a few times does wonders for your confidence levels. I'd faced down dragons, evil wizards, and creatures out of my worst nightmares—and won. Even with a magical brooch, Mimi was nothing.

"I still don't work for you," I said with a shrug. "I never said I worked for any of the event companies. I'm here for another purpose."

"I knew it!" she shrieked. "That crazy gossip blogger is trying to ruin me! He sent you here to infiltrate the place, didn't he?" She dove at me, grabbing my shirt collar and getting right in my face. "Tell me, you little bitch!"

"Takes one to know one," I said, locking my eyes onto hers, which was easy because they were only a few inches away. It would have been difficult to focus on anything else.

She straightened, released my collar, and drew back a hand as though to slap me, and that was exactly the wrong thing to do. For one thing, all the event staff had stopped what they were doing to watch the show, and I got the feeling that if she actually went through with the slap, she'd never be able to put on an event in this city, ever again. For another, my boyfriend was standing right behind her, watching her sternly after he'd ended his call to Rod, and he was immune to magic, so the protection of the Knot didn't affect him as long as he didn't use a weapon. She'd barely raised her hand before he jumped forward and grabbed her wrist.

But most important, she'd threatened me in the presence of my grandmother, and Granny did not take kindly to people messing with her grandbabies. I'd known that Granny wasn't as feeble as she sometimes pretended to be, but I had no idea how fast she could move. She'd have made a reasonable showing in the hundred-meter dash at the Olympics. Almost before Owen grabbed Mimi's wrist, Granny had managed to cross the room to insert herself between us.

I would have liked to fight my own battle instead of letting my grandmother come to my defense, but there was no stopping Granny when she got her dander up. This would be a world championship-level bitch-off, the wily old battleaxe squaring off against the entitled control freak. Mimi didn't stand a chance.

"You keep your cotton-picking hands to yourself, missy," Granny snapped, waving her cane for emphasis. "This is no way to treat people. Don't you know you catch more flies with honey than with vinegar? Besides, people with real power don't have to act like bullies. If you really were as powerful as you think you are, you wouldn't have to say anything. They'd just do things for you because they'd want to please you. You're only showing off your weakness."

Muffled laughter spread throughout the courtyard as the bullied staff got their vicarious revenge. I gave myself a moment to enjoy the epic battle, then returned my focus to the mission. Owen still had Mimi's right hand in his grasp, so her pocket was unprotected. I darted around Granny and reached for the pocket.

I wasn't the only one who'd had that thought. Sylvester and Lyle simultaneously lunged toward Mimi, deflecting my attempt. Meanwhile, the puritan minion knocked Owen aside. Owen refused to let go of Mimi's wrist, so he took her down with him when he fell. The minion brought the side of his hand down on Owen's wrist, forcing him to release Mimi. Mimi straightened, rubbing her wrist, then put her hand back in her pocket. I'd lost yet another chance at the brooch.

Owen was still on the floor. He pulled the tranquilizer dart from his shirt pocket, made eye contact with me to warn me he was about to act, then raised the dart and aimed it at the back of the minion's leg.

But Sylvester got in the way, making yet another go at the brooch. He didn't seem to be acting rationally anymore. There was no thought or plan, only raw need. His eyes blazed feverishly, and sweat dripped down his face as he clawed at Mimi's pocket, his fingers brushing against thin air an inch away—before he toppled over to lie face-down on the ground. He'd moved so quickly that Owen hadn't had a chance to pull the dart back. That meant we had only one dart left, but at least we'd learned that they worked on elves.

Mimi scrambled backward as Sylvester fell at her feet. If she'd seen past my disguise illusion, that meant she'd also seen the elves as they really were. No wonder she'd assumed they were the band. If she didn't know that magical races existed, then that was probably the only explanation she could think of for people with pointy ears and slanted eyebrows. The notorious oddness of musicians covered a lot of quirks.

"*What* is going on here?" Mimi screamed. "Why is everyone attacking me? It's sabotage, isn't it? They're trying to ruin my event."

"You can expect that sort of thing when you treat people the way you do," Granny said. "You make enemies, and eventually they'll find each other and team up against you. Happens all the time."

Mimi stared at Granny as though she was actually considering what she'd said. After a while, she said, "It's those breast cancer people, I'd bet. They can't stand some other problem getting any attention. They've probably joined forces with the AIDS foundations." She gave a sharp little laugh that was practically a bark. "And don't get me started on the 'wipe out malaria' people. This is just the sort of thing they'd do, though they'd probably release a swarm of mosquitoes in the middle of dinner." She turned to the minion with the checklist—who'd been watching these events with a shell-shocked expression—and said, "Make sure we've got mosquito repellent." For that one moment, she sounded totally sane and in control.

Then pacing and shouting as she waved her hands, she went back to raving, "They don't want me to be part of their little club. They think I'm just marrying for money and social position. Well, how did they get there? Are they any better because their *mothers* married for money and social position? I got a billionaire interested in me. That's an achievement." The entire time, her eyes jerked back and forth, like she was watching her perimeter. There'd be no getting close to her anytime soon.

While she carried on ranting, I slipped around her and helped Owen up. "Are you okay?" I asked him. He had an ugly red mark on his forearm, visible where he'd rolled up his shirtsleeves.

"This is turning out to be more challenging than I anticipated," he remarked. "But it does look like the stories about the paranoia the Eye can induce are true. We seem to be in the Lady Macbeth portion of the evening's adventures."

"Actually, this is normal Mimi, just amplified. When you treat people the way she does, you don't have to be paranoid to know that everyone's probably out to get you, or at the very least will celebrate when you fail."

"How long did you work for her?" he asked in disbelief.

"A little more than a year. And then you came to my rescue."

He took my hand and squeezed it. "If I'd known what you were going through, I'd have done so sooner."

"But you didn't even know me then!"

"I'd noticed you. If I hadn't been too shy to talk to you, I could have saved you sooner."

"You were still in plenty of time."

Mimi interrupted our romantic moment, whirling to screech, "You! You're the one responsible for all this!"

At first, I thought she was accusing me, since she was pointing in my general direction and I figured she'd already pegged me as the scapegoat of the day. But then I realized she was pointing just behind me, to the puritan minion who reeked of cologne.

"Ex-excuse me?" he stammered.

"Oh, don't you try to play innocent with me," she snarled, stalking toward him. She pointed at him with her left hand while her right hand fondled the brooch in her pocket. Owen and I took a big step backward to get out of her path. "It was so very convenient when my last assistant just happened to quit without notice and you just happened to be there to take the job." Her voice had lost the shrill madness of a moment before, and now she seemed to be channeling the Eye again.

"But it was all a setup, wasn't it?" she continued, now standing barely a foot away from the minion. Even if he had something to keep him from being affected by the Eye, he still shrank from Mimi's power over him. "You were put in position to sabotage me, weren't you? Who are you working for? Tell me!"

He sputtered and stammered, then finally blurted, "It's not about you. It's about a higher cause. You are merely the vessel to bring about a return to purity!" Then he clamped his lips shut and shuddered.

Yet again, Mimi was stunned speechless. This had to be a new single-day record. She probably would have been less surprised if he'd admitted that he'd been sent by a conspiracy of other disease-fighting groups to ruin her event. I wasn't sure what shocked her more, the indication that he was some kind of fanatic using her event to further his cause or the assertion that it wasn't all about her. The latter was a totally foreign concept for her. I thought we might have to explain it.

As if reading my thoughts, she whispered, "It's not about me? Are you sure? Because I do have enemies."

"Lady, we don't even know who you are," he said, sounding less enthralled. "You're just convenient."

That was the worst possible insult anyone could ever give Mimi. She pulled herself together, clutched the brooch in her pocket, then straightened her spine and looked down her nose at him. I halfway expected her to shout, "Off with your head!" but instead she merely said, "You're fired! Get out of here, now, or I'll have you arrested for trespassing." Her voice rang with the power of the Eye.

His fanaticism for his cause warred with the magical compulsion of the Eye as he struggled between trying to stay and trying to leave. The result was an odd quivering as he shifted his weight back and forth between his feet and twitched his shoulders.

"Well, go on!" she said with a haughty wave. "Your cologne is making my eyes water. God, but that stuff is vile, and practice a little moderation. You don't have to *bathe* in it." For a moment, I felt kind of bad for the guy, since the cologne wasn't his fault. That lasted about two seconds. After all, I'd sprayed him in self-defense.

The room had fallen totally silent while Mimi had her outburst, and all the workers turned to watch the minion leave. Mimi noticed everyone staring and shouted, "Well, what are you all looking at? Back to work! The guests will start arriving in less than an hour, and we're nowhere near ready. The tables still aren't set, the flowers aren't done, the bandleader is unconscious, and the lighting is all wrong. This is a disaster!"

Mimi's moment of crazy made her momentarily forget about us. When she rushed off to supervise the setting of the tables, Owen and I regrouped with Granny.

"So, we're down one elf lord and one puritan," I said. "That should make this a little easier."

"But you heard her, we've got less than an hour before the guests are here," Owen said, "and she's going to be especially guarded from now on."

"You know, at this point, I'm not sure anyone would so much as blink if one of us tackled her and took it away from her. They'd probably cheer for us."

"Okay, then. Let's do that."

I turned to stare at him in shock. "Seriously?"

"Yeah. I'm tired of this. We've tried everything else. I don't like her. And I'm sure you'd enjoy it."

"Oh, yeah," I sighed. "I spent a year dreaming about the chance to do something like this. Dreams do come true!"

All this time, Granny had been watching Mimi across the room. Actually, I wasn't sure if she was watching Mimi or tracking the Eye. "How are you holding up?" I asked her.

"I could use a drink, but the bartender isn't set up yet."

"I meant, are you feeling any strong thirsts for power, or anything like that?"

"Honey, I don't know what I'd do with real power at my age. Ruling the world would take too much energy. I'd miss all my TV shows."

"You managed some control over Mimi earlier," Owen said. "Do you think you could do it again? We just need to distract her enough to get her off guard."

She snorted. "Piece of cake. Her mind's pretty weak. I meant what I said about her doing all this bossing people around because she doesn't have real power. The moment someone truly powerful comes along, she'll hand over that brooch before she knows what she's doing, and she'll be the first one to sign up to be his flunky."

"I should have had you come visit me when I worked for her," I said wistfully. I rolled up my sleeves to match Owen's, then said, "Let's do this."

Together we advanced on Mimi, who was back to criticizing the ice sculpture. We had to step around Sylvester's prone body, which the elves had left where it fell. Lyle and the other elves had their heads together in a corner, probably hashing out their own plan. Earl kept trying to join the group, only to be shoved out.

We'd just passed Sylvester when Thor emerged from under the table where Owen had shoved him. He still looked a little wobbly and reeled as he walked. If Granny hadn't been certain that the bartenders hadn't set up yet, I'd have suspected him of drinking under that table. He staggered away from the table, dragging the tablecloth with him and sending the centerpiece crashing to the floor.

The noise got Mimi's attention, foiling our plan, but that wasn't the most immediate concern. Thor had seen his enemy lying helpless on the ground and was heading straight there—well, as straight as he could stagger—with his battleaxe in hand.

"No, you don't," Owen said, catching him by the collar of his jacket and taking the axe away from him.

"He owes me money," Thor slurred. I bent over to see if I could smell alcohol on him. Maybe he had a flagon of ale as part of his gear. My nose might have been dazed by so much forced proximity to that awful cologne I'd sprayed on the puritan, but I didn't smell anything. I supposed he really had been that addled by running into the magical force field around Mimi.

"Yes, but do you think you'll get your money if you decapitate him?" I asked.

"I wasn't gonna de–decap–decapa—cut his head off," he protested. "I was only gonna stick my axe in his back."

"That's not any better! It still would have killed him, and it's hard to get money out of a dead man."

"Not too much harder than getting it out of a live elf."

"You were planning to cheat him all along," I reminded him. "It wasn't his fault that you got cheated first. It was those magical puritans who stole the brooch from you. Go after them."

"Okay, where are they?" He swung his empty hands, then looked down to notice he didn't have his axe.

Owen hid the axe behind his back and said, "Why don't you come with me? Maybe we'll find one of those puritans for you." To me, he added, "Hold on for a second. I don't want him messing things up again." He marched the still reeling gnome over to Rod and handed Rod the tiny battleaxe.

While we'd been dealing with Thor, the elves had put whatever plan they'd come up with into motion. They moved as a group toward Mimi, Earl bringing up the rear and saying, "But remember—" before being cut off by Lyle.

It looked like Lyle was going to try Granny's trick of channeling the power of the stone through proximity. I didn't have high hopes for that, considering how susceptible he'd been to Mimi's orders earlier. He stood close to Mimi and said, "Give me the Knot!"

She looked at him in genuine confusion and asked, "What?"

"The Knot is ours. You must give it to us."

She put her hands on her hips. "Look, I don't know what's going on here, and I don't know what you're talking about. Now, you should probably go sober up your leader, then change into your tuxedos and warm up or tune up or whatever it is you vocal groups do."

"Yes, we should do that," Lyle agreed, turning to go, but one of his sidekicks caught him by the shoulders and spun him back around to face Mimi. He nodded thanks to his colleague, then repeated to Mimi, "Your brooch belongs to us."

Her hand went straight to her pocket. "My fiancé gave me this brooch. It belongs to me."

Lyle fought the compulsion to agree with her, then said, "But it was taken from my people."

"File a police report, then, but I'm not handing it over on your say-so."

While they argued, I scanned the room for any other puritan agents. If we spotted them trying to stop the elves from getting the brooch, then we'd know who to look out for when we made our attempt.

But it wasn't a person or even a group of people who took action against the elves. Something dark rushed down from the mezzanine, aiming at the elves. I instinctively ducked as it whooshed over my head, and then I got a good look at it.

It was gargoyles. Not MSI gargoyles, but the mossy, chipped, stained old gargoyles the puritans had sent against us earlier—the ones Granny had turned back into stone. Yet here they were, flying again.

"Great," I muttered. "Just what we need, zombie gargoyles."

Mimi saw them flying at her, and she reacted pretty much the way I'd expect someone who didn't know that gargoyles could come to life would react to seeing such a thing.

In other words, she lost it completely.

She screamed like the forces of hell were coming at her and fell on the floor, curling into a ball to shield herself. The elves had turned to magically fight the gargoyles that were attacking them. The event staff, however, didn't see the magically veiled gargoyles. All they saw was the band members gyrating oddly and their tormentor going into hysterics on the floor for no apparent reason. Some backed away from the crazy person, while others moved in for a better view. A couple snapped pictures with their cell phones.

I was surprised by how sorry I felt for her. Yeah, she probably deserved it, but she had no idea what was going on. I went over and knelt beside her. "Mimi?" I said gently.

"Katie?" She clutched at me, clinging to me like I was saving her from drowning. "You've got to help me. Save me from these things."

"Yeah, I think we'd better get you out of here. You've been under a lot of stress," I said. "Do you think you can stand up?"

"But those things … You see them, don't you?"

"Yes, I see them. They're really ugly gargoyles, aren't they?"

Reassured that I was seeing what she saw and not just humoring her, she let me pull her to her feet. "But they'll get me," she said.

"I can protect you from them." I nodded to Granny as I got Mimi off the floor and guided her away from the battling elves and the gargoyles. Granny took up a defensive position, blocking the elves from following. "Now, isn't it about time for you to get ready for the event?" I asked, keeping my voice low and calm. "I'm sure they can finish setting up, but you'll want to do your makeup and put on your evening gown. Where do you have your stuff?"

"I already had my hair done," she said mechanically.

"Yes, I can see that. It looks nice. But where are your clothes?"

"In the Patron's Lounge. We'll have to take an elevator."

"Okay then, you'll have to lead the way because I don't know where that is."

She guided me across the museum to an elevator, then directed me to the lounge, leaning heavily on me the whole time. I didn't know quite what to make of such a vulnerable Mimi. She'd only been nice to me in the rare times when she decided to play mentor and be my best buddy. Those times had never lasted, and I had a feeling that as soon as the shock wore off, she'd not only be back to her old self, she'd be worse because she'd be embarrassed about falling apart so badly.

The lounge had a nice powder room, and her evening dress was already hanging there. "Here, let's take your jacket off," I said. "Then you can wash your face without getting it wet." As biddable as a small child, she let me pull the jacket off her shoulders and guide her arms out of the sleeves. I folded the jacket carefully over my arm and told her to go use the bathroom.

While she was in the stall, I quickly switched brooches, pinning the real brooch to the inside of my skirt pocket. My heart raced as I completed the swap. After all we'd gone through, I couldn't believe it had been this easy. Granny really had been right about catching more flies with honey. Maybe if I'd been nice to Mimi earlier, we'd be out of here by now. We could even have staged our own gargoyle invasion.

Now to find that protective box. It would make things a lot easier if I could carry the brooch without it affecting everyone around me. I draped Mimi's jacket over the back of a chair and then dug through the bags lying on the floor, but the sound of flushing stopped me. Mimi came out of the stall, washed her hands, then splashed her face with cold water. She still looked pale and fragile, but she seemed to have a little more life in her.

"You'll need to touch up your makeup," I told her. "Which bag do you have your makeup kit in?" I moved as if to look for it, but she brushed me aside and got it herself.

I felt intensely aware of the brooch in my pocket while I watched her apply makeup. When she finished and took her dress into a restroom stall to change, I resumed frantically searching for the box. I still hadn't found it when I heard the latch on the stall door and had to stop digging. Mimi came out and did a catwalk turn for my approval. "Lovely dress," I said.

"I thought so. It was designed just for me," she said smugly. Yep, I thought, the old Mimi was on her way back. "Now, where's my brooch? I need to wear it tonight."

My heart pounding madly, I took the fake from the jacket pocket and handed it to her. "Here you go," I said. The gnomes had done an excellent job of creating a fake that was nearly indistinguishable from the original. In fact, I had a moment of panic that I'd mixed them up when making the switch, since I couldn't feel the magical difference.

She pinned the brooch to her gown, then checked the placement in the mirror. When she frowned at her reflection, I held my breath, but she only adjusted the angle before turning to me and saying, "Does that work? It's not too showy, is it?"

"No, it's fine," I lied. It was showy—rather gaudy, actually—but this wasn't a jewel for looks. It was a jewel for power. Well, the real one was.

She patted her hair, touched up her lipstick one last time, then said, "Now I suppose I'd better get back there. The guests will be arriving soon." She frowned, and I again held my breath, worried about why she was frowning. "You–you don't think they're making fun of me for that little episode, do you?" she asked hesitantly. "I mean, imagining gargoyles! How silly!"

"I'm sure they understand completely," I said. "They know the kind of pressure you're under."

"Yes, of course," she said, standing a little straighter. But she was still frowning.

It pained me to leave without the box, but we'd have to take our chances without it. I stuck close to her on the way back to the event space, hoping she wouldn't feel the loss of the brooch as long as it was nearby.

As we went down in the elevator, she said, "Katie, be honest with me, are you really undercover here, or is this the only job you could get?"

"Oh, I'm definitely undercover," I said. "I'm a terrible waitress. Let's just say it's a security situation."

"Who do you work for, FBI? CIA? Homeland Security?"

"I'm not at liberty to say, but there are initials involved."

"How did you go from being a marketing assistant to that?"

"My unique talents were recognized."

Her eyes widened. "Oh."

As we entered the gallery adjacent to the courtyard, we nearly ran into Owen, who was heading in our direction like he was on an urgent mission. As soon as he saw us, he abruptly changed course, turning his back to us to look at a piece of medieval artwork. I kept walking Mimi toward the courtyard, then said, "Now, are you going to be okay?"

She took a couple of deep, long breaths, then nodded. "Yes, I think so."

"Okay, then, have a good event, and I'll keep an eye on things for you."

As soon as she was gone, Owen and I rushed toward each other. "I got it!" I whispered when I reached him.

"Yes!" he exulted, throwing his arms around me and giving me a big kiss. Then he took me by the arm and said, "We'd better get out of here."

"What about the others?" I asked, glancing over my shoulder as he walked me toward the next gallery.

"We're safer away from them now that we have the brooch."

"My grandmother will never forgive you."

"She will if I keep you safe. And to do that, we have to get out before anyone notices that the Eye's gone."

Before we even reached the next gallery, Mimi's voice echoed through the museum, shrieking, "My brooch! It's been stolen!"

CHAPTER THIRTEEN

"That was sooner than I expected," Owen said, hurrying us into the next small gallery in the chain that led to the exit. It was full of religious medieval artwork, and I hoped some of that holy mojo would rub off on us. We needed all the help we could get.

We practically ran through the smaller galleries into a large, open space full of even more medieval art. It felt like we were running down the central aisle of a cathedral full of relics. Now we had a straight shot to the exit. Then there came a strange rustling, whooshing noise behind us, and I was afraid to look back, for fear of what I'd see. Owen didn't look back, either. He was running full-speed while on his phone with Sam. "Yeah, we've got it and we're coming out, so we'll need cover." There was a pause, and then he added, "Yes, I noticed." He pulled me quickly along as he ended the call. "Sam says the old gargoyles are on their way."

"I thought that's what I heard."

"Rod and Granny have them bottlenecked, but some got through. Sam's sending help."

I hoped help would come soon enough because the zombie gargoyles were now diving at us, and the only saving grace was that they were slow and clunky enough for us to dodge them. As we ran, I said to Owen, "Will the Knot protect me, even if I don't have any magic for it to work with?"

He ducked, then pulled me out of the way as a gargoyle dive-bombed me. "I don't know, but something tells me you'll find out soon."

Now I could see the Great Hall ahead of us. We were nearly out of the museum. That made me wonder something … "Where are the puritans?" I asked. "You'd think they'd want to stop us from ruining their party by running away with the brooch."

I should have known better than to say anything, since that was as good as summoning them. As soon as we came into the Great Hall, a group of men there rushed at us. They tried a magical attack first, obviously not realizing we were immune. The magic didn't do much to us, but we were caught between them and the zombie gargoyles.

That's when I learned that, no, the Knot didn't protect magical immunes. The gargoyles were able to clutch at my clothing and hit me when they dove at me. "This is not fair!" I shouted as I fought to fend them off. "I get all the bad effects of this thing without any of the good ones!"

The puritans soon overwhelmed us and had us pinned with our arms behind our backs, just as the front doors of the museum opened and the guests began arriving. Instead of dragging us away or trying to take the brooch from us, the puritans forced us to stand there as the rich and powerful entered the museum for the gala.

I screamed for help, but the puritans must have magically hidden us because the first few arrivals didn't seem to notice us. The Eye must have still had its usual effect because a woman in an evening gown I thought was rather frumpy veered abruptly off the red carpet and headed straight for me with a truly frightening gleam in her eye. I struggled against my captor while a man ran after the woman, shouting, "Senator! Senator! Where are you going?" He caught her before she reached me, much to my relief. She'd looked like she'd have gladly cut my throat to get to the brooch.

No sooner had she been herded away from us than a tall, powerfully built man with a million-dollar smile came our way. He didn't look quite as crazed, but he also didn't look like he could be steered away by a mere aide. I wasn't sure a brick wall would stop him.

A stone gargoyle, however, was another story.

Something winged dropped from the ceiling, coming between me and the powerful man. In the glare of the lights from outside, I couldn't tell at first if it was one of ours or one of the zombies, but then I noticed that it moved too fluidly to be a zombie. I was close enough to feel the tingle of magic as the gargoyle gave the man a jolt that sent him back onto the red carpet.

At the same time, other bursts of magic forced our captors to free us. "C'mon, kids, let's go!" a familiar voice said. I'd never been so glad to see Sam, and he'd come to my rescue many a time. "Out the back way," the gargoyle continued. "It would be a feeding frenzy if you took the Eye out the front door near that power-hungry throng."

While Sam's team held off the puritans and their zombie gargoyles, Sam escorted us through the side galleries, back the way we'd originally come in. There was no sign of the fierce fighting that had taken place there earlier. Obviously, the gargoyle corpses had all been reanimated, but the fire, water, and thorny vines were all gone, too.

We paused in the stairwell to catch our breath. I hoped I didn't look as bad as Owen did. His shirt was torn, he had a red patch on his jawline that would probably develop into a bruise, and blood trickled down his temple from a cut on his forehead. His clothes were disheveled, and his hair was even messier than it got when he was stuck on an intellectual problem and running his fingers through it. And yet, even though he was a total mess, he also looked disturbingly hot that way.

I was afraid to look at the condition of my tights, my hair probably looked like a bird's nest after the gargoyles had dug into it, and I had enough stinging, sore spots on my body to indicate that I probably had as many cuts and bruises as Owen. I decided that if I lived through this, I was taking tomorrow off.

"I should have looked harder for the box," I said. "That would have made this a lot easier."

"You got the brooch. That's the important part," Owen reassured me.

"So, now where do we go?" I asked.

"We need to get away from people."

"Yeah, I'm guessing we probably don't want to plunge into the Upper East Side with this thing," I agreed. "There might be riots."

"Into the park," he suggested. "This time of night, the population's pretty sparse."

"And the drunks and druggies aren't known for their ambition," I added.

Sam, who'd been keeping watch, said, "Okay, kids, time to go. I think some of our friends have made it past my guys."

With a groan of dismay, I forced myself away from the wall that had been holding me up. We ran down the stairs and into the parking garage. Sam had magically sealed the doors behind us, but the zombie gargoyles just burst through. Sam and his security gargoyles hampered our enemies while we ran up the driveway to the sidewalk and then aimed for the nearest park entrance.

There were still a few of the zombie gargoyles pursuing us as we raced down Fifth Avenue, but once we plunged into the park, we had some cover among the trees. We got off the paths and ran an indirect route, keeping to the tree cover and away from the lights. I hoped Owen knew where he was going because all I could tell in the darkness was that we had crossed Seventy-ninth Street.

I'd developed a stitch in my side, and I was gasping for each breath, but I kept running as well as I could, with Owen practically dragging me along. This was more intense exercise than I was used to, but Owen sounded like he was barely breathing hard. I could still hear gargoyles overhead, and I figured if they were ours, they'd give us the all-clear and guide us to safety, so I didn't have any choice but to keep running.

At least no late-evening joggers had yet tried to mug me to get at the brooch, and none of the brooch-crazy museum gala power brokers seemed to have followed us. Our situation wasn't ideal, but it could have been much worse.

Eventually, we lost the zombie gargoyles. We stumbled down a hillside, then Owen stopped me while he stepped over a low fence before lifting me up and over it. Nearby was a bridge that spanned a footpath, creating a tunnel. We ran under the bridge and paused, holding our breath while we waited to see if anything came in after us.

When it seemed like the coast was clear, Owen sank back against the side of the tunnel and I leaned on him, gulping for air in great, shuddering breaths. He put his arms around me, lightly at first, as though for comfort or security, but after we'd both settled down a little and I no longer felt like I was going to collapse, he pulled me against himself in a big hug.

"You did it!" he whispered. Then he gave me a big kiss before adding, "You're amazing! How did you pull that off?"

"It was incredibly difficult and dangerous. I should get a medal, or something."

"What did you do?"

"I was—get this—*nice to Mimi.*"

"Really?" He looked skeptical.

"I helped her calm down after that freakout when the gargoyles attacked. I made her take off her jacket so she could wash her face, and while she was in the bathroom, I switched the brooches."

"So you didn't have to hit her or tranquilize her, or anything?"

"I know! I'm actually kind of disappointed. Maybe I should have tranquilized her. Then I'd have had time to find that protective box so we wouldn't have everyone after us, and if she'd been unconscious for a while, it would have taken longer for her to realize she had the wrong brooch."

"It's better to have one more dart."

"But if I'd had the box, we wouldn't have evil zombie gargoyles and rich people and probably eventually elves and wizards chasing us."

"Getting the brooch was the goal, and nobody else was able to manage even that much."

"What do we do with it now? Last thing I heard, there weren't any active volcanoes in the greater New York area."

"I'm not sure that would work. That sounds like the sort of thing Merlin would have tried back in his day." He got out his phone and added, "Speaking of whom, I'd probably better call this in." He dialed the number, then held the phone so we could both hear the call. "We got it!" he said when Merlin answered. "Well, Katie got it. But we have it now. Should we bring it to the office?"

"No!" I couldn't help but flinch away from the phone, I was so shocked by the vehemence of Merlin's response. "That would be most unwise. A building full of powerful and ambitious wizards—including myself—would be the worst place for the Eye. I don't suppose you also got the protective box?"

I leaned closer to the phone. "No, I tried, but I didn't have much time to search."

"Ah, pity. Are you safe now?"

"For the moment, yes," Owen said. "I don't know how long we can stay here, though. We tried to get as far away from people as possible, but I'm sure they'll track us down before long."

"Stay there as long as you can. I'm creating a new box, and once the protective spells are complete, I'll have it delivered to you. When you have it encased, you'll be able to bring it to your manuscript room, where you can lock it in the safe with the *Ephemera*. That room is so carefully warded that the Eye should be secure there until we can find a way to destroy it."

"How much longer do we need to hold on?" Owen asked.

"I have at least an hour's worth of work to do. These wards are tricky, and I need to ensure that even I can't break them. It's a shame I don't have your assistance, as I recall you're quite good with wards."

"If I were able to help you with wards, you wouldn't dare let me anywhere near the Eye or anything designed to protect the Eye," Owen said. "Too many people would see that as suspicious." He took a deep breath, then said, "Okay, then, we'll try to hold on for an hour. Call me when you're ready to deliver the box to us."

When he ended the call and put the phone back in his pocket, I leaned against him again, and he settled his arm around me. "Do you think we can just hide out for an hour?" I asked.

"I doubt it. We may have about twenty minutes here, and then we'll have to find another hiding place. If we stay on the move and stay away from people, we might be able to last until we can get that box."

"Those are big ifs, considering that all we can do is run. We don't have magic, and it probably wouldn't be safe to let anyone with magic near the Eye. I'd rather fight our enemies than our friends."

"Yeah, I'm right there with you." He was silent for a moment, then he said, "You do know what our priority is, right? Keep that brooch safe and under your control, no matter what. Don't worry about me. Guard the brooch."

"I seem to recall that we've had a similar conversation before."

"And I was right then, too. You saved the day by focusing on the mission."

"Yay, me," I said weakly. "But you know that leaving you behind almost killed me. I don't want to ever be in a situation like that again."

"I'm not saying that I *want* to be left behind and attacked so the mission can be completed. But I think it's best if you have the brooch, and that means you've got to get the job done. And that reminds me, this is as good a place as any for that talk we've been needing to have."

"What talk?" I said, trying to play innocent.

"The one you've been avoiding. So, come on, Katie, tell me, what's wrong? You've obviously been unhappy about something."

"It's not you, not at all."

"Okay, then, what is it? Because if you don't tell me, then I'll assume it really is me, and then you know me, I'll mope. I might even clean my house."

I couldn't help but chuckle. "Oh, no, we can't have that!" I sighed, then said, "Okay, if you want to know, I think I kind of hate my job. It's so trivial with all that's happened to you and now this whole Eye business, but there you have it. I'm so bored I could scream. Not now, obviously, but this isn't part of my regular job. It's been sheer torture coming to work every day for the last few months, ever since we beat the last round of bad guys."

"Why haven't you said anything?"

"Like I said, it seems so trivial. And besides, I'm on at least my third assignment since coming to work for MSI, and I haven't even worked there a whole year."

"What is it that you hate, aside from the boredom?"

I had to think about that. The boredom was so mind-numbing that it was hard to get beyond it to see anything else. "Mostly, I don't think I'm getting to use my abilities. You recruited me because I'm immune to magic, and that has nothing to do with my current job. Anyone of any level of magical or nonmagical ability could do my job. I have the skills for it because the only job I could find when I moved to New York was as an administrative assistant in a marketing department. It's like, oh, I don't know, say that they put you to work just setting wards. That's something you're good at that you've had a lot of practice with, but it wastes your real skill, which is translating ancient texts and ferreting out the parts of the old spells that might be useful."

"I see your point. You are being wasted. Maybe you should talk to Sam about something in security. A magical immune might come in handy, and you definitely have experience in dealing with bad guys and solving crimes."

"Security? Really? I'm not really the security type, am I?"

"Let's see, in the time you've been with the company, you've caught intruders, revealed a spy, and helped bring down the bad guys while evading the opposition. Sounds like security work to me."

"That could actually be kind of cool," I said thoughtfully. "But you don't think I'll seem ungrateful to reject a job Merlin created for me?"

"The needs of the company keep changing." I felt his shoulder shrug where my head rested on it. We were both quiet for a moment, listening to make sure our enemies hadn't found us. Then he said, "I have to say I'm relieved. I thought you were unhappy that we weren't spending enough time together. I know I can get obsessive when I'm working on a project."

I wrapped my arms around him and hugged him. "Yes, I know you can get obsessive, which is why I try to find ways of working around it, like sneaking in early in the morning to bring you breakfast. If you weren't obsessive, you wouldn't be you, and I happen to like you a lot."

"We *will* take that vacation, I swear," he said.

"Yeah, I've heard that one before." But I was smiling when he kissed me. A tunnel under a Central Park bridge late in the evening wasn't a bad place for a makeout session—that is, if there weren't multiple factions out to get us. As if to remind us that we probably ought to be a little more focused on our surroundings, Owen's phone rang before things could get too heated.

It was Rod. "Are you two okay?" he asked.

"For now," Owen replied. "What happened back there?"

"I wish I could have found a way to record it because Katie would've enjoyed seeing it."

I stood on my tiptoes to speak into Owen's phone. "Oh, do tell!"

"Mimi made a huge fuss about her missing brooch, so they eventually brought in one of the NYPD officers working event security to take her statement. They couldn't take her too seriously when she was griping about missing a brooch that she was still wearing. She insisted that it was a different brooch, and the way she could tell the difference was that the real one made her feel better. Once the officer heard about her earlier meltdown, there was talk about calling Bellevue, but one of the museum trustees was there and talked them into just letting her lie down for a while. They may have given her a little something to help her relax."

"So we won't have to worry about Mimi coming after us for a while," I concluded with some relief. "What about the others?"

"Thor and Granny are with me. Sylvester finally woke up, and he and his group, including Earl, just left. I'm not sure how much time you have before they reach you. Sam's tailing them and we're trying to stay in range so we can help if you need us."

"Thanks for the warning. We should be on the move."

"I hope you've got a plan because you're eventually going to have a lot of people after you."

"The boss is working on a new protective case, and when he gets it to us, we should be okay. We just have to hold out until then."

"Maybe instead of following the elves, we should meet up with you."

"No, sorry, I'd rather not tell you where we are. It's not that I don't trust you."

"It's that you don't trust us around the Eye. Don't worry, I get it, but I'm not sure Katie's grandmother does. She's not happy."

"I'll deal with her later," I said.

"Are you sure you don't need help? I don't like the idea of you two out there alone, defenseless, with who knows what coming after you."

"Who's defenseless?" Owen said indignantly.

"Magic can't hurt you, but I can think of a lot of other things that could."

"Still, the fewer people who might be affected around me, the fewer I'll have to deal with. Or do you want me to have to hit you?"

"Okay, then," Rod said, "I'm here if you need me. We'll try to keep everyone else off your backs—from as far away as possible."

Owen ended the call and said, "We should probably move on."

"Yeah. It would be too easy to trap us in here—just close in on either side."

However, neither of us moved. It was comfortable standing huddled together, and I felt safe in the enclosed environment, even if it did make a perfect trap. Outside, the world was a scary place, full of people who were out to get us—and this time, that wasn't paranoia talking.

"So, maybe we should check to see which side is safest for leaving," Owen said after a while.

"If you insist," I said, forcing myself to pull away from him, and then instantly missing his warmth.

"You check that end, I'll check this end." He grinned. "Maybe you could consider all this part of your security job audition for Sam."

I reluctantly headed to the opposite end of the tunnel from Owen. I didn't like splitting up like that, even if I thought it was probably a good idea. I flattened myself against the tunnel's wall and peered out from behind the bridge's decorative edging. All I saw was a dim darkness. It wasn't pitch black, thanks to the lights from the city around us and the lampposts that lined the footpath, more of a dark twilight. I thought I heard faint footsteps on the road above, and I held my breath to listen, but they grew fainter until I could no longer hear them. I didn't hear anything else, other than distant city sounds, and I didn't detect any motion, either on the ground or in the air.

I turned back to look at Owen's end of the tunnel. He was doing the same thing I'd done, hovering at the edge of the tunnel to watch and listen. I could only see him in silhouette, but I thought he turned back to look at me. I gave him a thumbs-up sign, holding my arm away from my body so he might be able to see it. I waited for a similar signal from him. Instead, he jumped, and then I heard his footfalls echoing through the tunnel as he ran toward me.

Apparently, the coast wasn't clear on that side.

Obeying his directive to focus first on protecting the brooch, I ran out of the tunnel. He was faster than I was, so I figured he'd catch up soon enough, and I didn't want to risk being trapped.

After all our earlier running around, I didn't know where I was in the park or where I should go, so I stuck to the path for the time being. Owen caught up with me pretty quickly, and I reached out to catch his hand. "The elves," he panted. "They must have sensed the Knot and found us."

I risked a glance over my shoulder, but didn't see anything coming up behind us. I also didn't hear footsteps. That made it hard for me to force myself to run all-out, since I was still winded from the last footrace. The next time I looked behind us, I recognized Lyle's upturned collar as he raced toward us. He ran like a gazelle, and I wasn't sure his feet even touched the earth. No wonder I hadn't heard footsteps.

That gave me plenty of incentive to put on a burst of speed, although I suspected it would be fruitless. Owen had been holding back to keep pace with me, so he matched my speed. We were so busy running from Lyle that we nearly ran head-on into Sylvester, who seemed to come out of nowhere to block the path. We probably left skid marks as we stopped abruptly and turned to the side. The sides were also blocked, with Earl standing on one side of the path and another elf blocking the other way. Lyle then came up behind us, blocking our retreat in that direction. We were surrounded.

"You have my brooch," Sylvester said. "Hand it over!"

Owen regarded Sylvester calmly, acting as though he'd just run into him while out in the park and completely ignoring the fact that we were surrounded by elves. "But, see, your brooch got all mixed up with our stone," he responded. "So we're just going to get our stone out of the brooch, and then you can have your brooch. That is, if it survives."

"Don't get insolent with me, boy," Sylvester snarled. "I haven't forgiven you for knocking me out earlier."

"I wasn't trying to knock you out. You got in my way, and even if I hadn't knocked out, you wouldn't have been able to take the brooch. Don't you know how the Knot works?"

"Hand over the brooch!" Sylvester sputtered. He was deeply under the influence of the Eye, and I doubted he'd listen to reason. Even in the darkness, I could see his eyes glittering with need.

I instinctively flinched, but Owen stood firm. "If you want it, come and take it," he said. "I don't recall that you were very successful in your previous attempts."

I wasn't sure what Owen thought would happen when Sylvester called his bluff. The Knot wouldn't protect me the way it had protected Mimi. I turned to Earl, who stood his ground while fidgeting uncomfortably. I gave him my best pleading look, but I didn't expect much, even if he really was on our side. If he helped us, he'd blow his cover.

So far, Owen's bluff was working. Sylvester held back, watching us, unable to tell which of us had the brooch. His eyes shifted back and forth between us as he tried to decide who would be the most likely keeper of the brooch. Owen oh-so-casually put his hand in his pocket, as if to protect something valuable, and then Sylvester made his move.

CHAPTER FOURTEEN

Sylvester rushed at Owen, who stepped forward to meet his attack, catching him off-guard and grabbing his arm to use Sylvester's own momentum against him. The Elf Lord went flying, landing face-first on the path. The other elves hesitated, torn between keeping their positions and moving to help their leader. We darted through the opening Sylvester left.

Sylvester shouted, "Get them! Get the brooch!" and soon the other elves were after us. I didn't see how we'd avoid capture for very long. They could outrun us, they had magic, and they had us outnumbered.

The elves had reached us and one even had a grip on my arm when a noise in the bushes beside the path startled me. I thought at first it was just some animal, but then something sprang out of the bushes onto the path with a bloodcurdling war cry. When it went on to shout, "Sneaky, greedy, cheap elves!" I knew it had to be Thor. I wasn't sure, though, if he was attacking the elves or coming after the brooch. I jumped out of the way, just in case, and he ran past me into the group of elves. He swung his tiny battleaxe with a vengeance, but it didn't seem like he actually hit anything. The elves jumped nimbly out of the way before he could hit them, and then it took him a while to recover after the momentum from each blow swung him around in a circle.

Something dark came out of the sky, and I dove for the nearest bush. After so many attacks by the antique zombie gargoyles, I wasn't taking any chances. This one must have been one of ours, though, because it went for the elves. In the darkness, it was difficult to follow the fight. All I could see was a swarm of shadows. After taking down Sylvester, Owen guarded me, but at the moment, everyone was more focused on fighting each other than on going after the brooch. In fact, I wasn't sure they'd yet figured out which one of us actually had the brooch, only that it was in the vicinity.

The sound of heavy breathing nearby jolted me out of my hiding place.

"It's here, it's here, it's here," Sylvester muttered, sounding more and more unhinged. He pounced on the spot where I'd been just a second earlier. At that sound, Owen whirled away from watching the fight to pull me to my feet and away from the bush. Sylvester still came after me, his hands stretched out ahead of him and his fingers bent into claws. "It's mine," he rasped.

"Back off, buddy!" I ordered, on the off chance that I could use the Eye on other people even if it didn't affect me. It didn't work, or else Sylvester was too far gone under the power of the Eye itself to fall under the sway of the Eye's holder. He kept advancing, and when Owen and I fled from him, we nearly bumped into Lyle.

There was a loud popping sound, and I felt magic nearby as Sylvester suddenly swayed, then collapsed. Rod stood behind him. "Sorry it took me so long," he said. "I was trying to remember a spell that might work on an elf. Now, come on, we need to get out of here."

We evaded Lyle, only to find ourselves facing Earl. Rod flexed his wrists, preparing to fight, but then Earl grinned and joined us, shouting over his shoulder, "Help! I'm being kidnapped!"

"Are you *trying* to make them come after us?" I asked him.

"Do you really think they'd come to rescue me?" he replied without breaking stride. "I was just coming up with an excuse to leave."

We followed Rod into a rough, rocky, hilly area that felt like it was in the middle of the wilderness. I could still see the city skyline, so I knew we hadn't somehow teleported out of the park without me noticing. We stopped in a secluded area surrounded by trees. There were some large rocks, just the right size to sit on, and I availed myself of one of them because I wasn't sure my legs would hold me up any longer.

"I thought I said we didn't need help," Owen said, facing Rod.

"Yeah, but what I saw was you two with a bunch of elves on your tails. Admit it, you need us. You won't last another five minutes without magical support, let alone an hour or more."

"But who's going to help us against all of you?" Owen asked, his voice soft and solemn.

"Thor's having too much fun fighting elves to remember to come after the brooch, Earl just wants to keep it away from Sylvester, and you can tranquilize me if you have to. Remember, I came on this jaunt with that understanding."

We went on the alert when we heard a slight crunching sound, like footsteps on the rocky ground. "I've set some wards that may confuse them for a moment," Granny's voice said as she entered our hideout.

"Good thinking," Rod said.

Then I yelped as the end of her cane poked into my shoulder. "And as for you, young lady, I told you I wasn't letting you out of my sight, and there you went, rushing off on your own and getting yourself into trouble."

"What was I supposed to do?" I protested. "As soon as I got the brooch, I had to get out of there. If I'd gone back to get you I'd have been in even worse trouble."

"And obviously you avoided all trouble by leaving on your own," she said, and I could hear the smirk in her voice even if I couldn't see it in the darkness.

Owen sat next to me and put his arm around my shoulders. "The guests were already arriving, and we had a close call with a couple of them," he said. "I'm not sure what we'd have done if we'd had to face the guests, the puritans, the gargoyles, the elves, Thor, and Mimi, all at the same time. You held back some of them, so you were helping even if you weren't with us."

That mollified her somewhat. She still made a loud "Hmmmph" sound, but she dropped the argument and quit poking me with her cane.

After a few minutes of rest, I asked, "Will Thor be okay? It's just him against all those elves."

"And Sam," Rod reminded me. "Sam won't let him do anything too stupid, and we need Thor to keep the elves off us. They and the puritans are our biggest dangers. The power-broker types will only be strangely compelled. They won't actively seek it."

"How are you holding up?" Owen asked him. "Will I need the dart anytime soon?"

"I won't lie to you and say that I don't want that thing, but I can fight it. I'm getting some pretty vivid mental images of what I could do if I had it, and I think it might be whispering to me."

"Ew!" I said with a wince, then asked, "What's it saying?"

"It's hard to describe. Picture that little cartoon devil that sits on your shoulder. It's like that, not so much words as ideas, playing to all my deepest desires."

"I would appreciate it if you didn't share any details," Owen said, and I felt him shudder. "I heard way too much about your deepest desires when we were in high school."

"Not *those* deepest desires. Well, okay, maybe a few, but only because power does tend to draw beautiful women. I have to admit, it paints a really pretty mental picture."

"It whispers to me, too, but I am choosing not to listen." Earl said. "I am focused on my aim to keep Sylvester from having it."

"And I already told you I don't care much for that kind of power," Granny said. "I've got a mission of my own."

"Do you think this is the danger you predicted?" I asked. "Me in possession of this horrible thing that draws people to it and makes them thirst for power, but not getting the magical protection it gives other people?"

"No, don't think so."

"There's something worse than this?" I turned to Owen. "How much longer should we have to wait?"

Owen checked the luminous dial of his watch. "I know it's hard to believe, but it hasn't been that long. We still have almost an hour, and that was only an estimate."

"Then how long do you think we can hole up here before someone finds us?"

"That'll depend ..." Rod started to say before a soft rustling sound in the grass distracted him. The sound grew louder, and soon a faint glow spread out on the ground around the rock where Owen and I sat. I pulled my legs up and then climbed to stand on the rock. Owen joined me, his arm securely around me as we watched the glow build. Rod and Earl jumped onto nearby rocks, but Granny stood her ground. Oddly, the glow kept a safe distance from her.

"What kind of spell is this?" I asked frantically as the glow surrounded our rock.

"I don't know!" Owen said. "I don't recognize it."

"A seeking spell, maybe?" Rod asked. "Was there anything like it in your medieval book?"

"No, nothing like this. I don't think it's the puritans trying to find the brooch."

"It's not a spell," Granny said.

Now I could see that the glow wasn't an unbroken mass. It was made up of lots of tiny little lights, and each of those little lights was a creature. I'd seen beings like this, back home, when we'd enlisted the local magical folk to help us fight the bad guys. They were the nature spirits, what my grandmother called the wee folk, but I hadn't realized there were any in New York. Yet, here they were.

And they were all kneeling at the base of my rock.

A whispering sound rose into the air, like the sound a soft breeze makes when it blows through pine trees. After listening for a while, I was able to discern words. "Hail to thee, our queen!" they said over and over again as they bowed.

"You've got a fan club," Rod quipped.

"They must have been drawn by the Eye," Owen said, more seriously. "It seems to be an instinctive response. Small creatures like this can't help but respond to power."

"Will they try to take it away from me?" I asked, my flesh crawling as I imagined these things swarming over me to get to the brooch in my pocket. I thought that might be even more unpleasant than being tackled by Mimi.

"I don't think so," Owen said. "They're probably just basking in the proximity of the great power."

"It's still freaky," I said. "You're sure they're not dangerous?"

"Well, there is the possibility that they may draw the attention of other magical things," Owen said. "They've pretty much created a big, glowing 'Hey, over here!' sign that's visible from the air."

I instinctively looked up for signs of the zombie gargoyles. "Would it be rude to make them go away?"

"Try it. They think you're their queen."

"But the brooch doesn't work for me," I protested.

"Still, try it."

"It's worth a shot," Rod added. "I'm torn between trying to take the brooch away from you and worshiping you, myself."

I whirled to him, waving my fist. I would have lost my balance on the rock if Owen hadn't steadied me. "Don't even think about it!"

"And now I no longer want to worship you. See, it works! Now, try it on them."

"Okay, then," I muttered as I thought of what to say. I'd never been good at speeches. "Um, thank you all for coming," I said. "It's very kind of you. But you don't need to worship me. You can run along now."

Nothing happened. They just kept up that whispering and glowing. I never thought I'd be irritated with being worshipped.

"You don't have to be nice to them," Owen said. "They think you're their queen. Queens aren't nice. Pretend you're Mimi."

"If I do that, they'll shoot me with their tiny bows and arrows."

"No, they won't. Remember, you're their queen. You have power over them."

"Okay, then. Your homage is noted," I said as pompously as I could while keeping a straight face. "Now, be gone! Leave me!" That wasn't any more effective. I turned to Owen. "Maybe I should give you the brooch and let you try."

He flinched. "I don't want to touch that thing."

"It can't be any more dangerous for you than it is for me." I studied him for a moment, trying to read what I could see of his face in the eerie glow of all the little magical creatures on the ground. "Or are you feeling something from it? I know you want your powers back, but this would be really bad timing."

"No, but if I ever even act like I want the Eye, with or without powers, there will be plenty of people who think I'm trying to take over the world."

I gestured around us. "There's nobody here but us!"

"That we know of. I'm pretty sure I'm being watched, all the time, by officials and by other people, and the moment I show any sign of doing anything even remotely suspicious, they'll probably just shoot me without asking questions."

"You're being paranoid."

"Not really," Rod said. "He *is* being watched."

"Then if they won't listen to me, what do we do? If anyone's searching for us by air, they'll have found us by now."

Granny banged her cane on the ground and shouted, "Oh, get out of here! Shoo!" The glow receded rapidly, flowing away from us until there was no sign it had ever been there. When the rest of us turned to look at Granny, she shrugged and said, "It's all in the tone of voice. I deal with these folk all the time, though yours aren't as sophisticated as the ones we've got back home. Ours would have argued with me for a while or demanded a gift instead of just leaving."

I laughed. "You know, that may be the first time someone called something from a small Texas town more sophisticated—" I broke off as something came at me out of the sky, knocking me off the rock. I hit the ground hard, landing on the brooch, and that caused such a sharp pain that I cried out. The fall had knocked the wind out of me, though, so my cry came out as a mere gasp.

I was so dazed that I only got a vague sense of the others running around and shouting. I felt the ground shake slightly and heard a loud thud as something hit the ground hard, as though from a great height, nearby.

Then someone took me by the shoulders and shouted my name. I started to fight off my assailant, then realized it was Owen. "Are you okay?" he asked.

"I landed on the brooch," I said, wincing and shifting my weight so the brooch wasn't pressed against my hip. "I have a feeling I'll have a very interesting bruise in the morning."

He chuckled and started to help me to my feet, but then Rod shouted, "Incoming! They didn't just send the one."

"I hate these things," I muttered into Owen's shoulder as he pressed me back into the ground, sheltering me from the attacking zombie gargoyles.

"You two find cover," Rod ordered. "We'll deal with them."

We moved in a crouch toward a cluster of trees, weaving our way across the clearing like we were crossing a battlefield. I had the strangest feeling that we were being followed. When I turned to look, I saw that Rod was right behind us.

"Rod!" I shouted. "You're supposed to be fighting them, not following us!"

He froze, then shook his head. "Sorry! Fighting, yeah, that's it." Without another word, he turned and ran back to where Granny and Earl were fending off the attacking gargoyles.

"That's not a good sign," Owen said softly before leading me to an entirely different group of trees.

"Maybe we should take this chance to go off on our own again," I suggested.

It was a while before he answered, so I knew he was thinking about it. "No," he said eventually. "We'd be sitting ducks without their help. We shouldn't get rid of them until we know they're a danger."

"Rod was just breathing down our necks and reaching for the brooch," I pointed out.

"Yeah, but he snapped out of it as soon as you said something. It's when he *doesn't* snap out of it that I'll be worried. Do you still have the dart?"

I reached for my purse and then had a moment of panic when I didn't find it. "I think my purse is back at the rocks."

"Then that settles it, we can't just sneak away. We'll have to trust Rod. I don't think your grandmother will let him harm you."

The others were winning the battle against the zombie gargoyles, turning them back into stone—again. Soon, several more "boulders" decorated the landscape. When nothing else came out of the sky, Owen and I rejoined the others.

I kicked one of the de-animated gargoyles and said, "I wonder if smashing them thoroughly would keep them from being brought back to life yet again."

"Unfortunately, I left my sledgehammer in my office," Rod said.

"And the gnome is still gone," Earl added.

"I don't think his tiny battleaxe would do much for breaking rocks," I said.

"I was thinking about his head. I've heard gnomes' heads are made of rocks."

"Earl, be nice," Granny scolded. Then she pointed her cane at one of the fallen gargoyles, blue flame shot out of it, and the gargoyle shattered into mossy little bits. "Who needs a sledgehammer?" she asked. "And you call yourselves wizards. Hmph."

"I call myself an elf," Earl said, "but point taken."

Rod blasted a gargoyle, but before they could get to another one, I called out, "Hey, wait a second—if those wee ones were like an arrow saying 'Magic Brooch Here!' then what do you think all these pyrotechnics are?"

Rod said, "We'll finish them off, then hurry out of here."

While they blew apart the remaining gargoyle corpses—with enough glee that I suspected they were working off all the pent-up urges brought on by proximity to the brooch—I found my purse and made sure the tranquilizer dart was still there. Then we headed deeper into the Ramble part of Central Park.

I could get lost in the Ramble on a sunny day. The paths twisted around themselves enough that you didn't know where in the park you'd eventually come out. At night, in the dark, it was even easier to get lost. Fortunately, that was what we wanted. If even we didn't know where we were, we'd probably be harder to find. I wasn't sure how Granny managed, since some of the hills got pretty steep and the footing wasn't always solid. There were a couple of times I'd have fallen if Owen hadn't steadied me. When I looked back to see how Granny was faring, I saw that Rod and Earl were practically carrying her between them.

We moved briskly at first until we were well away from our previous hideout, then we slowed our pace. It wouldn't do to wear ourselves out. We finally found another relatively sheltered spot and stopped to rest.

"I wonder how long we'll be able to hold out here," I said, leaning my head on Owen's shoulder.

There was a noise like a herd of elephants tromping up the hill toward us, and Owen said, "Not much longer, I'd guess." He was already up and pulling me to my feet.

But it was only Thor, his battleaxe gleaming in the moonlight. I was relieved to see that it wasn't coated with blood—and then I wondered what that meant about the outcome of his battle. "Where are the elves?" Owen asked him as I sat down again.

"I have subdued them," Thor said proudly. "They shouldn't bother you again for a while." He patted his jacket pocket, which jingled. "And I have secured payment for our work. I had to go through all their pockets to get enough, and I may have to go back for another payment later if their watches don't appraise for what I expect, but for now, the elves' debt to us is cleared." He gave a formal little bow to Earl. "And you, good sir, are no longer my opponent."

"I wasn't the one who owed you money," Earl said. He hesitated, then added, "Sylvester didn't suspect anything about me, did he?"

"I don't think he noticed you were gone."

"What about Sam?" Owen asked.

"The gargoyle said he would keep an eye on things from the air and alert you to any potential problems."

"He didn't warn us about the zombie gargoyle attack," I said as a sick feeling developed in my stomach. "Do you think he's okay?"

Owen got out his phone and hit the speed dial key, then gave an audible sigh of relief when Sam answered. He updated Sam, put his phone back in his pocket, then reported, "There's a commotion at the museum. He thinks he saw Mimi running away. He tried to follow, but lost her in the park."

I jumped to my feet. "Mimi's on the loose? Then we'd better go. I've seen what this thing does to people who've had it only a little while. She was carrying it around all evening. She'll kill me if she catches me."

But she'd have had to get in line. Suddenly it seemed as though the entire forest around us had come to life, and this time it wasn't tiny little people. These were full-size, and they were closing in on us.

I knew there were regular fairies who hung out in the park, as well as gnomes and other magical creatures. There was even the occasional enchanted prince turned into a frog—Gemma was currently dating one of them. I just hadn't ever run into so many of them, all at once, or with such a sense of hostility about them.

"Don't worry, I've got this," Earl said softly, and then he started singing. There was answering elfsong from within the circle, and the sense of hostility faded.

"Don't you work for the Elf Lord?" a voice asked.

"I work for the free elves, but that work takes me into the Elf Lord's court," Earl replied.

"You have the Knot in your possession," another voice from the circle said. "As well as something more."

"We are guardians of the Knot and must keep it safe," Earl said. More softly, he said to our little group, "We'd better get out of the park as soon as possible because these people know what the brooch is and what they could do with it."

"But Mimi's coming!" I hissed.

"Mimi doesn't have magical powers." Raising his voice again, he said, "Now we must take our leave." He began walking forward, motioning us to go with him. The whole way, he hummed under his breath. There were answering hums as the circle parted to allow us to leave. They didn't try to stop us, but they did fall into step behind us, drawn inexorably to the brooch.

"They're still there, Earl," I whispered.

"Yeah, and that's why I said we have to get out of the park. I don't think they'll follow us into the city."

"But the power-hungry people are in the city!" I protested.

"They don't have magic. Trust me, you don't want these people coming after you."

"I'm immune to magic."

"But they may be able to channel the brooch just from being near you, the way Granny did."

"I bet I could get rid of them," Granny muttered.

"Please don't, Granny," Earl said, a pleading tone in his voice. "Even as powerful as you are, you couldn't take on all of them at once."

We finally came out of the lower end of the Ramble, onto Bow Bridge. As I recalled, it was cast iron. "Isn't iron supposed to be bad for fairies?" I asked.

"That's just folklore, stories people tell to make themselves feel safe," Earl said. He walked easily across the bridge, and so did the weird procession following us. We were heading into a more civilized part of the park, but I didn't know how civilized things would have to get before we lost our entourage.

Once we were across the bridge, we followed the path as it skirted the edge of the lake. It came out at Bethesda Terrace, and then we climbed the stairs to the street. We'd lost a few of our followers, but there were still enough to make the back of my neck twitch. Even though I couldn't draw power from it the way Mimi had, I put my hand in my pocket to make sure the brooch was still secure.

I was so worried about what was behind us that it took me by complete surprise when something jumped out in front of us, shouting, "I want it now!"

CHAPTER FIFTEEN

At first I thought it was yet another one of the park's wild inhabitants. The figure that jumped out at us was dirty and disheveled, wearing ragged clothes covered in leaves, and it waved a small tree branch over its head. In fact, it looked wilder than any of the beings who'd followed me through the park. Then I realized it was Sylvester.

His expensive suit hung in rags and his formerly perfectly coiffed hair stuck out in every direction, with twigs and leaves tangled in it. If he'd been shorter and wearing green, he'd have looked like some of the less-sanitized drawings I'd seen of Peter Pan.

Out of the corner of my eye, I noticed Earl slipping into the throng of park denizens, probably so his supposed boss didn't catch him hanging out with the enemy. I didn't think he was in too much trouble, though, because Sylvester was too far gone to notice anything but the brooch and anything that stood between him and the brooch.

The closer he came to us, the madder he looked. He was breathing heavily, sounding like a bull gearing up to charge. "Mine! It's mine! And you've got it!" he snarled. He advanced slowly, but then, all of a sudden, he ran at us, waving his tree branch like a club. Rod stepped out in front of him and hit him with a spell that left the air feeling charged with magic, but it didn't slow Sylvester down at all.

Owen caught my arm and we jumped out of the way, but no matter how we dodged, Sylvester kept up with us. The whole time, he made a musical keening sound in the back of his throat. It was part rage, part yearning, part mourning, and entirely creepy. I'd heard music that I thought ought to be classified as a weapon, but the elves really had music in their arsenal. The noise grew even worse as some of the park denizens took up his cry and added their keening to his.

Then there was a thud and a cry of pain, and I looked back to see

Sylvester lying full-length on the ground and Granny standing nearby, twirling her cane like a victorious gunfighter twirling his six-shooter. Rod rushed over and kicked Sylvester's branch out of reach, then Granny gave Sylvester a good whack on the back of the head with her cane.

Only when it appeared that the Elf Lord was completely unconscious did Earl emerge from his hiding place among the park denizens. "He's really taking this seriously, huh?" he said, kicking his boss's leg.

"He must have been around the Eye for a while between the time he found it and the time he sent it to the gnomes to be merged with the Knot," Owen said. "It's infected him. I'm not sure he'll ever be truly happy again without it."

"I wonder if he's got some residual protection from having owned the Knot," Rod said. "That spell should have dropped him. It *did* drop him when I used it on him earlier, but this time it didn't even slow him down."

"We'd better split before he wakes up," I said. We headed out, our strange retinue following us. They kept a respectful distance from me, but I still worried that one of them would pull a Sylvester and go mad trying to get the brooch.

As a result, I probably overreacted when I felt someone reaching for my right pocket. I kicked out while throwing an elbow, then cringed when I recognized Rod's voice, sounding strained with pain, saying, "Sorry! Don't know what came over me."

"Yes, you do," Owen said mildly.

"It told me to take it," Rod said. "It kept yelling at me in my head, until I had to do it."

Owen moved around me to protect my right side. "Now you'll have to get through me," he warned his friend.

"That may not stop me," Rod admitted.

"Then I'll try not to break any bones."

"I would appreciate that."

"But try to pull yourself together, okay? We need your help, but we don't need another liability."

To emphasize Owen's point, Granny gave Rod a light whack across the legs with her cane. "You can focus better than that," she scolded. "Ignore the brooch. You don't strike me as the kind of young man who'd take orders from jewelry. Show some backbone!" She punctuated her pep talk with yet another tap from her cane.

Shouts behind us made me pause to look back to see a commotion in the crowd. I couldn't help but scream as Sylvester came rushing out of the crowd of elves and fairies, tossing them aside to clear his path as he ran right at us.

"What is he, some kind of pointy-eared Terminator?" I complained as Owen moved me out of Sylvester's path. The Elf Lord's momentum kept him going on the wrong course for a moment, and in that spare moment, I dug into my purse. "I vote we use the dart."

"It's our last one, and Rod's already giving us trouble," Owen argued without taking his eyes off Sylvester. He moved me aside again while I continued rummaging in my handbag, searching by feel for the dart case.

"But Rod's been pretty easy to snap out of it. So far, neither magic nor physical force have been enough to stop Sylvester, but we know the tranquilizer kept him out for a good half hour. It might not last as long this time, but maybe it'll keep him out long enough for us to deal with this." My fingers closed on the case, and I took it out of my purse just as Owen had to pull me away from Sylvester again.

Then the Elf Lord came to a stop as he seemed to notice for the first time that we were surrounded by elves, fairies, and other magical folk. He swayed slightly, then raised his voice and called out, "My people! They've stolen something that rightly belongs to all of us! You must help me get it back!"

"We aren't your people!" someone in the crowd shouted in response. "We answer to no lord!"

That set Sylvester off again. With a wordless scream of rage, he turned and ran at us. "Do it!" Owen shouted.

Granny bought me a couple of seconds with another whack of her cane that I wasn't sure Sylvester even felt, though it did break his stride. When Sylvester came at me, I jabbed the dart into his neck.

He didn't fall immediately. Instead, he stood still for a moment as his eyes lost the wild, mad look. I was afraid the potion wouldn't work on him any better than the spells had, and I'd let him get way too close to me. Then he fell forward, his arms going around me like we were dancing, and finally he lost consciousness. He would have brought me down beneath him, but Owen and Rod extricated me from his grasp as he fell.

A cheer rose from the crowd when the Elf Lord hit the pavement. "She has defeated the tyrant!" someone cried out, and then they all began singing. It wasn't the tight harmonies and unearthly beauty of the elfsong I'd heard before. This song had a wild, undisciplined quality to it, but the way the crowd swayed in unison as they sang was hypnotic.

"All hail the conqueror!" they sang. "We must serve the one who frees us! Adore and acclaim our glorious queen!"

Then I realized they were singing about me. "Whoa! Hey! Stop!" I called out. "I thought you said you served no lord! You don't want a queen! Especially not me. I'm human, and I'm not even magical!"

That didn't sink in. They kept singing, moving closer to me, some of them reaching out to touch me, not going for the brooch, but just brushing their fingers against my sleeve, my hair, or the hem of my skirt. I skittered out of the way, protesting, but that didn't stop them.

"If they won't listen to me, then why are they worshipping me?"

"If it makes you feel any better, I think they're worshipping the stone, and you happen to be holding it," Owen said.

"I can see why Sylvester wanted the Eye. It definitely would have eliminated any resistance, and with the Knot added to it, no one would have been able to take it away from him."

"That's what he was doing?" someone nearby blurted, and I turned to see that Lyle and one of the other elves had arrived, panting and breathless. They looked down to see their ruler lying on the ground, and I tensed, anticipating their response, but they merely stepped over him on their way to me.

"You didn't know?" I asked Lyle. "Sylvester had the Knot and the Eye, and he was the one who commissioned the brooch."

"It's true!" Earl said, stepping forward.

"Shut up—" Lyle started to say, then he frowned at Earl. "How would you know?"

"Because no one notices I'm around. Nobody listens to me. That means I hear everything, and I know what Sylvester was doing." His voice rose, taking on a mad shrillness. "But we won't fall under his rule! We will remain free! He won't get the brooch. He doesn't deserve it!" I didn't think Earl had planned to announce his true allegiance, but it didn't sound like he was thinking clearly at the moment.

Already seeing where this was likely to go, I moved out of the way of the arguing elves, but I didn't move quickly enough. Earl spun and came at me. "It should be mine! I could rule! I'd be better than Sylvester. I wouldn't oppress people. I'd let people finish a sentence!"

"Earl, you don't want to do this," I said, backing away from him and trying to keep my voice calm and soothing.

"Yes, Earl, be reasonable," Owen added, sticking by my side. "You're not like Sylvester, so you won't give into it. You don't have to listen to it. You know how to cut it off. Just tell it to shut up."

Earl squeezed his eyes shut and shook his head, muttering, "Shut up, shut up, shut up!" as he did so. When he opened his eyes, the worst of the madness was gone, and he let out a long, deep breath. "Sorry about that," he said. Then his eyes widened and he cried out, "Behind you!"

I turned, not sure what horror might be coming after me this time, but it was only Rod, reaching toward my pocket. Owen snapped, "Rod! Not now! Get a grip!"

Rod wiped sweat off his brow with a shaking hand and said, "I'm good, I'm good. But I think I'll go stand over there."

When we returned our attention to Earl, the madness was on him again, and he rushed at us. "Rod, now would be a good time to help us," I said desperately. "You know, a little protective magic? That is, if you can draw your attention away from the brooch."

Before Earl reached me, he jerked and flinched as Granny's cane connected with his back. "Snap out of it, son," she said. "Honestly, I've never seen such a weak-minded group of people in my life, and that includes the biddies at the beauty shop back home who believe everything they see on the Internet and then forward it to everyone."

Earl hung his head and said sheepishly, "Sorry, Granny." Then he slunk back into the crowd, keeping his distance from the stone.

All the while, the fairies and elves kept singing as they danced in circles around us, which added an odd contrast to the events. I waited for Lyle and the others to go on the attack, but instead they, too, joined the chorus. "Let's get out of here," I muttered to Owen, who resumed his protective position on my right side as we headed toward Fifth Avenue.

I worried that the procession of singers and dancers following me would attract even more unwanted attention. This was about as far as I could get from stealthily sneaking through the park. I felt like I was in an old musical, where suddenly everyone in town joins in the song-and-dance routine, knowing the words and the dance steps, even though they're total strangers. Only, I didn't feel like dancing, and I didn't have the energy to sing.

I turned out to be right about drawing attention, but it wasn't the kind of attention I'd expected. The park's true wildlife was emerging from its hiding places. Birds flew overhead, and small furry things came out of the bushes and hedges. I didn't want to think about what kinds of things lived in the city park, but I doubted they were all cute and cuddly.

"I feel like I'm in some demented Disney movie," I said to Owen. "If they start making little outfits and singing to me, I may join Sylvester in la-la land."

"They must sense the raw power of the Eye and be drawn to it instinctively," he said.

"Then we have definitely *got* to destroy this thing. If it's doing this on its own, without anyone directing it, then what could it do if someone actually tried to use it to gain power?"

"Merlin said it started wars."

"That is *not* reassuring. I never imagined myself as a Helen of Troy type who could be the cause of a war."

"It wouldn't be about you. It's all the stone. You just happen to be holding it at the moment."

"That 'at the moment' disclaimer isn't reassuring, either."

A loud "ribbit" stopped me just before I put a foot down on a frog. Then I saw that there were several sitting expectantly at my feet. "I'd bet you've found the enchanted frogs," Rod observed. "They must be transformed wizards who sense the power."

I sidestepped the frogs and hurried away, trying to move quickly enough that they couldn't keep up with me. "Uh uh," I said, shaking my head. "Been there, done that, and I'm not doing it again. I know too much about what that can lead to. Besides, I've already got my prince." I favored Owen with a smile, which he returned.

"Seems cruel to leave them like this, though," Granny said. "I suppose I could help them out." She bent to pick up one of the frogs, but it let out a horrified croak, and then all the frogs fled. "Suit yourself," she called after them. "It's your choice." She snorted, then added, "You're probably older than I am."

That was funny enough to make me laugh in spite of the dire circumstances. "You know, in the morning, I'm going to wonder if I dreamed this whole thing," I said. "This is the kind of nightmare I have where it's so vivid that when I wake up, I think it really did happen until I remind myself of all the absurd, impossible details. Only this time, the absurd, impossible details are real."

"You'll have enough bruises to prove it was real," Owen said.

"Oh, yeah, that one on my hip will be especially vivid. Can a bruise leave a scar?"

A cry of pain nearby told me that Rod had tried to creep up on me again, and Owen had knocked him aside. "He'll have a few bruises, too," Owen remarked.

"Sorry!" Rod called out.

"Distract yourself," Owen suggested. "Think about baseball statistics or sing commercial jingles to yourself."

"I'll give it a shot." He combined the solutions and sang "Take Me Out to the Ball Game" at the top of his lungs. If the singing elves and fairies hadn't drawn attention, then that was sure to.

"Do the police not patrol the park at night?" I asked, glancing around. "I'd think they'd be drawn to this thing along with everyone else, and they've got guns."

"There's at least one patrolman in your entourage, but he's currently dancing with a fairy," Owen said. Then he suddenly spun me around into a dance hold and waltzed a few steps. "Why let them have all the fun?" he said. "Enjoy your moment to be queen."

"Well, no one is currently trying to kill me," I admitted. So far, the fairies and elves were willing to merely bask in my glory—well, the glory of the Eye—and their presence seemed to be keeping the power lusts of others somewhat at bay. Earl and the other elves from Sylvester's crew were following me instead of chasing me, and even Rod seemed to relax once he got into the spirit of things.

I wasn't a great dancer, but Owen, who had been brought up by the kind of old-fashioned people who would have made sure he knew what to do at a formal ball, was a good leader, and soon I was almost able to forget the imminent danger long enough to enjoy the fact that I, Katie Chandler, a woman who was so ordinary that it came back around to extraordinary, was waltzing through Central Park at night with a handsome man while a horde of adoring followers serenaded me, pledging their undying devotion.

It was too magical to last. So, of course, it didn't.

Earl emerged from the crowd, his eyes showing the same kind of madness that Sylvester had. Instead of being lulled or distracted by the singing, he seemed to have decided that he wanted these people to follow him the way they followed me. "Listen to me!" he called out, raising his voice above the song. "You're following a mortal woman, a woman with no magic! It's the Eye of the Moon you follow, not the woman."

Someone in the crowd laughed, and that laugh gave me shivers. "We knew that. Did you think we were so foolish as to follow an ordinary girl? We follow the stone. She rules us."

I looked up at Owen as we stopped dancing. I knew they weren't really following me, but it stung to realize that they knew it, too. More alarming was the fact that they had pledged their loyalty to a stone. That meant they'd willingly follow whomever held it.

Earl figured that out pretty quickly, himself. "You should follow one of your own," he said, and then he rushed at me. "Give it to me. It isn't yours!"

"It's not yours, either," I replied, moving out of the way. Then I played dirty. "Who do you think you are, *Sylvester*?" I asked with a sneer. "Are you that hungry for power that you'd do exactly what he tried to do? You're even letting it affect you the same way."

He froze, then shook his head. "I'm not like him! I'm not!" Then he turned to Granny. "Please, help me! I can't stop listening to it, and it's telling me that if I had it, people would hear me, for once. They'd do what I told them. They'd let me finish sentences." He was pleading now, and I saw tears glistening on his cheeks. "I don't want to be like Sylvester."

"Come here, boy," she said, her voice gentle. "Bend down. You're such a beanpole I can't reach you." He went to her and leaned over. She reached up and touched the middle of his forehead with one finger. "Sleep now," she ordered. His eyes closed, and then he slowly crumpled to the ground, where he curled up on his side. All the muscles in his body relaxed as he gave a little sigh.

"They're so cute when they're asleep," Granny remarked as she watched him. "Now, we'd better get away from here before that stone proves more powerful than my spell. He doesn't seem as far gone as the other one, but it's best not to take any chances."

We were near the edge of the park now. The traffic noises from Fifth Avenue almost drowned out the unearthly singing behind us. My—make that the stone's—entourage had thinned somewhat as the less civilized park denizens withdrew. I noticed that there were fewer animals following us, too.

"Do we really need to leave the park?" I asked Owen. "These people are creepy, but they don't seem to be going after the brooch, and, who knows, maybe they'd do something to protect it if someone else tried to take it."

"On the other hand, if someone else does take it, they'd follow them just as readily, so it may be too risky to hang around here."

"Riskier than being out there?"

He turned to look toward the busy street, then back at the crowd of magical folk. "I don't know. I don't think there's a right answer, just a bunch of answers that are all wrong in different ways. I suppose it won't hurt to stay here as long as we can, and then we can leave if we need to."

We stopped, and then I edged closer to Owen as the crowd caught up with us and circled us, still singing to the stone. The air crackled with magic, and I wondered what those spells would have done to me if I weren't immune to magic. They didn't seem to affect Granny, but Rod swayed along with the crowd. As long as that stopped him from trying to get the brooch, that was okay with me.

Then I realized that there was one member of our party unaccounted for. "Where's Thor?" I asked.

"I don't know," Owen replied, scanning the crowd. "Did he stay with Earl?"

"They had a truce, but I don't think they'd yet become friends. Maybe he wandered off since he got his money. That was his main goal."

"Yeah, and money's probably more powerful than the stone to a gnome." But Owen didn't stop scanning the crowd. "It's not like a gnome to blend in with elves and fairies, so he probably is gone," he added.

"Granny!" I called out. "Have you seen Thor?"

"He was here with me a minute ago," she said.

"Oh?" Now I was worried.

"He was very politely escorting me. Not that I needed any help."

"Then where is he now?" If meek, gentle Earl had turned on us, I worried about what Thor would do. He'd gone after Mimi with his battleaxe, but the Knot had protected her. I had no such protection. My calf muscles twitched in anticipation of an axe blow.

A war cry rang out in contrast to the sweet singing, and I screamed and jumped. "Thor!" shouted Granny, her voice ringing with iron.

The war cry stopped, and I saw Thor swaying on the edge of the crowd, directly in front of us. "I need it," he whispered.

"You have your money," Rod reminded him. "Remember money? Put your hand in your pocket and jingle those coins."

Thor did so, a look of pleasure so intense that it was nearly obscene coming over his face. While he enjoyed a special moment with his money, Rod crept over and reached to grab the axe. Unfortunately, he didn't make it in time.

As though sensing Rod's approach, the gnome jumped to attention, got both hands on his axe, then ran right at Owen and me, shouting, "The brooch is mine! It will bring me much gold!"

Some of the elves and fairies in the circle rushed forward, surrounding him and keeping him away from me. A melee ensued as the elves and fairies fought first against the gnome and then against each other. The stone seemed to feed on and encourage hostility, and soon the love-in atmosphere was gone.

"Okay, *now* we get out of the park," I said to Owen. We had to fight our way through the other side of the circle. Hands grasped at me, but I kept moving, glad I'd thought to pin the brooch to the inside of my pocket so it wasn't easy to take. If I moved quickly enough, they didn't have time to unpin it before I swatted their hands away.

The battle cry rang out again, and Owen shoved me forward, but at his yelp of pain I rushed back to find him on the ground, his hand clasping his calf. Thor lay motionless nearby with Granny and her cane standing over him.

"Oh my God, Owen," I cried out as I knelt beside him. "Are you okay? Did he get you?"

"Just a glancing blow," he said through clenched teeth. "It's not deep, and I don't think he hit the Achilles tendon."

I touched the wound and my fingers were immediately covered in warm, sticky fluid. "You're bleeding pretty badly," I said. "We've got to get this bound up."

Granny joined me, already digging in her copious tote bag. "I'm sure I've got something in here," she muttered to herself. To Owen, she said, "Pull up your pants leg, son, and let me get a look at it." She pulled a vial out of the bag and poured a liquid on the wound as she said, "I'm not sure how well this will work on you without magic, but at the very least, it'll kill germs." I clutched Owen's hand as he hissed in pain. Then she pulled a length of cloth out of the bag and said, "I'll have to buy a new pair of support hose, but these'll do for a bandage for now." She wrapped the hose securely around his leg, tying them off and tucking in the ends before pressing her hands on the bandage and murmuring a few words. "There, that should hold back some of the bleeding. I don't know if the spell will help, but it can't hurt."

Owen started to get up, but I put a hand on his shoulder. "No, rest for a moment. They're leaving us alone for now. I guess all the blood scared them away."

"There are things that are drawn by blood, and you don't want to meet them," he said, his voice shaky even though I could tell he was trying to sound strong and steady.

"Let me guess, they're power hungry, too."

"Of course."

"Look, maybe you should stay here," I said. "I can go on. Granny can protect me. We shouldn't have to hold out much longer."

"I'm not leaving you alone with that thing."

"What good will you do? You won't be able to walk much, probably won't be able to run, and you don't have magic."

He shrugged his shoulder out from under my hand and pushed himself to his feet. "I can walk just fine. And I'm not leaving you alone, so don't waste your breath arguing."

"I won't be alone."

"No, because I'll be with you." He took a step toward me, demonstrating that he could walk. He barely limped, but I could see the pain on his face. I was about to argue some more, but his phone rang.

"Hey, Sam," he said. "What is it?" His eyes widened as he stared past me, and then he slowly said, "Uh, I think they're already here."

I turned and saw a whole gang of puritans, including Mimi's ex-minion, approaching us, and they looked like they meant business.

"Get here as soon as you can," Owen said into his phone. "It looks like we'll need backup."

CHAPTER SIXTEEN

I counted at least ten puritans. Granny and Rod moved in to flank Owen and me, but we were still badly outnumbered. With Thor and Earl out of the picture, we were down to a skilled wizard who was one of the world's greatest illusionists, a crafty old woman well-versed in folk magic and adept with a cane, and two magical immunes, one of them wounded. The only physical weapon among us was Granny's cane. I wondered if I could get my hands on Thor's tiny battleaxe.

When Sam reached us, presumably with some allies, that would even the numbers somewhat. I had an army of followers, but I wasn't sure if they cared who held the Eye. They'd defended me from Thor, but I suspected that if someone got past them to take the brooch, their allegiance would switch in a heartbeat. I glanced over my shoulder and found that we were nearly alone, most of the park denizens having melted into the darkness upon the outsiders' arrival. So much for my loyal subjects, I thought.

"Okay, now what?" I whispered. "Back into the park?"

"They'd come after us," Owen replied.

"I could make us invisible," Rod suggested.

"They've already seen us," Granny pointed out.

Indeed, they were heading straight for us, and Thor's battleaxe wouldn't have helped much, even if I'd grabbed it, because these guys were armed with guns.

The lampposts cast a sinister glow on the barrels pointed directly at us. "You're right, they are hypocrites," I whispered to Rod. "I thought they were opposed to modern technology. At the very least, shouldn't they be using crossbows?"

"You're trying to apply logic to fanatics," Owen said, sounding strangely calm. I would have worried that he'd gone into shock from blood loss, but he was always like that in a crisis. The worse things were, the calmer he got.

His voice was at Minnesota winter levels of "cool." Our situation was dire, indeed.

"Hand over the brooch," the ex-minion said, gesturing with his gun.

While Owen got cool under pressure, I got mouthy. It was a failing that had gotten me in trouble more than a few times. "I thought you were trying to stop people from using technology instead of magic," I said. "Obviously, you don't practice what you preach."

"All tools are acceptable for purifying the world," he said stiffly.

"That's a very clever justification," I said. "I bet you can rationalize just about anything."

"You have no use for the brooch, so there's no point in you losing your life over it," another one of the puritans said, sounding perfectly reasonable, almost friendly.

"I have plans for it," Owen said, sounding equally friendly and reasonable.

"Ah, yes, Mr. Palmer," the friendly puritan said, nodding. "I can see why you might desire the Eye. You've certainly been persistent in seeking it. But I understand that it would do you no good now. Or do you hope to use it to restore your powers?"

"I may not be able to use it, but I know people who can, and, quite frankly, I think they'll do a much better job of stirring up the kind of chaos you want than that woman would have," Owen said.

I was sure he was bluffing. We'd been through too much together for him to have fooled me about the kind of person he was. Taking it on faith, I chimed in. "Yeah, I used to work for her, and you'd have only had a petty charity circuit power struggle. What we have planned is much, much more spectacular. You'll get a lot more attention for saving the world this way."

"That is, if you can defeat us," Owen said mildly with a slight shrug. I really, really hoped he was bluffing and that the stone wasn't working on some tiny residual trace of magic in him.

While I knew we were just trying to convince the puritans that we weren't a threat to their plans, not everyone in what remained of the crowd did. There were a few gasps, and while some people stepped forward, ready to challenge us, others slipped away into the darkness. Out of the corner of my eye, I saw Rod giving Owen a worried stare. He'd known Owen since they were kids, so surely he didn't believe Owen could possibly go bad—or did he have a better understanding of Owen's background than I did?

The puritan acted less convinced that Owen posed a danger than Rod did. "I would have expected you to try to destroy it," he said. He reminded me of Merlin—a professorial type who might have been a mentor or a favorite uncle. Ideological differences aside, he, Merlin, and Owen might have gotten along pretty well. They could have geeked out over the same medieval magical texts.

"Merlin tried to destroy it soon after it was created, but nothing he tried worked," Owen said. "There's no magical way to destroy it, and no way to defend against it."

"That's where you're wrong, my boy. Do you see us lusting for power and grabbing for the Eye?"

"You're holding guns on us and demanding it," I said. "So, yeah."

"We do not desire the Eye for what it is, only for what it will allow us to do."

"And I have my own plans for it, which don't directly contradict yours," Owen said. "Maybe we could work together and plan this a little better."

The man laughed, but his laugh had a patronizing tone. It reminded me of the way I reacted when my nieces and nephews made up silly jokes they thought were hilarious but that made no sense whatsoever. It was a laugh calculated to appease a child. "You, work with us? You are the very people we oppose."

"Do you think I'm on the same side as the people who put me on trial for being born?" Owen asked, and either he was a better actor than I could have imagined or there was a germ of truth in what he said because he spat out the words with an uncharacteristic bitterness that I found disturbingly convincing.

Not sure I liked the way the conversation was going, I jumped in with a question. "I'm curious, how will turning the Eye loose on the world purify magical society?"

"Katie!" Rod protested, sounding truly concerned.

"Well, we're either going to hand it over to them or team up with them, and I need more information to make that decision." Besides, as long as the puritan was talking, his people weren't shooting.

"Ah, a very conscientious young lady you have there, Mr. Palmer," the puritan said with a genial smile. "One must think of the consequences of one's actions. We merely mean to demonstrate the superiority of pure magic over magic that's been bastardized over the centuries. Then people will see what they've lost by forgetting the old ways. They'll turn to us to learn how they should live."

I had to fight to keep from grinning. I couldn't believe my gambit had worked. I'd always thought it was a movie cliché when the villain felt the need to expound on his entire evil scheme while he had the hero in his clutches, but when you get a fanatic to talk about his object of fanaticism, it's hard to get him to shut up. "But you've got something up your sleeve, right?" I said. "It's not like any old medieval magic is any better at dealing with this thing than newer magic is."

I must have pushed it too far because his face lost all traces of friendliness. "What is it to you?" he asked, his lips twisting into a snarl. "You aren't magical at all. You're an abomination. Back in the days of true magic, when a child like you was born, it was left to die rather than pollute the magical race."

I wheeled on Owen. "Seriously? That wasn't in any of the magical history books you gave me to read."

"It's the first I've heard of it," he replied.

"That's because you've lost touch with your own history!" the man shouted. This was better than asking questions to stall. He was on an even bigger rant now, sputtering with rage as he outlined, in great detail, the true history of the magical race and how that history was being covered up by today's corrupt magical leaders. It was a boring lecture, but staying focused wasn't a problem. The mad professor's gun-toting buddies were enough to keep me awake and alert.

I thought I saw something approaching in the sky and hoped it was Sam—and about time. I forced myself not to look up as I squeezed Owen's arm slightly to alert him, then nudged Granny on my other side. The moment the gargoyles dove, Granny struck her cane on the ground, and vines stretched out of the bushes to tangle around the gun-toting puritans. "Too bad this park doesn't seem to have any poison ivy," she muttered as she guided the plants with her cane.

"Quick, this way," Rod said, tugging on Owen, who tugged on me. "I've got you veiled, and I've got a dummy illusion working for cover. That is, assuming you really want to get away."

"Don't tell me you believed that!" Owen said, sounding truly wounded.

"Just checking. Now, go!" We ran, Owen leaning heavily on me, while the gargoyles, Rod, and Granny engaged the puritans.

So far, none of them had fired their guns. I didn't know if that meant they were less comfortable with the technology than they acted, or if they knew that shooting at magical people would be a waste of ammunition. There had to be a spell for blocking bullets. Unfortunately, Owen and I had no such protection. Immune to spells, yes, bullets, no.

The Eye allowed the puritans to track us in spite of Rod's illusion. They didn't know who had the brooch, but they knew where it was. One of them grabbed me. I shouted a warning and then put up a fight. With three older brothers, I knew a thing or two about scratching, clawing, hitting, and kicking. I kicked my captor in the shin with the hard heel of my shoe, then stomped on his instep while driving my head up under his chin. That left me with a headache, but the shout he gave and my sudden freedom made me suspect he hurt worse.

A quick glance showed Owen tussling with another puritan, but before I could get to him, someone else grabbed me. I was really getting tired of this, I thought as I lashed out with an elbow to my captor's ribs, then twisted around to jab my knee into a sensitive portion of the male anatomy. "Hands off me!" I ordered.

I winced when a familiar voice said, "Sorry, Katie!"

"Rod! *What is your problem?*"

"You should give it to me," he said urgently. "Then it would make me invulnerable so I could fight off these guys and save us all."

I crossed my arms over my chest. "It told you to tell me that, didn't it?"

He grimaced and rubbed his temples with his thumbs. "Yeah, sorry."

"Well, nice try, but I'm not falling for it."

He cried out a warning and shoved me aside. At first, I thought it was another ruse, but then I heard the bang of a gunshot and something whizzed past my ear as he knocked me to the ground.

"They're shooting!" I gasped. "They're really shooting at us."

"On the bright side, they're not very good shots," Rod said as he shielded me with his body. I started to shove him aside and get up, but I heard another gunshot and ducked again.

Then I felt something on my side and said, "Rod, do you want to keep that hand?"

"Huh? Yeah. Why?"

"Then get it away from my pocket."

"Oh, sorry!"

We crawled to a nearby tree to take cover. I searched for Owen in the mob of puritans and gargoyles. As if reading my mind, Rod said, "I'll go get him."

I was worried. Maybe the second gunshot hadn't been aimed at me, and maybe it had hit its target. Owen didn't have magic, was hurt, and wasn't his usual agile self. I couldn't see him, but he was shorter than most of the puritans, so I prayed that he was simply hidden among the fighters.

Granny's voice rose over the din of the scuffle, but I couldn't tell what she was saying. And then I realized that she wasn't speaking English. I didn't know she spoke any other language, and this wasn't one I recognized. It sounded wild and ancient.

Soon, a soft glow appeared in the nearby hedges. The creatures Granny called the wee ones had returned, but they'd come at her command this time. I knew she'd claimed to commune with these kinds of creatures back home, but I hadn't realized she spoke their language. They swarmed up the legs of the puritans, hampering their movements and making them easy prey for the gargoyles attacking from above.

Out of this tangle of people, creatures, and plants came Rod, supporting Owen. Rushing to meet them, I let out a little sob of relief at seeing Owen without any bullet holes. I draped Owen's arm around my shoulder to support him.

"You two should get out of here while we've got them distracted," Rod said. He called over one of the gargoyles to escort us, and we hurried toward the edge of the park, away from the fighting. We didn't get very far, though, because even in the middle of a magical battle, our enemies sensed the departure of the Eye and came after us.

"Persistent, aren't they?" Owen remarked. He sounded beyond his usual crisis cool, and I wondered if maybe he was growing giddy from pain and loss of blood.

"Well, they are fanatics. They're not known for giving up easily," I replied.

MSI gargoyles swooped in to shield us, and we dove for cover as bullets ricocheted off stone. I hoped the gunshots didn't hurt the gargoyles. If bullets chipped them, did the wounds heal?

Granny and Rod joined us, Granny still directing plants and magical creatures to do what they could against the puritans. "I hate to say this, sweetie," she said to me, "but I'm not sure you're up to this."

"What do you mean?" I asked indignantly.

"You're helpless against these people, with no magic to protect you. You may not be the best bearer of the brooch."

I placed a protective hand in my pocket, feeling the reassuring presence of the knotted gold with the smooth stone in the middle. "But I can't do anything with it other than keep it safe. I can't say the same about you."

"It's not talking to me," she said, her voice sharp with exasperation. "I wouldn't use it. I'd just be able to protect it because there'd be nothing they could do to me to take it. You'd be able to get it back when you needed to."

I shook my head. "Granny, no. A magical immune needs to keep it because we're the only ones who can be trusted with it."

"Are you saying you don't trust your own grandmother?"

"I'm saying I don't trust *anyone* where this thing is involved."

"It sounds to me like it's working on you," she said, frowning in concern at me. "Why are you so reluctant to hand it over to me, even though that would save your life and keep it out of the hands of the enemy?"

"It *can't* work on me," I protested. "It's telling you to say these things, isn't it?"

"Don't be silly. It's not affecting me." But her eyes glittered with desire as she approached me, and I knew she'd succumbed, too.

She was so focused on the stone that she wasn't fighting the puritans. Two of them slipped past her and headed toward me. Rod and Owen scuffled with them, but one of the puritans grabbed me.

I struggled against him, but he must have had a younger sister because he knew all my tricks. Then an ice-cold voice said, "Let her go."

I looked up and found myself looking down the barrel of a gun, but the gun was pointed just above my head at my captor, and it was held by Owen, who must have won his scuffle and come out with a prize.

He held the gun steadily, his eyes narrowed in concentration. Even when he'd been an extraordinarily powerful wizard, Owen had been one of the most gentle people I'd ever known. He was the kind of guy who took in stray kittens, for crying out loud. I wasn't sure I could imagine him pulling the trigger, but if I didn't know him and if I'd seen that look in his eyes, I'd have taken him seriously.

My captor did. He released me, and I hurried to Owen's side. "Now, back away," Owen ordered. The man hesitated, and Owen's voice sharpened. "I said, move!"

"He might have made a good hostage," I whispered as the man backed away, but Owen shook his head.

"No, it's all about the cause. They'd probably shoot their own guys if they had to."

"Could you shoot?"

He didn't answer, and his gun didn't waver as we slowly backed away from the puritans. "Sam, take their weapons," he ordered. The gargoyles stopped dive-bombing and instead snatched the guns out of the hands of our enemies.

"Do you know what you're doing, son?" the mad professor asked, friendly again. Sam confiscated his weapon and brought it to me. I hefted its unfamiliar weight in my hands. I'd fired air rifles and even a small shotgun, but I wasn't sure about aiming a handgun at a human being, no matter how threatening or deranged he was. I braced the gun in both hands, glaring down the barrel at our enemies.

"I know exactly what I'm doing," Owen said. "I'm foiling your evil scheme."

The man laughed that patronizing laugh again. "Evil? *You* accuse *me* of evil? That's rich."

"I never knew my parents, so you can't blame me for their actions, and I'm not trying to stir up strife to further my cause."

"But blood does run true, doesn't it? Don't tell me you've never been tempted to use power, even if your power has been corrupted. All of this is your fault, you know."

Owen's cool faltered and his voice cracked as he blurted, "*My* fault?"

"Merlin was our great hope, the one who could have restored us to the true ways. When he returned, we knew he would purify the magical world. But you were the one who brought him back. You made him a modern wizard. You influenced him to put the past behind him."

"You obviously don't know Merlin," Owen said with a harsh laugh. "He's a scholar, so he set out to learn what he'd missed, and he chose to adapt to the modern world. I may have taught him to use the Internet, but he was the one who decided to put the past behind him—where it belongs."

If that revelation disconcerted the puritan, he didn't show it. Then again, that type seldom let the truth get in the way of their beliefs. Instead, he gave Owen a cold smile and said, "You may be right about one thing."

"Just one?"

"You may not be evil. You're certainly too weak to be effective even if you are evil. Otherwise, you'd have fired that gun by now. But you're reluctant to take a life, aren't you?"

I aimed high and to the right of him, where I was sure I wouldn't hit anything, braced myself for the recoil, and pulled the trigger, just for the pleasure of watching him scramble backward. "*I'll* shoot," I said. "Next one is aimed better."

"You were high and to the right," Granny criticized.

"It was a warning shot," I argued, exasperated. "I wasn't *trying* to hit anything."

I saw movement out of the corner of my eye and heard a loud bang, but before I could react, the world went still. I looked down to see Rod kneeling, his hand on the ground. Then I looked up to see a bullet hovering in mid-air a few feet away from me. I wouldn't have had time to duck if Rod hadn't intervened.

"I'm not as good at this as Owen is, so get out of here, now," Rod said through clenched teeth. "Granny and I will keep them here."

Owen's shirttail had come untucked long ago, and he stuck his pistol in the back of his waistband, letting his shirt cover it. I put mine in my purse. There were laws about carrying concealed firearms in this city, and both of us were disheveled enough to look suspicious, but I didn't want to face whatever might be out there without a weapon.

I took Owen's arm, and the two of us ran for the park exit. He wasn't limping as badly now, but he had a hop-skip gait that favored the wounded leg. As we came out onto Fifth Avenue, I said, "Maybe we could get a cab. We'd be mostly alone and more or less protected for a while, at least until the cabbie is driven mad with a lust for power, and I think we're safest if we stay on the move."

"Good plan," he said, stepping forward to hail a cab. Several in-service cabs passed us by. A good look at him in the bright city lights showed why. Yeah, he was still ridiculously good-looking, but he also looked like a wild man, with his hair disheveled, his clothes torn and dirty, and blood everywhere. I probably looked just as bad.

"We'll never get a cab. Let's walk," I suggested. "We need to get away from here before they catch up, and Sylvester could be waking up any minute now."

He put his arm around my shoulders again, leaning on me while acting protective. "I should call the office and see if that box is ready." He got out his phone, hit the speed dial button, then waited what seemed like forever for a response. At last he said, "We're hanging on, but this is getting dicey.

How much longer?" He listened, then said, "Okay, but please hurry." He put the phone back in his pocket and said, "He's putting the finishing touches on it now."

"Finishing touches means what, exactly? Like, a few minutes, or half an hour?"

"Magic isn't an exact science. But soon, I'm sure."

"And then it has to be delivered to us. I vote we start heading in that direction."

"We're already heading in that direction."

"Oh, right. Sorry. I'm really tired."

He gave me a squeeze. "I know. But you're doing great. I'm not sure I could have pulled the trigger the way you did."

"I didn't hit anything."

"But I couldn't do that much."

He stopped abruptly, his arm tightening around my shoulders to force me to stop, as well. I started to ask him what was wrong, but then I heard the rustling sound in the plants on the other side of the park wall. We were close to a park entry, and the rustling was heading toward the wall's opening. Moving as one, Owen and I slowly backed away. I didn't know what he was thinking, but I figured that since all the magical and nonmagical wild things in the park had been drawn to the gemstone in my pocket, I wasn't being paranoid or egotistical to think that rustling was coming after me.

The rustling grew louder as it drew closer. It sounded like a herd of wild rhinoceroses was heading my way. I was on the verge of turning and running when a figure shambled out of the park. At first, I wasn't sure it was even human. It was covered in leaves and other debris and looked like it had risen from the floor of an ancient forest. Then I saw something shimmery beneath the leaves and wondered if it was some magical creature of the park. And then I realized it was a woman in an evening gown.

It was Mimi. She looked like she'd cut straight through the park to reach me, not bothering with footpaths and climbing up, through, and down any trees that got in her way instead of going around them. "There you are," she said when she saw me, sounding remarkably friendly. "I've been looking everywhere for you. Now, what have you done with my brooch?"

CHAPTER SEVENTEEN

Mimi didn't have the level of extreme crazy I would have expected of her in this situation. She seemed almost reasonable, more reasonable than her usual self, actually. I knew from many a staff meeting that the reason wouldn't last long. Things would get ugly soon.

Our best hope was to maintain the calm as long as possible. "Mimi, you're wearing your brooch," I said. "See, there it is on your dress, just under that leaf."

She glanced down and brushed the leaf away, then frowned and looked up at me as she gestured at the brooch she wore. "*This* isn't my brooch."

"It looks just like the one you had back at the museum. I saw you take it out of your jacket pocket and put it on."

"Someone switched it—and it could only have been you." She jabbed an accusing finger at me.

I forced myself not to react defensively, remembering her talent for sensing fear or weakness. "What do you think is different about it?"

She hesitated, then said with a shrug, "It's just different. The real one made me feel strong. People obeyed me. This is nothing more than a piece of jewelry. It doesn't do anything for me."

"Maybe you're tired. You can't feel powerful all day." I kept my voice kind, calm, and soothing, the way I had after the gargoyle attack in the museum. "You've been through a lot. That would sap anyone's strength. Did everyone stop doing what you told them to do?"

She frowned. "No, not really. But they had to do what I said because I was in charge." She actually seemed to be listening to me. She certainly didn't have the crazy gleam in her eye that everyone else got around the brooch. "You could be right," she added with a sigh.

"I am right. You should go back to the museum before you miss the rest of your party. You're having a big gala tonight, aren't you? You put in so much work. You deserve to take credit for it. Drink some champagne, dance a little, enjoy yourself."

She nodded. "Yes, I should do that." Then she frowned at me. "What on earth happened to you? You look awful. Come on, you should come back to the museum with me. You both look like you could use a drink."

Now I was suspicious. Mimi was never this nice. She'd been bearable when she was in shock after the gargoyle attack, but she still hadn't really been nice to me. When I worked for her, I could have come to work missing a hand and she'd have criticized my typing speed. Not to mention the fact that she didn't seem to have noticed what a mess she was. This was a woman who practically had to be tranquilized when she snagged her tights. Something was definitely wrong.

"No, thanks," I said, taking a big step backward and pulling Owen with me. "We're on our way home so we can relax. We're not really up to a party right now." And that was the absolute truth. I wanted nothing more than to take a long, hot bath, put on my pajamas, get in bed, pull the covers over my head, and stay there for about a week.

"You're probably right," Mimi said.

I turned to walk away, talking to her over my shoulder. "Well, it was great running into you again. Good luck with your party!"

I didn't think it would be so easy to escape from her, and I was right. Even though she talked about going back to the museum, she came after us—in the opposite direction from the museum. I was also right that it was weird for her to be so nice to me. The Eye must have been telling her what to say so it could get back into the hands of someone who would use it. Now she had that scary gleam in her eyes, and I knew that reasoning with her wouldn't work. She lunged at me, clawing at my clothes. "Where is it? Give it to me! I know you have it!" she shouted.

I tried to fight her off, resorting to the usual chick fight moves of hair pulling, kicking, and scratching. Owen wrapped his arm around her neck to try to pull her off me, and then she screamed, "Help! Police! I'm being attacked!"

"*You're* attacking *me*!" I protested.

"Because you stole my brooch!"

"You're wearing your brooch!"

"This isn't the real one!"

"Take it to a jeweler, he'll tell you it's real." At least, I suspected he would. I didn't think the gnomes would have tried to make the switch on the elves unless they had something that would stand up to appraisal. Not that it mattered, since she wasn't listening to reason. She could feel the difference, and that sense of power had become a need, a hunger.

With either uncanny knowledge or extreme luck, she lashed out with her high heel and caught Owen's injured leg. He blurted something that I suspected was a naughty word in some ancient, esoteric language. In his moment of shock, she broke free from him, knocked him down, and lunged at me again. There was a horrible tearing sound, and then she gave a cry of triumph. She had the brooch.

She held it above her head, cackling like a mad scientist in an old B movie. "Hey!" I cried out as I jumped to grab the brooch from Mimi, ignoring the torn lining hanging out of my skirt pocket.

"You did take it!" she shouted, holding the brooch out of my reach. "I knew it! I'm not insane! I *was* missing my brooch!" She pinned it on her dress, next to the fake brooch, then stepped to the curb to hail a cab.

"Don't let her go!" Owen warned. He was still struggling to get to his feet, but he waved my help away.

I rushed to stand beside Mimi, hoping that my bedraggled appearance might be enough to scare away cabs, even if she did now have the power of the Eye and could probably summon them. "Go away!" she said to me, a ring of command in her voice.

"No!" I said cheerfully. "I don't think so."

She turned to look me in the eye. "I don't need you now that I have my brooch back, so *go away*," she said, emphasizing each word.

"What was that? I didn't hear you."

Owen limped over to join me. "Let's herd her away from the street," he whispered. I looked at him and could tell from his slight smile that he had a plan.

"Hey, Mimi," I said, taking a step toward her. "Did I ever tell you what it was like to work for you?"

When I was nearly toe-to-toe with her, she took a reluctant step backward. "Get away from me," she said, reaching up to rub the brooch.

Owen moved around me to stand in front of the curb, and then stepped up onto the sidewalk, forcing her back another step. "I hear you weren't a very nice boss," he said.

She backed away, frantically rubbing the brooch, like she expected a genie to come out of it and help her. "I said, get away from me."

"I told you there was nothing in that brooch to give you power," I said, enjoying this way too much. "You only imagined it. You're still as weak as ever."

"No, no!" she sputtered, missing her footing as she backed away and nearly falling. Her voice rose shrilly as she cried, "Get away from me! That's an order!" When we didn't relent, she turned and ran toward the park entrance we'd so recently left.

"Keep her in sight," Owen said, speeding his pace in spite of his limp. I took his arm to support him, and the two of us went after her, running like contestants in a three-legged race.

"I'm assuming you've got a plan," I said as we ran, "because in case you didn't notice, we lost the brooch. We were supposed to get and *keep* the brooch, not lose it. We're back to square three!"

"Square three?"

"Well, we know who has it and we know where it is, so we're not on squares one or two. But the important part is that *we don't have it anymore!*"

He must have gotten a better second wind than I did, because he managed to outline his plan while running and without panting. "The Knot doesn't offer either of us any protection. Anyone could have eventually stolen it from us. But it does protect her. *We're* the only ones who can take it from her. So, let her carry it for a while, just as long as we keep her away from the magical puritans and any power brokers who'd cause problems in its presence. Then when we get the box, we take the brooch back from her and immediately put it away for safekeeping."

"Wow, you *are* brilliant, but if we want to keep her away from the puritans, we're driving her in the wrong direction."

He pulled his arm from around my shoulders. "Then get in front of her. Drive her into the city. I suspect it would go to her head if the park people worshipped her."

"Oh, you have no idea."

I sprinted in front of Mimi, blocking her approach to the park. We were a little too close for my comfort, considering I could still hear the scuffle inside the park. Pretty soon, they were sure to sense the proximity of the Eye and come looking for it. It might take them a while to figure out it had a new owner. They'd go after me before they discovered Mimi, and she might get away while I was defending myself.

I was lucky that Mimi had no desire to go into the park, after all. She headed toward the museum. All I had to do was hurry her along to get her past the danger zone. That wasn't too difficult. Convinced that I was chasing her to get the brooch back, Mimi jogged in a mincing trot, hampered by her heels and her long, slim skirt. "Stop following me!" she snapped at me. "You can't have the brooch back."

"I'm not following you. I just happen to be heading uptown," I said, trying not to grin from the sheer joy of irritating Mimi.

While I wrangled Mimi, I heard Owen behind me on his phone, saying, "Sam, we could use some air support out here." Soon, there was a faint stirring of air above me.

It was just in time, because a spectacularly well-dressed crowd was coming down the sidewalk from the museum. The power-hungry gala patrons must have been drawn by the brooch, and we were about to be menaced by a mob in formal wear. It looked like what would happen if a riot broke out at the Oscars.

"Oh, look, my party came to find me!" Mimi said. "They love me so much."

We couldn't let that bunch get near the brooch or we'd have another melee. "Sam!" I shouted.

"I've got 'em, doll," the gargoyle said. Then he called out, "Rocky! Rollo! You deal with the crowd." To me he added, "Let's get her away from here."

There was a traffic light with a crosswalk nearby, and I dragged Mimi toward it. When the "walk" light came on, Sam dropped out of the sky and said, "Hey, sweetheart!"

Mimi gave a piercing, panicked shriek and ran out into the street. Owen and I followed her, Sam flying above. When we reached the opposite sidewalk, I turned back to see that the park gang had come out, and the museum party mob had nearly reached the intersection. We ducked around the nearest corner as the light changed and cars started moving past us again.

"Do you think they saw us?" I asked Owen.

"My guys set up a veil," Sam said. "The gang from the museum may have caught a glimpse, but they didn't see where you went, and that bunch of fanatics shouldn't have seen anything."

"They'll sense the stone, though," Owen said. "They'll find us eventually."

"But if they can't see us, it might take them longer to find us," I said, desperately hoping I was right. It was the only hope I had to hold on to.

I was surprised by how long Mimi was able to keep running, even in a tight dress and high heels. Then again, she never missed a spin class, so she probably had enviable stamina. I was running out of steam, and Owen, with his bad leg, trailed behind me. Only Sam kept an easy pace, staying just above her. Come to think of it, that probably had as much to do with her stamina as her time in the gym. If I didn't know Sam, a gargoyle chasing me would give me plenty of incentive to run until I keeled over.

Fortunately, this part of town was relatively quiet at this time of night. It was mostly residential, with doctors' offices on the ground floors of the swanky apartment buildings. The street was nearly deserted. If the people in the apartments above were affected by the proximity of the Eye and driven to come after it, then we'd be long past by the time they made it down in the elevator. Luckily, Mimi was too focused on running to remember to scream for help.

She slowed as we neared Madison Avenue. The window of a designer boutique distracted her. If the shop had been open, I was sure she'd have gone in and demanded that they give her everything she wanted. As it was, her eyes grew wide and she practically drooled with her face pressed against the glass like a kid perusing the thirty-one flavors in an ice cream parlor.

I was immensely grateful for the opportunity to stop and catch my breath. Being the chaser instead of the chased wasn't any easier. It still had the same effect on my heart, lungs, and muscles. Sam perched in a nearby tree and Owen and I hung back while Mimi window-shopped. She seemed to have forgotten we were there.

The respite gave our pursuers time to catch up, though. The sound of running footsteps approached, and Owen and I ducked into the shadow of a spindly sidewalk tree. A moment later, I saw that it was Rod and Granny, but without the puritans.

Owen gestured for Sam to keep an eye on Mimi, then we stepped out of the shadows to meet Rod and Granny. "What happened with the others?" Owen whispered.

"They're confused, wandering around like they're looking for something," Rod said.

"What about the museum party people? Did you see them?"

"They were milling aimlessly. It may take them a while to get a fix, since they don't know what they're looking for." Then he frowned and stared at me. "You don't have the brooch anymore. What happened?"

I gestured over my shoulder at Mimi. "She got it back."

"Damn! I guess there's not much we can do to help."

"I might be able to talk her out of it this time," Granny said.

"No, don't!" Owen hurried to say. "We're keeping an eye on her, but it's probably better for now if she has it."

"We're using her as a brooch mule," I explained. "Since it works on her, nobody but us can take it from her, and that means they're not attacking us. Which, believe me, is a really nice change of pace."

"We'll get it back when it's time," Owen said. "We just have to keep her away from anything that would stir up problems."

Rod nodded. "I see. That's actually pretty clever."

"I wish I could say we planned it," I said, "but we're making the best of a bad situation."

"Hey, gang!" Sam called out softly, "She's on the move." He stayed hidden in the trees to avoid panicking her again.

Mimi, tiring of the sights in that window, moved on to another one. We followed from a safe distance, like wildlife experts on a nature show, tracking a skittish animal through its native habitat.

Just then, Mimi shrieked, even though Sam was nowhere in sight. She'd come to the intersection with Madison Avenue and had run smack into the ragged remnants of the group of puritans that had attacked us in the park. Her ex-minion was front and center, with the mad professor standing beside him. They must have circled around on the adjacent street to cut us off.

With Mimi wearing both brooches, we couldn't throw them off the trail by staying nearby and pretending to have it. For the first time in my life, I hoped that Mimi retained her essential Mimi-ness and could keep these guys at bay.

"I fired you legitimately!" Mimi said to her ex-minion. "That's no reason for you to go get your cronies and stalk me. You'll get paid for the hours you worked, but I'm not giving you your job back."

"It's not a job I want," he said. "I want that brooch."

She put her hands on her hips. "You've got some nerve! What is this, a holdup?"

He gambled on the possibility that she didn't know that the brooch made her invulnerable and pulled a gun on her—apparently our gargoyles hadn't disarmed all of them. "As a matter of fact, it is," the ex-minion said. "Now, hand over the brooch and I won't shoot."

I held my breath, wondering what we should do. Should we intervene? The last thing we needed was the puritans getting the brooch. Next to them, Mimi was little more than a controlling bitch.

But the Eye's hold on Mimi was too strong. She put her hand up to the brooch, cupping it protectively, and shook her head as she backed away. "No. It's mine. You can't have it. You can't take it from me." Her voice grew shriller as she shouted.

"Are you willing to die for it?" the ex-minion asked, curling his lip menacingly.

She held her head high and looked down her nose at him as she said, "Go ahead and try."

He made the mistake of firing, in spite of what he knew about the brooch's properties. Everything after that seemed to happen in slow motion. Mimi screamed at the sound of the gunshot and ducked, but the bullet was too fast for that to do any good. It flew straight at her, but less than an inch away from her it deflected as though it had hit a bulletproof barrier. The ricochet hit one of the puritans, which I felt was just desserts.

Mimi stood openmouthed, still clutching her brooch, as the wounded puritan fell and some of his comrades went to his aid. "I'm bulletproof!" she said in awe. "I knew this brooch made me powerful. It saved my life." To her ex-minion, she snarled, "Now try to take it from me. You can't hurt me."

She had him there, and I could see from the look on his face that he knew it. I didn't know if they'd planned for her to end up with it, but if they had, they'd picked entirely the wrong woman. She was too strong to let it go to anyone who could really use the power, but she was too petty to do much with the power other than boss people around. About the only difference the brooch made for Mimi was making her bulletproof.

It was now late at night, and we were in a part of town not known for its nightlife, but we were also on a major street in a part of town not normally known for gunfire. Since there had been a gunshot, a crowd was forming. Most people just craned their necks to see what was going on, but I recognized a certain look in the eyes of some of them and elbowed Owen. "We need to get her away from here."

We didn't get a chance to act before someone made a lunge for the brooch. Mimi knocked the man aside, then faced the crowd. "Don't get any ideas! Now, get out of my way. I've had a long day, and I'm going home."

Most of them—even some of the puritans—did get out of her way. She strode through the path they cleared, but then as soon as she had passed them, they fell into formation behind her as she headed down Madison Avenue. Some of them wore evening attire, but I couldn't tell if they were part of the museum mob.

"Oh, this is not good," I muttered. If we took the brooch while she was surrounded by people, we'd then be back where we started, with all of them trying to get it from us. We needed to get Mimi alone.

"Rod, could you pull the time trick again?" Owen asked.

"Maybe, but not for long, and after that I'd be totally wiped."

"Okay, wait for my signal. We need to get to a place where we can get away with Mimi. Sam, some veiling after that would be nice. And let's hope that the brooch's magical immunity works the same way it does for us. It won't help if she's frozen, too."

Owen and I worked our way through the crowd to flank Mimi. The puritans had lost all interest in us now that we no longer had the brooch, but I wasn't sure how long that would last after they realized we had Mimi.

Once Mimi was between us, Owen signaled Rod and then everything went still. We grabbed a protesting Mimi by the arms and ran into the street, weaving our way between frozen cars. The spell wore off just before we reached the other side. We put Mimi between us and the oncoming traffic, hoping that she'd work as a human shield since the cars couldn't hit her. Brakes and tires squealed, and there were some close calls, but Mimi didn't seem any the worse for wear. Once across the avenue, we ducked back onto the side street and ran, dragging Mimi along with us.

"Katie, what are you doing?" Mimi asked once she calmed down enough to recognize me.

"Rescuing you," I replied. "Those people back there were bad news."

"But they couldn't hurt me. Didn't you see that I'm bulletproof?"

"They wanted to take your brooch," I reminded her.

"But they can't! They can't do anything to me. All I wanted was to go home, and I'd be safe there. I didn't need your help."

"Yeah, but do you really want an army of stalkers finding out where you live?"

That thought alarmed her, and her eyes bulged with horror. "Oh! No, I wouldn't want that. But I do have a good doorman. He wouldn't let them in the building."

"I don't think he's bulletproof, and neither is your fiancé."

"Probably not," she admitted.

Mimi was capable of being meek for only so long, especially when she was being magically influenced. Before we made it to Park Avenue, she tried to pull away from us. "I don't need you anymore," she said, jerking her arms out of our hands. "I'm invincible. You're just trying to get my brooch back, anyway, and let's face it, Katie, it doesn't suit you."

"Yeah, you're probably right," I said. "It's way too tacky for me." I reached to grab her again.

But she was already rushing for the curb to flag down a cab, so she didn't hear my insult. A cab cut all the way over from the far lane when she beckoned, with much honking of horns and at least one fender bender along the way. Owen and I barely reached her before she got in the cab. She could compel the cabbie to take her away from us, and then we'd lose the brooch. "You don't want to do that," I said.

"Why not?"

"Did you see the way this guy drove? You'd be putting your life on the line if you got in his cab."

"But I'm invincible!"

"To bullets, maybe, but do you want to risk being disfigured in a car accident?"

I'd hit the right button, and she stepped back from the cab, letting it go. We still had the accidents to deal with, and the drivers came out of their cars to argue over fault. One of them got that now-familiar gleam in his eye and left his car in the middle of the street to come toward Mimi.

"What do you want?" she demanded, standing her ground. "That wreck wasn't my fault. I can't help it if the cab driver was an idiot. I was hailing a closer cab."

Meanwhile, the driver of the closer cab was also heading over to yell at the man approaching Mimi. "You'll pay for this!" he shouted. "You cut in front of me."

The other man turned to argue, and when Mimi shouted, "Stop it and get away from me," the cabbie immediately left while the other man returned his attention to Mimi. The look in his eyes was truly frightening, and I didn't blame her for giving a startled squeak, turning, and then running away.

Not that I was happy about having to run again, but I gathered my resources and forced myself to take off. Owen looked even less enthused. I imagined his leg was killing him by now. He lagged behind as I chased Mimi.

At the next intersection, I ran into Rod and Granny, who'd caught up with us. "After her!" I panted, relieved to hand the baton over to someone else and catch my breath.

Sam glided down to give her a good scare and send her down a side street where there was less traffic, and therefore fewer opportunities for her to cause more mayhem. Unfortunately, that meant she ran a block, then darted straight into traffic crossing Park Avenue. The cars all barely missed her, thanks to the Knot's protection. Granny raised her cane and brought traffic to a halt so she and Rod could follow. I couldn't tell if she'd used magic or played the little old lady card. Then again, this was New York. She had to be using magic to stop traffic.

Owen and I had no such magical advantage. The best we could do was follow in their wake and hope that Granny's spell didn't wear off before we got across the street. It did. We barely reached the median, then had to wait for the signal to change before it was safe to make it the rest of the way across the avenue.

"This isn't close to where she lives, is it?" I asked Owen.

"I think it's a few blocks down from here," he replied.

"Then she's not heading home." As soon as the light changed, we ran across the other side of the avenue and down the side street. I barely caught a glimpse of Mimi, Rod, and Granny rounding a corner and forced myself to put on a burst of speed to give chase.

It was as though the brooch also gave Mimi superstrength and endurance in addition to power and invulnerability, because I didn't think there was any other way she could keep up this kind of pace while running in three-inch heels, no matter how many spin classes she took.

When we reached Rod and Granny, I started to thank them for giving us a chance to take a break, but my thanks died on my tongue when Granny's cane shot out and blocked me. "Oh no, dearie, it's mine," she said, and the raw hunger in her eyes made my stomach sink.

Before I could say anything, Rod whirled on Granny. "Wait a second, grandma, it's mine. It's been my magic keeping her away from the others."

"Ha! Like you'd know what to do with that thing. I'd use it wisely. You'd just pick up chicks with it."

While they argued, Mimi was getting away. "Sam, stay on her!" Owen called out. He and I edged our way around the combatants and sprinted after Mimi. We'd lost our magic users, but they were of no use to us now. It was down to us, the nonmagical people who could remain sane around the brooch.

Unfortunately, Mimi had a good head start. "Mimi?" I called out when I lost sight of her. "Are you okay?" I didn't get an answer, so I shouted, "Sam, have you got her?" He didn't answer, either.

Owen caught up to me and said, "Where is she?"

"I don't know. I think Sam's still with her."

We kept going, checking in doorways as we passed, in case she was hiding. There was no sign of her the whole block. Soon, we reached Lexington Avenue, which was busier. In all that traffic, she could easily have disappeared. She could have hailed another cab.

"I think we've lost her," I said.

"Sam's still with her. He's hard to shake."

"Well, there's no point in us running until we hear from him, right?" I said.

"Very good point." We stopped, both of us breathing heavily.

"How's the leg?"

"I barely feel it anymore."

"Either you're lying or that's a very bad sign."

"I've got bigger things to worry about than pain."

A bench would have been nice, but I wasn't sure I'd ever be able to stand up again if I let myself sit down. Owen and I just leaned wearily on each other as we waited for word.

Finally, Owen's phone rang. I heard Sam's voice on the other end when Owen answered. "Sorry, kids, but I think I lost her."

CHAPTER EIGHTEEN

I wanted to bang my head against the nearest brick wall. We'd gone through all that to get the brooch and keep it safe, and now we'd lost it again?

"Keep looking, Sam," Owen said into the phone. "She can't have gone far. You know the signs to look for." When he ended the call, he said with a weary sigh, "Okay, maybe letting her keep the brooch for a while wasn't the best plan."

"On the bright side, how long has it been since anyone's attacked us?"

"Good point."

We stood there for a moment, both of us swaying slightly as our bodies fought to force us to rest. "I suppose we ought to search, too," I said after a while.

We began walking, keeping our eyes open for signs of Mimi's presence. There seemed to be a higher-than-normal number of fender benders, so either Mimi had hailed another cab or she'd crossed the street. In case it was the latter, we crossed over. We hadn't gone far when we heard raised voices coming from a nearby coffee shop, where it looked like an altercation was in progress.

Owen and I exchanged a glance. "Do you think …?" I asked.

He shrugged. "It's worth a shot."

We went inside and found Mimi holding court, surrounded by young people whose backpacks suggested they were students at the nearby university. She was berating a waitress for bringing the wrong kind of creamer for her coffee.

"Jackpot!" I whispered. "Now what do we do?"

"That box should be ready soon, so we might as well wait and watch. She can't get out of here without going past us. Are you hungry?"

"Starving," I said, my stomach seconding the motion with a rumble. We'd done so much running and fighting, and the late lunch was hours away.

We took the table nearest the door, and Owen ordered coffee and pie for both of us. The waitress gave us a funny look. I figured we didn't look much grungier than any of the other late-night patrons, so long as no one noticed the blood on Owen's leg, but we also didn't exactly look like reliable, upstanding citizens. Owen put enough money to cover the bill and a generous tip on the table, and that seemed to ease the waitress's concerns.

I winced at the sound of breaking crockery as Mimi forcefully rejected whatever they'd brought her. "I'm sorry, I'm so sorry," her waitress groveled, backing away. Mimi's court of students rushed to do anything she demanded. One stood behind her, picking the leaves and twigs out of her hair. Another knelt under the table, washing her feet and lower legs.

"She's got ultimate power, and she's using it to boss around waitresses and college kids," I said, shaking my head.

The waitress brought our coffee, and Owen took a long sip. I couldn't tell if it was the fluorescent lighting in the cafe, but he looked awful, his face a sick, greenish pale color. "What would you do if you had that kind of power?" he asked.

I sipped my own coffee while I considered his question. "I don't know. It must tap into your basic personality rather than your plans. I doubt she'd have thought she'd be so petty with it. She would have wanted to rule the city social set, to be the Mrs. Astor of the twenty-first century. With me, it would probably be something pathetic like getting people to give me their seat on the subway and hold doors for me."

"That's not pathetic. It's nice that you'd only use that kind of power for making people treat you with common courtesy."

"But it means I'll never rule the world," I said with a melodramatic sigh.

"Ruling the world is overrated. It would really cut into your leisure time."

I laughed. "Do you even know what leisure time is?"

He gave me a wry smile. "I once translated the definition from an ancient dictionary in an arcane tongue."

The waitress brought our pie, and it took every ounce of willpower I had not to inhale it. "What about you?" I asked after a few bites, mostly to pace myself.

"I'd probably use the power to make people leave me alone."

The sound of coughing made me turn slightly in my chair. The cougher at the next table looked vaguely familiar, but I couldn't place him. It was probably just one of those Central Casting regulars who seem to be required by law to inhabit every coffee shop. I waved over our waitress to ask her to bring him some water to help ease that cough.

When I returned my attention to Mimi, she was up and heading toward the door. As annoying as Mimi might have been to the staff and other patrons, things would likely get much worse if she got back out into the city.

Under my breath, I said to Owen, "We've got to keep her here. Follow my lead, and don't overreact."

He'd just started to ask, "Overreact?" when Mimi reached our table and then walked past without even noticing me.

Although it went against all the survival skills I'd developed while working for her to draw her attention to me, I called out, "Oh, hi, Mimi!" She stopped and turned to glare at me. Her cluster of sycophants moved to surround our table, looming threateningly over us. I fought off an instinctive shudder and forced my voice to remain bright and cheery. "Imagine seeing you here. This isn't your usual sort of joint. I never thought I'd see you in a place that doesn't take reservations."

"You're following me!" she accused.

"Yeah! Following her! You shouldn't do that!" her groupies chorused.

"I'm eating pie," I countered, pointing to the evidence with my fork. "It has nothing to do with you."

"I'm getting tired of your games. I fired you. Now stay away from me."

"You've never fired me. I quit because I got a better job. And I wasn't working for you tonight."

"You were stealing my brooch. That's what you were doing, and I won't let you do it again." She executed a sharp turn that would have delighted my high school band director, gestured for her court of admirers to follow, and headed for the exit.

Motioning for Owen to stay in his seat, I jumped up and ran to block the doorway. "I'm not done with you," I said, barely suppressing a giddy giggle from living out the kind of scenario I used to dream about in staff meetings.

Mimi and I stood nose-to-nose as her groupies clustered behind her. She arched an eyebrow. "What could *you* want with *me*? You were just some underqualified secretary who dragged me down."

Although I'd been trying to antagonize her, I felt my cheeks blaze. "Dragged you down?" I sputtered. I was only buying time, I reminded myself. Nothing she said really mattered. "I kept that department afloat. I bet you had to find yourself a rich fiancé after I quit because you no longer had anyone around to clean up your mistakes and make you look good. You had a résumé that impressed your boss, but you were lousy at your job and cruel to your staff. Somebody would have eventually seen you for what you were." The surge of adrenaline from finally saying these things to her face made me shaky, and I braced myself against the door so the shaking wouldn't be quite so obvious.

Now Mimi's face was turning red. "How dare you speak to me like that?" she demanded. "Don't you know who I am?" Her groupies closed in, echoing Mimi. I felt like the nerd being cornered on the playground by the school mean girl and her friends.

"Yes, I know who you are," I said, forcing myself not to show fear even though I was deliberately poking a snake with a sharp stick. "You're the worst boss I've ever had—and that includes the one who turned into a literal ogre when he was angry. At least he couldn't help it."

She gave me a venomous smile, and I braced myself for what would come next. I'd seen that look before. "What would you know, you little hick? You thought your insignificant state school business degree and your 'experience'"—she made air quotes—"working in some small-town store qualified you in any way to work in the big leagues? You were lucky to get a job at all."

I had to bite the inside of my lip to keep tears from welling in my eyes. I *had* been lucky to get a job, and if the MSI opportunity hadn't fallen into my lap, I might have still been working for Mimi because I hadn't had any luck finding anything else. Most of the Manhattan employers had seen my qualifications the same way she did. "I got a better job quickly enough," I shot back in a voice that was shakier than I liked. Never mind that the job had nothing to do with my résumé and everything to do with a genetic quirk.

"And yet you were working as a caterer and stealing jewelry," she said with a smirk. Then she waved to her groupies. "I've had enough of this. Come on, I want to get home. You can escort me and keep the rabble at bay."

Her followers shoved me aside, and Mimi and her entourage swept out the door. As soon as I caught my balance, I went after her, running to get in front of her before she went very far. "I'm still not done with you," I said, panting. I noticed that Owen and some of the other patrons, including the cougher, had also left the coffee shop. I gave Owen a nod to say, "I'm okay," then returned my attention to Mimi. I needed to buy time, but how much time did I need? *Where* was that box?

"Write me a letter," Mimi said, stepping around me.

I rushed at her, grabbing her arm. "I said I wasn't done." But then her groupies surrounded me, dragging me away from her.

Owen stepped in, and I was glad he didn't have magical powers anymore or else the lot of them might have been turned into something worse than frogs, judging by the look in his eyes. "Get your hands off her," he snapped. Even without magic, his voice and glare were enough to make them back away.

"This is harassment and assault, and you've already stolen my brooch," Mimi shouted. She turned to her nearest groupie. "Call the police!" she ordered. The groupie obediently got out a cell phone and dialed.

"I think she's outlived her usefulness as a brooch mule," Owen muttered.

I didn't disagree, but I wasn't sure how to get it from her when she was surrounded by fawning admirers. Worse, it seemed like everyone who came down the sidewalk ended up joining her entourage. The only saving grace was that none of them were trying to get the stone for themselves. They were only falling under Mimi's sway.

It sounded like the groupie was having a hard time convincing the 911 operator that this was a real emergency. With any luck, the operator would assume it was just a drunken spat. The last thing we needed was the police getting involved. Mimi glared over her shoulder at the groupie, who was inarticulately trying to explain why the situation was so urgent, and then she stepped forward and shoved me. "You'd better go now if you know what's good for you."

I drew myself to my full height, which was several inches shorter than Mimi, and said, "Why should I? I have every right to be on this sidewalk."

The groupies closed in, surrounding Owen, Mimi, and me, and I doubted we'd get out of there alive as long as Mimi had the brooch and was able to boss them around. One of the groupies imitated Mimi in shoving me, and Owen intervened. Mimi then grabbed his arm and jerked him away. "Hey, if anyone's assaulting and harassing anyone, it's you doing it to us," I protested.

"She's a thief! She has to be stopped!" Mimi shouted to her followers.

I had one last bit of ammunition, a secret I'd kept during my stint as Mimi's assistant because I'd thought sharing it would only make me look like an office gossip and probably wouldn't hurt Mimi at all. But the fate of the world was at stake, and I needed to get her off-balance. "Does your fiancé know that you got and kept your job because you were sleeping with your boss—while you were engaged to someone else? That's why you were in a job you couldn't really do and needed your flunkies to cover for you. The current fiancé seems like a nice man. Maybe someone should tell him."

Off-balance was what I wanted, and off-balance was what I got. Mimi went into the worst case of "evil Mimi" I'd ever seen. I almost wondered if maybe she'd drunk the ogre potion and really was going to turn green and grow fangs. As it was, her eyes turned red and bulged out of her face, and I could have sworn her head spun all the way around. "I have had enough of you!" she shrieked. Moving so quickly that I barely noticed her upraised hand, she slapped me hard across the face. I always thought it was a figure of speech when people said they saw stars, but I saw stars and my ears rang. I instinctively raised my right hand to retaliate as the stars were replaced by a haze of red—something else I'd thought was a figure of speech. Mimi caught my wrist, but I instinctively formed a fist with my free hand, drew back my arm, and hit her square in the jaw with all my might. She toppled over, taking me with her, and we hit the ground.

The brooch was there for the taking. But which brooch? I couldn't feel the difference between the real one and the fake one, so I grabbed both of them, tearing them off Mimi's shredded evening gown. I shoved them into my undamaged pocket before wrenching my wrist from Mimi's grasp.

Owen reached through the scrum of groupies piling onto the fight and pulled me to my feet. "We'd better get out of here," he said. I wasn't about to argue. With the brooch out of Mimi's possession, the groupies lost their focus, so they didn't try to stop us. I hadn't knocked Mimi out, merely dazed her a bit, and she was already sitting up. As we ran away, I heard her scream of rage.

"The subway!" I said, pointing out an "M" sign on the next block. "Mimi'll never look for us in there. I'm not sure she knows how to use the subway. She may not even know where those stairs lead."

"But it's full of people," Owen cautioned.

"Right now, I don't care. I just want to get away from her, and that's the fastest way."

Since we didn't have a magic user with us to get us through the turnstiles, we had to scramble in purse and pocket for MetroCards. A downtown train was just pulling into the station when we reached the platform, and we jumped on board the nearest car. As the doors closed, I let myself breathe a sigh of relief.

But then a hand stuck between the closing doors, forcing them back open, and Mimi entered the packed car. She didn't see us at first. As the train started moving, we scooted to the far end of the car and mingled with a cluster of people waiting at the door. Mimi spotted us just as the train pulled into the next station. As soon as the doors opened, we jumped out and ran down the platform to another car, waiting until the last second to duck inside.

The people there stared at us with suspicion and alarm. I glanced up to find that we were standing directly under the "If you see something, say something" sign, and we certainly looked like the kind of something people were supposed to say something about. "Whew, that's the last time we cater a party for those people," I said loudly as I sank wearily onto a nearby seat. "Things got way out of control."

Owen raised an eyebrow as he joined me on the seat. So far, so good. No signs of power lust. Anyone riding the subway at this time of night was probably too tired to want power.

"Do you think there's a chance we could get all the way to the office?" I asked Owen in a whisper.

"Do you think she'll give up?" he whispered in response.

"Of course not."

When there was no sign of her at the next station, I thought we had it made. I should have known better.

The first hint of trouble was a muffled yapping as a tiny dog being carried in an oversized purse got excited. That didn't necessarily mean anything, I knew, but then a small child who'd been dozing against his mother's shoulder woke and stared at me with an all-too-familiar look in his eyes. He wormed his way out of his mother's arms and crossed the car to stand in front of me. "Gimme!" he demanded.

"Jacob!" his mother scolded. "Get back over here and leave the lady alone."

"It's *mine*," Jacob protested, reaching small, grubby hands toward me. I shrank away and was grateful when his mother came out of her seat to take him by the arm and pull him back with her. He continued to whimper and squirm in her grasp.

I glanced around the car to gauge other potential threats. A trio of young men in hooded sweatshirts gave off menacing vibes, but they weren't even looking in my direction. The dog owner was too busy grooving to music coming through her earbuds to notice her dog's yapping. A couple of teenagers were making out at the other end of the car, oblivious to anyone but each other.

I tensed when I noticed a cop sitting across the aisle on the far end of the car. Normally, a cop's presence would have made the subway feel safer, but I worried what might happen to an armed person in a position of authority if he came under the Eye's influence. Not to mention the illegal weapon in my purse. So far, he didn't seem to be reacting, though. He looked nearly as tired as I was, so maybe at the end of a shift he didn't care about power.

The last person on the train I expected to be a problem was the elderly lady sitting on our side of the car. She was a frail little thing, the type Granny sometimes pretended to be when she thought it would give her an advantage. This woman sat dozing, her string shopping bag resting on the floor between her feet and her support hose sagging around her ankles. An equally elderly man whose white hair stuck out in sparse tufts around his ears sat beside her.

And then she woke with a start. At first I thought she'd realized she'd missed her stop, but then she turned to look at me with cold, glittering eyes. She leveraged herself to her feet, leaning heavily on her metal cane, and made her way to me. Without warning, she lifted the cane and whacked me across the shoulder with it.

"Ow!" I cried in protest. Owen moved to intervene, but I pushed him back. The last thing we needed was for him to be seen fighting an elderly woman.

The woman pulled back the cane for another try, but one of the hoodie crew rushed over and grabbed it. "Yo, lady, that's not cool," he said. Then he turned to the old man. "Can't you make your woman stop this?"

The woman struggled with him over the cane, and Owen and I slid the length of the bench to avoid the scuffle. The woman was now yelling at the top of her lungs.

The cop stirred himself to get up, head our way, and ask, "What's the problem here?"

"This lady went crazy and started hitting that girl over there," the young man said, pointing at me. I rubbed my sore shoulder as the cop turned to look, and then I groaned when that familiar gleam came into his eyes. He advanced toward me, his hand going to his weapon. I clutched Owen's hand, unsure what I could do. I doubted that claiming the cop was under supernatural influence would help if I got arrested for attacking a police officer.

The train slowed as it approached a station, and the cop swayed to keep his balance. As soon as the train stopped, Owen jumped up, pulling me with him, and we bolted through the still-opening doors and onto the platform. While he steered us through the station, I looked back for followers. I didn't see the cop, and I wasn't worried about the old lady keeping up with us.

"I think we're clear," I told Owen. "Where are we?"

"Grand Central. Keep moving. We aren't clear as long as we're around people."

"We're in Manhattan! We can't get away from people."

"I have a plan."

"Yeah?" I asked with some trepidation. He was leading us to the subway exit into the main railway terminal, and I was afraid of what his plan might be.

"Who knows the tunnels around here better than I do?"

"The people who work in them?"

"Possibly, but I may even know a few they don't, and I've got a few tricks."

I came to a stop, bracing myself to force him to stop, too. "I can see where this is going, and I don't think it's such a great idea. There are dragons there!"

"Not anymore. Remember, we sent them all to a sanctuary. Those tunnels make a great hiding place. We can hide out until that box gets to us."

"Are you certain about the dragons?" I asked. "Do you know for sure that you got every last one?"

"I can't guarantee it, but all the ones I knew were accounted for."

"That's what makes me nervous. If there were any you didn't know, then they would be wild, and you don't have the power to tame them anymore."

A voice rang out behind me, shouting, "Give me my brooch!"

With a sick dread of what I was sure I'd see, I turned to see Mimi plowing through the sparse late-night crowds in the station. Her eyes were wild, like a creature beyond reason. "I think I've seen this horror movie," I muttered as Owen gave my arm a tug and started us running for the turnstiles at the station exit. I gave up resisting. A dragon that might or might not be there was preferable to having my power-crazed former boss hot on our heels.

We made it out of the subway station and up into the terminal itself, with Mimi behind us every step of the way. We ran across the concourse, down to the food court and then up again by another stairway, then back down again on the other end. The terminal wasn't entirely deserted, but it was late enough that there weren't too many people and there were fewer trains. When we seemed to have lost Mimi for a moment, we ran around a plastic "platform closed" barrier and down an empty platform. This part made me nervous, since we didn't have magic to hide us from station officials.

At the end of the platform, we scrambled down, avoiding the tracks, and headed deeper into the tunnel until we reached a break in the wall that led into another chamber. Mimi was nowhere in sight, so it was with great relief that I followed Owen through the gap and into a pitch-black cavern.

"Are you sure about the dragons?" I asked Owen. This chamber certainly smelled like dragons. It reeked of sulfur and charred wood.

Instead of answering me, Owen asked, "Do you still have that little flashlight in your purse?"

I dug blindly for it, trying to ignore the weight of the gun in my bag. When I found the light and switched it on, it didn't shed much light in the vast darkness. The tiny spot barely helped us find our footing. The light bounced off something shiny, and as we drew nearer, I saw that we'd stumbled upon a uniquely modern and urban treasure trove.

It consisted of old subway tokens, blinged-out cell phones, a few hubcaps, some keychains, and a couple of roadwork barriers with reflectors on them. There must have been at least one more of those barriers farther back in the cavern because I caught a glimpse of the light reflecting off it.

But then it moved. And blinked.

"Okay, maybe we missed one," Owen said, backing up.

"And this one isn't tame?" My panicky whisper echoed off the cavern walls.

"Likely not."

We edged away from the blinking eyes, back toward the entrance to the train tunnel. The dragon didn't move. With any luck, it hadn't noticed us.

Then a screech came from behind us. "Katie! Give me my brooch!"

We froze, caught between Mimi and a dragon. I wasn't entirely sure which was worse. Mimi was crazed under the spell of the Eye and would probably stop at nothing to get it. The dragon was huge, had long, sharp teeth, and breathed fire. It was a toss-up.

CHAPTER NINETEEN

I flicked off the flashlight, hoping that would keep Mimi from finding us, but she was drawn to the brooch, and the sound of her footsteps drew closer and closer. "Run!" Owen ordered, yanking on my arm, but he was dragging me *toward* the dragon, which I thought was nuts, but he had weight and momentum on his side, so I had no choice but to run with him. A burst of flame filled the cavern ahead of us, stopping me in my tracks, but Owen kept pulling me.

The dragon moved slowly, like it was just waking up and wasn't accustomed to being disturbed. We ran past it, with Mimi right behind us. She caught me by the back of my shirt collar, yanking me backward. Her fingers groped for my pocket, and I slapped them, then jabbed my elbow into her solar plexus. I scrambled away, but I wasn't quick enough. She got me in a headlock and held me tight. With the last bit of breath I had, I cried out to Owen for help, and then I heard a terrible roar in my ears.

Next thing I knew, I could breathe again. I was still being held tight, and I fought against my captor until a gentle voice said in my ear, "It's okay, Katie, it's me." I realized that it was Owen holding me and I sagged against him. However, there was still a roaring sound, and now it wasn't coming from inside my head.

I looked up and saw the dragon rushing toward us, its flame lighting the cavern and showing off even more troves of shiny treasure. "This definitely isn't one of yours," I told Owen as I started running, dragging him with me.

Mimi had finally noticed the dragon and was screaming her head off. "Hush, you'll make him angry," I shouted at her. I didn't know whether or not that was true. I just wanted her to shut up. At least she was too busy screaming to attack me, which was a plus.

"It's a dragon! A dragon! They don't exist!" she shrieked.

Then the need for the brooch overcame her fear of the dragon, and she lunged at me, clawing at my pocket. Owen grabbed her by the shoulders and sent her sprawling into a treasure pile, then took my hand as we ran from both Mimi and the dragon.

"I have an idea," he said. "Come on, where is it? I know it's around here somewhere." He had picked up the flashlight I must have dropped when Mimi attacked me and shone its meager beam around in the darkness. I wasn't sure exactly who he was talking to or what he was talking about, but I went along with him, hoping he was telling the truth about having a plan.

Finally, he said, "Aha!" He switched off the flashlight, pushed me down, and shoved me against a wall. I felt a gap and crawled through it, hoping that what lay on the other side wouldn't be any scarier than what we were escaping.

It was just as dark on the other side as it had been in the cavern, but I didn't smell sulfur, which meant this space was dragon-free. I considered that a distinct improvement. It was also Mimi-free, at least for the moment. Now I knew why Owen had turned off the flashlight. He hadn't wanted her to see the exit.

"You're leaving her in there?" I gasped when he joined me.

"She tried to kill you!"

"Well, yeah, but that's a dragon in there!"

"I know. I hate to do that to the dragon, but we don't have a choice. We can come back and rescue the dragon after we safely box up the brooch. Until then, you know she's going to keep attacking. Now, come on, let's get out of here." He switched the flashlight back on and began walking, and I reluctantly followed him.

I'd never thought I'd feel bad for Mimi. If anyone ever deserved to become dragon chow, it was Mimi. "She and the dragon should have plenty to talk about," I said in a feeble attempt at a joke. "They have a lot in common. They can exchange tips on making friends and dealing with people." In spite of my quips, I was still uneasy about leaving her.

"It's my decision," Owen said firmly.

It was for the greater good, I told myself. I knew that if it came to it, I'd have to leave Owen behind to protect the brooch, so why not Mimi? "Do you know the way out?" I asked, changing the subject.

"I think I do."

"You *think*?"

"If we get too lost, I'm sure someone will eventually be drawn to that brooch and find us."

"That isn't very reassuring."

We reached a wall, found a gap in it, and crawled through. That brought us into a railroad tunnel that, thankfully, was also sulfur-free. I couldn't help but keep glancing over my shoulder. I wasn't sure if I was afraid Mimi would come after us or afraid she wouldn't.

Finally, I saw light ahead, and it wasn't an oncoming train. It was the platform where we'd started. "We're there!" I said, giving Owen a quick hug for joy.

Owen's phone rang, the sudden noise making both of us jump. His magically souped-up phone really did work everywhere. He handed me the flashlight and took his phone out of his pocket. I couldn't hear the other side of the conversation or see his face as he talked, but from what I could piece together, the box was ready. "We're in Grand Central, and we're safe for now," he said. "But it would be nice if you could hurry. 'Safe' isn't lasting very long for us, and I'm not sure how much more we can take."

As he put the phone back in his pocket, he said to me, "It's on its way. We're almost done with this, for now." He put his arm around me, and I leaned into him gratefully.

We reached the end of the platform, and I helped him up. He was limping pretty badly now. We headed arm in arm for the exit to the concourse, but as we passed a pillar, someone leapt out from behind it, jerking Owen away from me and tackling him.

I tried to pull the assailant off Owen, but I couldn't get enough leverage to shift him. Owen shouted, "Katie, go, now!" After one more fruitless tug, I reluctantly ran for the exit, my hand held protectively over my pocket full of brooches.

I had a decent head start, but I doubted I'd be able to outrun a man, so I forced myself to put on as much speed as possible. The farther away I was before he realized that the brooch had gone, the better.

And then when I reached the "platform closed" sign in the doorway, I chanced a quick glance over my shoulder and saw that no one was chasing me. Even though the magical brooch that drew everyone to it with an intense lust for power was getting away, Owen's attacker was still focused on Owen. This wasn't about the brooch.

I paused, hesitating. The first priority was keeping the brooch out of the wrong hands, but if this guy didn't want the brooch, then I wasn't exactly going against the mission to stop and help Owen. I'd had to leave him in danger once before. I wasn't going to do it again.

With a deep breath and a silent prayer for strength, I turned and ran back, as hard as I could. As I drew closer, I heard the attacker shouting at Owen, "I should have known you'd destroy your rivals for the Eye of the Moon!" I flung myself at him, using my full body weight to knock him off Owen's back and onto the ground, where I kept him pinned down with my knee in the small of his back.

"I thought I told you to leave," Owen said, sitting up and pulling the gun from his waistband to level at his attacker.

"He wasn't after the brooch. He was after you," I said.

"You still should have gone."

"Yeah, because you were winning that fight so decisively."

Ignoring me, Owen said to the attacker, "I've got you at gunpoint, so don't try anything funny. Katie, get off him. Now, sit up slowly and keep your hands where I can see them."

I eased myself off the guy and resisted the urge to fan myself at the sight of Owen playing the steely cop, which was hot enough to stir me in spite of my fatigue. The attacker sat up, holding his hands in the air. He'd seemed so menacing and angry in his attack, like some ninja commando, but he turned out to be just an ordinary-looking man.

In fact, he was *extraordinarily* ordinary-looking. I used to joke that I could get away with bank robbery because any description of me would also fit half the city, but compared to this guy, I'd stand out in any crowd. He was utterly nondescript—average height, average build, brownish hair, brownish eyes, no distinguishing features, no scars, birthmarks, or tattoos that I could see. He wore a beige trench coat over a dark suit that, depending on the light, could probably look black, navy blue, or a variety of shades of gray. You could stand face-to-face with this guy and then not be able to pick him out of a lineup later.

And yet, he looked vaguely familiar.

"I should have known you were up to no good," he said. He didn't sound like someone being held at gunpoint. He sounded rather pleased with himself. "You've certainly been determined in your quest to obtain the Eye. I can only imagine what you'd want with power, control, and invulnerability." His bland face remained perfectly neutral. He might as well have been chatting about the weather.

The assailant's fingers twitched slightly, and Owen said, "Don't even try a spell." Then he sighed wearily and asked, "What makes you think I have plans for the Eye?"

"You said you had plans for it, and you've worked very hard to keep it in your possession."

Owen grimaced and shook his head. His ruse to make the magical puritans think he wouldn't get in the way of their plans had backfired. But that meant this guy must have been there in the park. I didn't recognize him, but it had been dark and there had been so many people and things there. There was still something familiar about him, though. I knew I'd seen him *somewhere* recently.

Abruptly, his bland, neutral face twisted into a mask of sheer hatred, his eyes narrowing, and furrows appearing in his forehead as his lips thinned to a harsh slit. "What do you want with the Eye and its power?" He spat the words at Owen.

"I want to keep it out of the wrong hands," Owen said with his characteristic crisis calm.

"Not to mention foiling an evil plot to stir up the magical world," I said, moving to sit beside Owen in a show of solidarity. Sitting may not have been a position of strength, but it was stronger than falling, which was what might have happened if either of us had tried to get up and run. "You aren't another one of those magical puritans, are you?"

"I have nothing to do with those fanatics," the man said with a shake of his head.

"Then who are you?" Owen asked. "What do you want with me?"

"My name is Raphael Maldwyn." He paused for a moment, like he was waiting for Owen to react. When Owen showed no sign of recognition, Raphael went purple with rage. "You don't know who I am? My name means nothing to you?"

Owen shook his head. "I'm sorry, nothing is coming to mind. It's been a really rough day. How about a hint?"

His name didn't mean anything to me, either, but I finally realized where I'd seen him. "Hey, you were in the coffee shop! The one sitting by us who had a coughing fit. You must be the person Sam thought was tailing us. You were using illusions and Sam noticed the magic." I wondered if I'd seen him anywhere else, but as busy as we'd been, chasing and being chased, I doubted I would have noticed any individual who hadn't physically attacked us. Was he the man I'd seen outside 21? I hadn't had a good look at his face, but his coat was familiar. Then again, it was just a bland, generic trench coat.

"Following you has been a challenge," he admitted. "You've been on the move all day, surrounded by your guards, and then there were the other people following you."

"Yeah, if you wanted to follow us today, you'd have to take a number and get in line," I said.

"Since you have the Eye, I can prove that you're up to your parents' tricks, and then you will be dealt with," Raphael said.

"I never even knew my parents," Owen said, his voice heavy with weariness. "I think my father died without knowing I'd been born, and my mother gave me away as soon as I was born. They didn't get a chance to influence me."

"And yet you have a weapon pointed at me."

Owen's gun wavered. He was in a no-win situation. He couldn't exactly protest his innocence and pure motives while holding someone at gunpoint, but without the gun, he was vulnerable to the madman with a vendetta.

Taking advantage of Owen's moment of hesitation, Raphael moved his hands in the form of a spell as he muttered words. I felt the magic building around us. He kept at it until beads of sweat formed on his brow. When several minutes went by with no result, he finally gave up and stared at Owen. "How do you resist me?" he asked.

"No magic. Not even enough to allow you to use magic on me. The Eye doesn't do me any good. *Now* do you believe that I don't want it for myself?" Owen very deliberately put his gun down and spread his hands in a gesture of helplessness.

"This is a trick!" Raphael shouted. Before either Owen or I had a chance to react, he lunged forward, grabbed Owen, and jerked him to his feet, shaking him violently. He was half a head taller than Owen and not nearly as weary or as badly hurt, plus he was crazy, so he was at a distinct advantage. I was afraid he'd kill Owen with his bare hands.

That wasn't something I could just sit by and watch happen. Forcing myself to my feet, I took the gun from my purse and aimed it at Raphael's head. "Let him go!" I commanded. The order didn't make its way through the fog of crazy. I thought about firing a warning shot, but I wasn't sure I could do that without causing a ricochet or drawing a security guard who'd ask questions we couldn't answer. Instead, I stepped forward and ground the barrel of the gun into the back of Raphael's neck. "I said, *let him go*."

That got his attention. Unfortunately, it didn't get his obedience. He did take one hand off Owen, but only to gesture casually. The gun jerked in my hands, like it was trying to escape my grasp. I held on as tightly as I could, my knuckles growing white with the strain, but it was no use. The gun slipped out of my fingers and flew into Raphael's hand.

"Damn!" I muttered. I was so used to magic not working on me that it hadn't occurred to me that magic could work on objects I held. That perhaps explained why weapons weren't used too often in magical fights.

Raphael shoved Owen roughly against the nearest pillar and pointed my gun at him with one hand while frisking him with the other. "Where is the Eye? What have you done with it?" he demanded.

"He doesn't have it. He never has," I said. "If anyone's power hungry and holding onto this dreadful eyesore, it's me, not Owen. And in case you're worrying, I have no plans to give it to him."

"Yes, she has been very stubborn about it." All three of us turned to see who'd spoken. The puritans had caught up with us. They must have tracked the Eye like magical bloodhounds. The mad professor led the group. "It took us some time to find you," he said. "I see you've taken the Eye back from that foolish woman."

He came toward us, ignoring Raphael, and although he claimed that the Eye didn't affect him, I thought his eyes had a suspicious glint in them when he got close to us. "Yes, I believe the girl has it once more. Give it to me, young lady, and things will go much better for you."

"Keep away from her!" Raphael said in a commanding tone, much to my surprise. He released Owen and stepped in between me and the puritans. Owen moved around to my side, and we exchanged a puzzled look. "You have no right to the Eye," Raphael continued.

"Neither do you," the lead puritan said.

"I'm not trying to take it."

"Then may I ask what your interest in the Eye is?"

"I am not interested in the Eye. My interest is in bringing Owen Palmer to justice."

"Then I would think you'd want to get the Eye out of his sphere of influence. He may not be holding it, but his girlfriend is, and do you have any doubt that she'd comply if he told her to give it to him?"

While they debated, Owen bent to whisper in my ear, "When you get a chance, go into the tunnels and hide. You know which ones are safe."

"I'm not leaving you here with these lunatics," I said.

"You agreed earlier that the important thing is keeping the brooch safe."

"It doesn't seem to be in immediate danger," I said, not budging from my position.

"We don't want these people getting their hands on the Eye," Owen said. "So, go. It won't be long until we have help."

"The puritans would just chase me, leaving you alone with the guy who hates you," I said. "I'm not seeing an upside to leaving you, for either of us."

"Katie, go!" His voice was sharp with urgency.

I crossed my arms over my chest. "I'm not going anywhere. We'll get through this together, and if we're lucky, they'll take each other out."

During this whole debate, another one of the puritans had edged his way around the platform, and he made a lunge at me. I jumped out of the way, protesting loudly. That got Raphael's attention. He hit the attacker with a burst of magic, then held his hands over his head and said something in a foreign language. "He's setting wards," Owen whispered to me.

"Well, maybe he's not so bad, aside from hating you," I said.

But it was too much to hope that we'd be safe for a moment. Raphael glanced over his shoulder at us, and then his eyes changed. He already had the mad gaze of the fanatic, but then he took on a look I knew all too well after the events of the day. The Eye had its hooks into him. It really seemed to love a fanatic. This would have been a great time for that protective box to show up, I thought.

But because we were apparently not allowed to do anything the easy way, the box didn't magically appear. Raphael turned and came at us. "I could use the Eye to bring about justice," he said softly, his eyes boring into me.

Owen and I backed away from him. "Okay, maybe I should have run," I said. "Now what?"

Owen didn't get a chance to answer because Raphael was on me, moving so quickly I couldn't jump out of the way. I lashed out with my feet and elbows, but it didn't help. He got his hand into my pocket and came out with a brooch, then raised it over his head in triumph.

"Oh no, not again," I moaned.

"This time, I don't think it's such a good idea to let someone else have it," Owen muttered.

Then Raphael lowered his hands to peer suspiciously at the brooch. He must not have got the real one, and while he was still figuring that out, we made a run for it.

Raphael didn't notice us escaping, but the puritans did. They came after us, and Raphael was too distracted by trying to channel the brooch to maintain his wards. We were soon surrounded.

"Katie, give me the brooch and get out of here," Owen urged.

"Are you insane?" I protested. "For one thing, they'd kill you, and for another, that would be playing into that psycho's hands. You'd prove him right if he thinks you're taking the Eye."

Raphael gave a cry of agony. At first I thought it was because he'd realized that he had a fake brooch, but then he grasped his head with his hands, like he was in pain. "No!" he cried. "I have evil in me! I should have resisted temptation." He threw the fake brooch on the ground. Most of the puritans dove after it, scuffling with each other as they fought to get to it first. The mad professor and a few others weren't fooled. They kept my arms pinned. Owen and I struggled, but we were both hurt and exhausted and they were crazed with power lust.

Suddenly, my arms were free, though I kept swinging them for a few more seconds before it dawned on me that I'd been released. Raphael stood behind the puritans, holding his arms out and chanting something that seemed to have frozen our assailants.

"Thanks!" I panted.

"I will resist!" he said. I wasn't sure whom he was addressing. Probably himself, I thought. His hair was damp with sweat, and his face showed the strain he was under.

But his eyes had that odd gleam in them. He blinked it away a few times, but the lure of the Eye was too strong. He lowered his arms and approached me. Owen took my arm, and together we backed away, down the platform. The spell broken, the puritans were moving in on us, as well.

We were almost at the end of the platform, and I could have sworn I heard a distant shrill voice from somewhere down the tunnel shouting, "Where's my brooch?"

And then they were all on us. "Go! Into the tunnels!" Owen shouted as the puritans swarmed him. I didn't make it to the platform edge before the puritans, sensing the brooch's departure, left him to go after me.

"Wait a second! I know what to do!" Owen shouted. "Katie, toss me the brooch."

Squirming in the grasp of one of the puritans, I yelled, "I thought we discussed this."

"I think I can destroy it." I followed his glance and saw the "high voltage" sign near the tracks. I suddenly knew what he had planned. They hadn't had high-voltage electricity back in Merlin's day, so it might do the trick to destroy the Eye.

But the puritans had my arms pinned, so I couldn't throw it. One reached a hand into my pocket. Then there was a loud popping sound, the puritans literally fell away from me, and I was free. I wasn't sure what had happened, but I didn't wait to find out. I grabbed the brooch from my pocket, rushed to the edge of the platform, then threw the brooch as hard as I could, aiming to slide it under the third rail. Thanks to having to play pitcher for my brothers' batting practice, my aim was true.

A second before it landed, Owen shouted, "Get out of the way!"

The brooch was sparking ominously under the edge of the rail. With no puritans hampering me, I spun away from the platform's edge, but Raphael stood poised there, like someone working up the courage to jump off the high dive. His face was a mask of agony, twisted into revulsion. "I am wicked. I have failed," he said, his voice flat with resignation.

I realized what he was about to do, and Owen must have come to the same conclusion, for both of us lunged toward him at once, grabbing him by the shoulders and pulling him back from the edge.

A second later, an explosion rocked the platform. The blast knocked me off my feet and up into the air. I hung suspended in space for what felt like forever. When I hit the ground, it was with a force that knocked the breath out of me.

As I lay on the platform, fighting to breathe, something landed on the ground beside me. I was barely able to focus my eyes enough to see that it was a small wooden box lined in velvet.

Then everything went black.

CHAPTER TWENTY

I woke gradually and reluctantly, at first aware only of being terribly uncomfortable, but too tired to do anything about it. Every bone, muscle, and joint in my body ached so badly that lying on a warm cloud probably would have hurt, but I was lying on something cold and hard. I thought I'd feel better if I could move to a more comfortable place, but the signals wouldn't travel from my brain to my body. The most I could manage was a twitch or two. Maybe if I rested awhile longer, I could get up, I thought. Or, if I was really lucky, someone might come along and move me. At the moment, I didn't much care who it was, so long as they moved me somewhere soft and warm and didn't expect me to do anything for a long, long time.

At the same time, I felt an odd tingling resonating throughout my body. It was like I was lying next to the speaker towers at a rock concert, but I didn't hear any noise. There was only a faint background buzz that might have been voices, or it could have been a really loud fluorescent light fixture.

Gradually, the buzz modulated until it made sense. It sounded like a name—my name. "Katie! Can you hear me?" the buzz said.

"Go away. It's too early to get up," I mumbled, trying to roll over and curl up into a ball.

Something stopped me, gripping my shoulder to keep me in place. It felt as cold and hard as the surface beneath me, not like any human hand. That was weird, I thought, weird enough that I needed to see what was going on.

Opening my eyes required more energy than I had, so I tried opening one eye and made it about halfway. Everything was blurry at first, but then my vision cleared and I saw a strange face looming over me. The strange face was familiar, and then my brain scrolled through a lot of events very rapidly, like it was fast-forwarding through a video, and I recognized the strange-yet-familiar face. "Sam?" I asked.

"Whew, I was starting to wonder if you'd come back to us, dollface," the gargoyle said. He got an arm and a wing under my shoulders to help me sit up.

I saw then that I was on a railway platform. My brain finished fast-forwarding the recap of the past day, and I knew I was at Grand Central. "What happened?" I asked.

"I got here just after it happened, but it looks like you two destroyed the Eye. There seem to have been some aftereffects."

I rubbed my temples, trying to ease the splitting headache. "I threw the brooch under the third rail," I said. "There must have been an explosion."

"Yeah, looks like there was a massive magical shock wave. Everyone on the platform was out cold."

Everyone, he'd said. "Owen!" I blurted, frantically looking around. I saw a motionless form not too far from me and willed my aching body to crawl over to him.

"He's okay, just knocked out like you were," the gargoyle reassured me.

I searched for a pulse, unwilling to take his word for it. In this lighting, Owen looked really awful, his skin a sickly pale color where it wasn't bruised, bloody, or covered in ten-o'clock shadow. His pulse was strong and steady, and his eyelids were already fluttering. "Owen!" I said, gripping one of his limp hands. "Come on, honey, wake up."

Without opening his eyes, he asked, "Did we do it?"

"Sam says we did."

"There's a melted blob of gold with a cracked stone in it lying on the tracks," Sam confirmed. "And it doesn't have a trace of magic in it."

"Good. It was just a crazy theory, but I'm glad it worked." Owen struggled to sit up. I slid my arm around him, and we leaned against each other, both of us too tired to do more than that. I wondered if it would be too much to ask someone to send wheelchairs to take us to a car for the ride home. I wasn't sure I could walk more than about three steps.

I closed my eyes and enjoyed not having anyone attacking me. Owen's voice stopped me from falling asleep. "What's that?" he asked.

I opened my eyes and noticed the small box that had been lying between us. "I think I remember seeing it fall right before I blacked out," I said. "It must be that box we were waiting for."

"Yeah, our people got here about a split second too late," Sam confirmed. "But looks like you didn't need it, after all."

"Oh, thank God!" A harsh voice caught our attention, and I looked up to see a frightfully bedraggled Mimi climbing onto the end of the platform. "I thought I'd never get out of those tunnels." She was limping, wearing one high-heeled shoe, the other nowhere in sight. Her skin was smudged with soot, her dress was torn into rags, and her hair looked like she'd stuck her finger in a light socket on a really windy day. "Now, where's my brooch? It should be somewhere around here. I found my way out of the tunnels by aiming for it, but now I don't seem to feel it anymore."

"How did you get out?" I asked.

"I just told you, Katie, I aimed for my brooch." Even in her exhausted state, she sounded condescending.

"What about the dragon?"

She sighed and shook her head. "Katie, there's no such thing as dragons. Now, about my brooch? It was a birthday gift from my fiancé, and I'd like it back. Don't make me call the police."

I spotted the fake brooch lying nearby on the platform. "There it is," I said. "Take it. I promise I'll leave you alone now."

She limped over to it, bent to pick it up, then pinned it on her tattered dress and took a few long, deep breaths. Then she frowned in disappointment. "Something's wrong," she said. "I don't feel the power."

"The power was in you all along," I said, feeling like I was reenacting the end of *The Wizard of Oz*. "You don't need a gem to be a bit—I mean, to be in charge. You need to find your own power."

She scrunched up her face, like she didn't quite believe that, then she shrugged and limped away toward the concourse. Owen and I turned to watch her go, then Owen said, "I hope the dragon's okay."

"You'd probably better send someone with magical powers to check on it," I said. "I know I'm not going back in there." Then my brain finally caught up to the current situation. With Mimi gone, that accounted for one of our nemeses, but what about all the puritans and Raphael who'd been on the platform with us when the Eye was destroyed? Sam had said everyone was knocked unconscious.

I glanced behind us and saw all the puritans just starting to stir. They were surrounded by MSI gargoyles. "What will happen to them?" I asked Sam.

"The boss figures that attempting to start a magical war puts them in Enforcer territory. He's staying out of it, on account of the Eye being his creation in the first place. The Council's not happy about having to take action, but it'll do them good to have to take a stand on something."

"What about him?" Owen asked, gesturing toward where Raphael lay, still motionless.

"I dunno. Who is he?"

"He seemed to have had some issue with my birth parents. He should probably be taken to the infirmary and kept under watch. I think he was suicidal. We barely pulled him back from jumping onto the tracks before the brooch exploded."

"Okay, I'll have our people deal with him," Sam said.

There were some popping sounds as the magical Enforcers materialized on the platform. I'd spent too much time evading them during the summer to be entirely comfortable with their presence, even though they were supposedly on our side this time. Their leader came over to us. "There was a report of an insurrection movement?" he said with a suspicious glance at Owen.

"Over there," Sam gestured with a wing. "Those guys could have destroyed us all if these kids hadn't stopped 'em."

The Enforcer signaled to his men, who bound the barely stirring puritans with silver chains, then disappeared with their prisoners. I gave a big sigh of relief when they were gone. If I never saw the puritans again, it would be too soon. I just hoped they didn't come up with any more crazy schemes for purifying the magical world.

The lead Enforcer stayed with us. "Is there anything else we need to know?" he asked, his attention on Owen.

"Merlin can tell the Council everything," Owen said. "And, no, I wasn't part of it, I wasn't a target. I never touched the Eye, and I wasn't the one who destroyed it. You can also tell your people to take the next few days off from following me because I'll probably be sleeping."

The Enforcer raised an eyebrow, but he said nothing before he disappeared. "Should we have mentioned Raphael?" I asked.

"He didn't really do anything," Owen said. "In fact, he helped protect us. I'd like to see if we can help him rather than turn him over to the Council. He needs the infirmary, not Council detention."

"Speaking of the infirmary, we'd better get you two to the office," Sam said. "Or maybe to a hospital, since magical healers won't be of much use to you."

"That gash on your leg will need medical attention," I said to Owen before he could protest.

There was a commotion at the entrance to the platform, and in came Granny, followed by Earl, Thor, and someone else who looked vaguely familiar but whom I didn't immediately recognize. Granny came right up to me. "Young lady, I told you that you needed me with you, and you just ran off." Her voice was sharp, and she punctuated each phrase with a poke of her cane.

"You were trying to take the brooch," I said. "I *had* to leave you. And I'm okay. Well, I will be when I've had a hot bath, an aspirin, and some sleep."

"The brooch must be safe. I don't feel it anymore," Granny said.

"It's destroyed," Owen said. "It shouldn't be a problem ever again. But just in case …" He tried to get to his feet, and I forced myself to stand to give him a hand up. The guy with Granny stepped forward to help. Owen looked at him, frowning. He must have had the same familiar/unfamiliar sense from him that I had. "Rod," he said, "I thought you were going to drop that illusion."

A second later, what little color he had left drained entirely from his face as the implication of that caught up with him. It took me a second longer to realize that I, too, was seeing Rod's illusion that he wore to make himself appear more handsome. But illusions didn't work on me, and they hadn't worked on Owen since he'd lost his powers last summer.

"Owen?" Rod whispered.

Owen didn't seem to hear him. He held his hand out in front of him, and soon a soft glow formed in his palm. "The blast when the Eye was destroyed, it must have done something," he said, his voice shaking.

"Yeah, I think a good blast of magic like that could be enough to reboot the system," Sam said.

I was afraid to ask what might have happened to me. If I saw Rod's illusion, then I'd lost my magical immunity. The blast must have turned me ordinary—normal ordinary, neither magical nor immune to magic. It looked like I'd be stuck in the marketing department, after all, in a job where my magical status didn't matter. I was glad I was too tired to cry because that kept me from embarrassing myself by bursting into tears.

I'd learned the hard way that when something odd was going on with me, I needed to say something instead of trying to hide it, even if I didn't want to face the truth of it. I waited until Owen seemed to have grasped the impact of having his magical powers back before clearing my throat and saying, "I see Rod's illusion, too."

Owen immediately stopped what he was doing and rushed to my side, taking my hands. "Are you sure?" he asked.

"Yeah," I said, forcing my voice to sound firm and brave. "It's just like that time when the potion took away my immunity." I managed a casual little shrug and a wry grin. "I guess I'll have to give up that idea of working in security. A 'normal' person won't be much use there."

"I'm not so sure about that," Owen said. "The line between powers and immunity is a fine one. If the explosion restored my powers …" His voice trailed off, and he squeezed my hands. "Okay, I need you to concentrate. Hold your hands out like so—" He turned my palms upward. "Now, imagine your hands growing warm, so warm that they're glowing." I closed my eyes and did as he directed. That weird buzzing tingle that had been running through my body since I woke up intensified. "Good," Owen's voice said softly. "Now let the glow lift into the air." I tried doing that, then opened my eyes to see what was happening.

Small, faint balls of light hung in the air in front of my face. "Did I do that?" I squeaked.

Owen squeezed my hands. "You did that."

"Yep, that's why I had to come," Granny said with a knowing nod. "You'll need me here to help you adjust. I don't want you to turn out like your brother. If I'd guided him as he learned to use his powers, maybe he wouldn't have been such an idiot about it."

"You mean, I have magic powers now?" I asked.

"Looks like it," Owen said.

"For good?"

"I don't know. I'll have to do some research." For Owen, that was like saying he'd have to eat chocolate cake. His eyes were already sparkling.

Still holding my hand, he walked with me to the edge of the platform, then gestured with his fingers. The ruined remains of the brooch flew into his hand. He swayed slightly as it touched him. "It still has a little juice in it, but it's limited to direct contact," he said. "To be on the safe side, could someone please hand me that box."

Rod brought over the box, and Owen placed the ruined brooch inside, then closed the lid and sealed it. He waved his hand over it, and the whole box glowed briefly before the light dimmed and it became just another wooden box.

"But you had no magic!" a voice cried in protest. Raphael was awake and staring in horror at Owen.

"I didn't then, but it looks like you were right about the Eye restoring power," Owen said. "I assure you, that was entirely unintentional."

"Wow, this is like something out of a Shakespearian tragedy," I said with a grin. "The thing you did to stop something you feared would happen turned out to cause the thing you feared. If you'd left Owen alone, he might have just put the brooch in the box and never learned that it could restore his powers. Not to mention the fact that we were so near the blast because we were saving your life."

If I'd expected undying gratitude or an apology, I'd have been sorely disappointed. "You should have let me die," Raphael said morosely, hanging his head. "I turned out to be as weak as anyone. I, too, fell under the sway of the Eye and lusted for power."

I went over to him and patted him on the shoulder. "Hey, nobody's perfect. It was the Eye. I'm not sure anyone could have resisted it. Even my own grandmother tried to take it away from me."

"And I'm no weakling," Granny said. "Come on," she added, nudging him with her cane. "Everything will look better after you've had a good meal."

"We'd all better get back to the office so we can let the healers at you two," Sam said. "I sent for a car. It ought to be here by now."

"This is where we part ways," Thor said with a bow. "I got payment for our work and saw to it that the brooch didn't fall into the wrong hands, so my work is done." All of us glanced at each other with some amusement, since he'd had very little to do with protecting the brooch and had even injured Owen while trying to get it for himself. But it seemed rude to quibble at a time like this. Thor took Granny's hand and added, "It has been an honor fighting at your side, good lady." Then he headed off into the concourse.

Rod took charge of Raphael, and we all started to leave the platform, but someone behind us cleared his throat. We turned to see Earl standing there, looking sheepish. "I don't suppose you're hiring," he said. "I probably don't have a job after attacking my boss, and I think I blew my cover as a spy in his court. I may even need to hide for a while if he figures out I tied him up before he woke up."

"So, that's why he didn't join the party," I said.

"I'm sure we can work something out," Owen said. "Come with us. Merlin will want to talk to you." He paused and smiled. "He may even want to listen to you. He'll want more information about what Sylvester's been up to."

It was probably a good thing I was too tired to think much about what had just happened to me or I'd have been like a kid on Christmas morning with a complicated new electronic toy that had come without instructions. I'd have wanted to play with my new powers, but I wouldn't have had the slightest idea how to use them or what to do with them.

I knew I had a lot of work ahead of me, and I didn't know what Owen having his powers back meant for him, since it would make people even more suspicious of him and it would stop his research on the *Ephemera*. But I figured we could worry about all that the next morning. Make that next week. It was already very early Friday morning, and we deserved a break. I suspected even Owen would take the whole weekend off.

It was too bad my grandmother had come to stay. It was the first time in ages when Owen didn't have any pressing problem to work on and would likely be under orders to stay home and rest. We were both too tired to get up to anything interesting, but it would have been a great time for a good, long cuddle and some privacy. The glance we exchanged on the way to the car told me he felt the same way. A warm tingle flowed upward from our joined hands as he laced his fingers through mine.

If this was what was possible when we shared a magical connection, then it appeared that I had a lot to look forward to—whenever my grandmother finally left town.

ABOUT THE AUTHOR

Shanna Swendson is the author of the Enchanted Inc. series of humorous contemporary fantasy novels, including *Enchanted, Inc.*, *Once Upon Stilettos*, *Damsel Under Stress*, *Don't Hex with Texas*, and *Much Ado About Magic*. She's also contributed essays to a number of books on pop culture topics, including *Everything I Needed to Know About Being a Girl, I Learned from Judy Blume*, *Serenity Found*, *Perfectly Plum* and *So Say We All*. When she's not writing, she's usually discussing books and television on the Internet, singing in or directing choirs, taking ballet classes or attempting to learn Italian cooking. She lives in Irving, Texas, with several hardy houseplants and a lot of books.

Visit her Website at www.shannaswendson.com.